D0386437

The stranger's eyes glinted through the slits of his mask. The next thing Jocelyn knew, his hard mouth descended on hers in a deep, devastating kiss. Gentle. Ruthless. Irresistible. He kissed her throat, her shoulders, then slid his mouth lower to suckle the tips of her breasts.

"Let's do away with our masks, shall we?" he murmured. "As a matter of fact, let's do away with the dress you're wearing."

"It's *you*," she said in a strangled voice.

"Of course it's me," he murmured.

And Jocelyn did not need to ask his name. Because she knew. Mask or no mask, she knew.

"Devon Boscastle." She stared up into his beguiling face as he wrenched off his hood and removed his mask. His beautiful mouth quirked into a grin.

"Jocelyn." He added insult to injury by breaking into laughter. "It is *you*."

Also by Jillian Hunter
(published by Ivy Books)

THE SEDUCTION OF AN ENGLISH
SCOUNDREL
THE LOVE AFFAIR OF AN ENGLISH LORD
THE WEDDING NIGHT OF AN ENGLISH
  SCOUNDREL

THE WICKED GAMES OF A GENTLEMAN

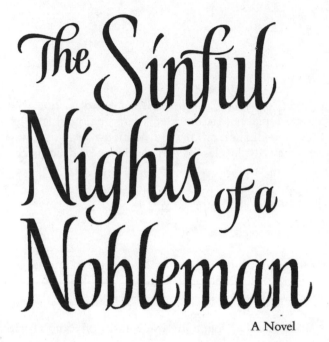

The Sinful Nights of a Nobleman

A Novel

Jillian Hunter

BALLANTINE BOOKS • NEW YORK

The Sinful Nights of a Nobleman is a work of fiction. Names, characters, places, and incidents are the products of the author's imagination or are used fictitiously. Any resemblance to actual events, locales, or persons, living or dead, is entirely coincidental.

Copyright © 2006 by Maria Hoag

All rights reserved.

Published in the United States by Ivy Books, an imprint of The Random House Publishing Group, a division of Random House, Inc., New York.

IVY BOOKS and colophon are trademarks of Random House, Inc.

ISBN 978-0-7394-7374-0

Cover design: Carl Galian
Stepback art: Jon Paul

Printed in the United States of America

For Juliana, with all my love

The Sinful Nights of a Nobleman

Chapter One

To all outward appearances, Lord Alton Fernshaw's annual house party in the Essex countryside was a dignified affair. If one inquired of a random guest why he or she had trundled all the way from London to the castle estate, the most likely, and fictive, response would have been to enjoy the concerts, the extravagant raffles, the elaborate sporting events that brought back the glory of medieval days.

Few, in actual fact, attended Alton's party for the cultural upliftment offered, or to compete in the vigorous athletic competitions. It was the pursuit of passion that beckoned the energetic youth of the beau monde.

By the dessert course of the Friday-evening supper that began the house party, most of the guests had singled out which gentleman or lady they wished to pursue.

By Saturday morning, Eros, son of Venus, had

discharged nearly all of his golden arrows. Some hearts had already begun to bleed. Some had taken wing.

The well-experienced servants of the estate, from the elderly majordomo to the youthful maids, stood at the ready to accept bribes in the cause of amorous conquests. Chambers could be changed with complete discretion at a moment's notice, doors unlocked at a whim. A footman would gladly serve as a loyal guard during a garden tryst for hours on end.

Lord Devon Boscastle and his acquaintances made no bones about why they'd accepted Fernshaw's annual invitation. Devon planned to excel at a more provocative game than jousting at a mock tournament, chivalric pretensions be damned. He'd already selected his partner and, to judge by the come-hither looks she was casting him across the crowded salon, Mrs. Lily Cranleigh was as eager for a liaison as he was.

She lifted her glass of champagne at him as if in a toast, and smiled.

Before he could respond, she turned on her heel and walked to the door without a backward glance, her gray silk half-mourning dress clinging to her lush hips, her swansdown boa draped over one flawless white shoulder.

Well, that was an opening if ever he'd been issued one.

He waited several minutes before following. There was no advantage in appearing too eager even though both he and the licentious widow were unattached.

Let the lady smolder a little longer. He'd been quietly pursuing her for weeks.

It was now his turn to tease.

He turned, deep in pleasant thoughts, and found himself unexpectedly face to face with another, far less friendly, female guest. A young country miss with whom he shared a transient if embarrassing bit of history.

Jocelyn Lydbury.

Once upon a time, before Devon had completely ruined his own reputation, Major-General Sir Gideon Lydbury, Jocelyn's father, had cast his eye upon Devon as a potential husband for his only daughter.

Devon had been asked to the ancestral country pile for a lavish dinner. The problem was, he had completely forgotten to attend because he'd been carousing in the low dives of London. After all, he'd just enlisted in the cavalry and thought it quite possible that he'd be killed or injured his first year out. He'd seen no point in planning a future.

Sir Gideon, who did not share in this fatalistic view, immediately let the whole of London know that he had not appreciated the social insult, war or no war. The matter might have blown over had the man not taken a seat in Parliament and gained the political support of Devon's eldest brother, Grayson, the Marquess of Sedgecroft. Even now, from time to time Sir Gideon reminded Grayson that he had not forgotten the slight.

And, of course, Grayson, in turn, reminded Devon.

Devon assessed the woman before him with an experienced glance. Her hair was not the ordinary brown he'd thought it was, but a deep burnished-gold becomingly swept back from her face in an elegant coil. Her face was one that the years had rendered more appealing than he remembered. Her dark eyes held his gaze.

"Jocelyn," he said, a practiced smile in place, "what a nice surprise. I didn't realize you were one of Fernshaw's guests." In his mind she was an unsophisticated debutante who should probably remain shielded from the risqué goings-on that one expected at a party like this.

"You aren't here by yourself, are you?" he asked curiously. "I haven't seen your brother anywhere. I seem to recall he used to follow you like a shadow."

Her skeptical gaze swept past him to the door through which Lily Cranleigh had made her enticing exit. "He's right there in the corner. You were too preoccupied watching the notorious widow, I expect." She gave him a rueful look. "Some people never seem to change, and obviously you are one of them. Good evening, Devon, and good-bye."

"Have you changed?" he asked, challenging her coolness.

She answered him with surprising honesty. "I hope so. For one thing, I should like to think I'm a better judge of character than I was a few years ago. I don't invite just anyone to dinner these days, at least. I'm more discriminating in who I ask to slight me. Is that what you were wondering?"

"I suppose I deserve that," he said with a rueful smile.

She laughed softly. "Well, let's not hope you get everything you deserve."

"Now that was cruel."

"It was actually kind. I don't imagine men like you deliberately go about doing hurtful things."

He shook his head. Of course he hadn't meant to hurt her, but it was obvious he had. God knew she'd have come out even worse if he had accepted her father's invitation and actually courted her. He didn't think he could ever be the sort of man who'd live up to a decent young woman's idea of love.

Which didn't mean he'd object to sharing his views on that subject with her. He was pleasantly surprised by the touch of cynicism that he sensed beneath her soft appeal. What had made her so? he wondered. Weren't her father and brother the overprotective type?

"How long has it been since I offended you?" he asked in an undertone. "And is there nothing I can do to make amends?"

The last question escaped him unbidden. He'd felt no previous desire to atone for his past behavior. Why the devil bother now?

Jocelyn Lydbury.

Too tempting up close for a country wallflower. Four years had certainly made a difference for the better in her, or perhaps it was only his perspective that had matured.

She wasn't lushly attractive in the flagrant sense, as was his widow. But there was something about her, a subtle but intriguing quality that made him wonder what he'd missed.

An aloof, untouchable young lady. Virtue to his vice, demure to his decadence. Good breeding stock to put it crudely. He'd always thought of her as a one-day girl—the sort of girl a marriage-minded man would desire in the distant future when and if he ever had the urge for a stable association.

Which Devon didn't.

Besides, she was far better off without a man like him, no matter what she or her father might have thought. She had clearly never recovered from his offense, and aside from apologizing, there wasn't anything else to do for it.

Her next question, however, prompted him to wonder if he'd overappraised his place in her life.

"What makes you think you offended me?" she asked in mischievous amusement.

His dark eyebrows lifted in reaction. Perhaps he should have paid closer attention to her in the past. She had a long-limbed, slender body that curved softly in all the right places to whet a man's appetite. He was sure she hadn't shown this intriguing sense of self the few times they'd met.

"I know that to slight you was rude," he said. "But the war was on, and—"

She glanced around his shoulder, apparently distracted by something across the room. "You slighted my father," she said with a dismissive laugh. "And you don't have to do anything to make amends except . . . "

He felt a rather irritating sting of curiosity and wondered if he'd grown too accustomed to easy conquests. "Except what?"

She looked at him levelly, then whispered, "Except to let me go *now*. Devon, I do not wish to offend you, but you are really in my way. Please allow me to pass. I don't want to be seen talking to you."

"What?"

"You did wound me before if that makes you feel better."

"Why would it make me feel better?" he asked, mildly outraged. "I can't believe—"

"Believe it," she broke in. "I'm not angry anymore. I just wish to . . . to not talk to you. Honestly, everything is fine. It's over, that's all. I've forgiven you."

He studied her with a reluctant smile. He knew he ought to let her go her innocent way, and he would, but it wasn't in his Boscastle nature to allow an offense against a lady to remain unpaid. He'd hurt her, thoughtless bastard that he had been. He wasn't sure he was any better now, but these days he tried to put more thought into his actions. It was true that he still indulged in sinful pleasures, but with a trifle more discretion, which was why he'd come to Alton's party. . . .

The thought triggered another possibility.

"Do you have an assignation, Jocelyn?" he inquired in a low voice.

One delicate eyebrow rose. "Is that all you think about?"

"Well, what do you think about?" he asked, aware that she had evaded the question.

"About finer things. About integrity and literature, and— I don't want to talk about it. Or to you. You're going to get me in trouble, and you know it."

He had to smile; the set-down was duly deserved but unexpected. He wasn't inclined to force a bud into bloom, no matter how promising, although he probably wouldn't have minded being discharged half so much if he hadn't felt he merited a scolding. And if he hadn't realized that Jocelyn's attention was focused on Lord Adam Chiswick, a good-looking blond cavalry officer who'd served in a different regiment than Devon's, but who didn't have a brain in his handsome head.

He grinned, murmuring, "There are more assignations in the air than dust motes in my grandmother's drawing room."

She gave him a knowing smile. "Speaking of

which, your widow won't wait for you forever. A number of your friends are seeking her companionship at the party. You've fierce competition for her favor. I think you should step up the hunt if you don't want to lose her."

He straightened. She had even white teeth, the faintest scar on the curve on her right cheekbone, and a forthright way of speaking that shouldn't have appealed to him, but did. "You didn't wait for me, did you, darling?"

"No," she said softly, "as difficult as it may be for a Boscastle to believe. But let us not harbor ill feelings. I told you, I've forgiven you."

"And forgotten me?"

"Yes." She bit the edge of her lip. "Well, almost."

He moved aside. She brushed around him, her slender body so visibly tense that naturally he wished to soothe her.

"Perhaps I don't want to be forgotten," he said in an undertone, catching her elbow in his hand.

She laughed in disbelief. "Perhaps you don't have a choice."

"Are you challenging me?" he asked, his heavy-lidded gaze holding hers.

"Only if the weapons are either pistols or swords."

"Be careful with Chiswick, won't you?" he murmured as he released her arm. "I think you may be a little too much for him to control." He paused. "You might need a man with more practical experience."

She stared back at him with a faintly patronizing look. "As if I would take the advice of a rogue like you."

He laughed without the least offense. She might have convinced him of her disinterest had he not heard the faintest quaver in her voice. "Jocelyn, it is only because I'm a rogue that I am qualified to warn you."

"Adam is a perfect gentleman."

"That's the worst kind."

"What do you mean?" she asked guardedly.

"All the devilry builds up in that sort of man. Look at him. Right now I'll warrant he's seething inside like a volcano."

"Is that right?" she said with a cynical smile.

He schooled himself to look completely serious. "Trust me, if a man does not let a little steam escape here and there, he's liable to explode and give everyone around him a nasty burn."

"I dislike challenging your profound theory on the building of . . . passion, Devon, but not all men are as full of steam as you and your brothers."

"I could expound on the theory in private if you're interested," he said quietly.

"Before or after Lily Cranleigh?"

He hesitated, surprised but not about to admit that Lily had been the farthest thing from his mind. His unexpected encounter with Jocelyn had completely absorbed him.

"Consider my offer," he murmured, not certain himself what he meant but leaving the door open.

And finding it closed firmly in his face. "I don't wish to be hurt again," she replied with a rueful smile.

"And I don't wish to hurt you."

He rested his elbow up against the wall. Where he stood, he could almost feel the warmth of her shoulder and soft, enticing breasts. He imagined he could see the rim of a pink half-moon nipple beneath her gown, and even if it was only his imagination it made his mouth water. Her lips parted slightly, but the pattern of her breathing did not change.

She turned, then paused, glancing back at him. Their gazes met, engaged, withdrew. How innocent was she? he wondered curiously. Had she and Chiswick been lovers for long, or was this her initiation night?

Fernshaw's parties were famous for igniting torrid love affairs.

He shrugged off the thought. To whom she gave her virtue, or when, was certainly none of his affair. He had relinquished any claim he might have made on her four years ago.

"It was nice to see you again, Jocelyn. You really are more lovely than I remembered."

"Thank you for saying that, Devon," she retorted, her grin implying that they would at least part on amicable terms. "It's reassuring to know that you're a worse rogue than I remembered, too."

And that she had escaped him.

She didn't need to speak aloud the thought for him to guess that that was what she was telling herself. He smiled. She'd be right, too, God love her. He had not been a man for marriage four years ago, and he was less of one now.

Chapter Two

❦ ❧

Jocelyn could not fathom how a man's smile could offer such angelic beauty and unrepentant decadence in the same instant. Or why, knowing as she did what a licentious heart fate had so unfairly put in his magnificent frame, she would even feel the least attraction to the devil.

She told herself, as she had a hundred times over, to thank her lucky stars that Devon Boscastle had rejected her four years ago, thereby sparing her a lifetime of lonely tears and shame. Yes, she had cried when he hadn't accepted her father's invitation. But then so many dewy-eyed debutantes had secretly been in love with Devon. Perhaps deep inside her some wistful glimmer of that emotion would always linger.

But she wasn't sure she even believed in love. Too many years witnessing her parents' unhappy marriage had slowly crushed her hopes. It was terribly unbecoming for a woman to embrace such a cynical view of life, but her father's cruelty had eroded her most cherished hopes.

And once she had hoped to be Devon's bride.

It was perfectly obvious that the elusive sinner had not remedied his roguish ways one iota. It made her feel rather smug and mature to discover that she could flirt with him and walk away unaffected.

Well, at least he hadn't noticed that seeing him again had kicked her heart into an unsteady tempo.

Fortunately, her heart was beating quite evenly now, despite the fact that she had just glimpsed Lord Adam Chiswick at the end of the hallway. She turned and examined the Flemish tapestry that draped the wall.

She had come to the party, at her father's unexpected encouragement, to procure a wedding proposal. And Adam was the first man in years to earn Sir Gideon Lydbury's approval.

Her father was a man impressed with power and all the trappings of a privileged life. It appeared he had no intention of letting his age deter him. He escorted his lovers about London as an emblem of his prowess. He had desired a link to the Boscastle family several years ago, and he had courted the support of the marquess for both political and personal ends.

But to this day, Gideon had not forgotten the insult that Devon had given his daughter, nor had he allowed Jocelyn to forget it, either. In truth, he had dwelt on the rejection perhaps even more than she had.

When Devon had been caught last year after a bollixed attempt at holding up a courtesan's carriage during a misplayed prank, her father had gloated and predicted Devon's downfall to anyone who would listen. Especially to Jocelyn, who found herself a captive audience during their frequent carriage rides back and forth from the country.

"Did I not warn you he was the wildest of the family?" he would demand, forgetting that it was he who had chosen Devon as a potential husband, and not Jocelyn. "Are you not glad now that I did not force his hand?"

To which Jocelyn would merely sigh or nod, or do both simultaneously while gazing outside at a world whose freedom beckoned more by the day. Her father could be both emotionally and physically cruel. He did not strike her now as often as he had when she was very young, but he rarely restrained himself from verbal abuse.

It was evident that Jocelyn had no choice but to escape, and marriage was the most convenient option, even if she harbored no illusions about wedded bliss.

Adam had promised to give her a surprise before the end of Lord Fernshaw's party. Her closest friends predicted that he was about to tender a long-awaited marriage proposal. He'd only hinted at tying the knot before, but she suspected that he was ready to settle down. Quite frankly, she was ready to propose to him herself.

One of the advantages in having spent her debutante years as a wallflower was that she'd been allowed the time and opportunity to study the game of romance. She'd watched as several of her previously calm-headed friends had fallen prey to gentlemen on the prowl.

She might even have been the sort to succumb to seduction herself had her own father not been so blatantly unfaithful to his late wife, Jocelyn's mother. To Jocelyn's disgust he had continued conducting affairs up until and after her mother's death.

Even now he made no secret of the fact that he currently supported two mistresses, one of whom was expecting a child.

Another child. Still, no matter how cruel or shallow-minded he was, her father had never been a man to shirk responsibility, and she had to concede he'd done his blustering best to prepare Jocelyn for her future.

The best governesses. The best boarding schools. The best wardrobe. The best fiancé. Or second-best, the Boscastle he had chosen having delivered that unforgettable snub four years ago.

The second-best choice was suddenly attempting to sneak up behind her. And she was attempting to act surprised as Adam's arm encircled her waist and ungracefully spun her around.

"There you are," he whispered, burying his nose

in her hair. "Umm. You smell like blancmange. I think I shall have to go back to the table for dessert. Smelling you makes me hungry."

"Now that's a romantic confession," she said with a laugh. "Is that your tactful way of telling me I've spilled food on myself?"

"Have you?" His prominent chin brushed her cheek. "How disgusting you've become, Miss Lydbury. We shall have to buy you a bib and spoon-feed you before long."

She lifted her face to his, wrinkling her nose. He might not be as exciting as one of the Boscastle brothers, for which she ought to be grateful. He did not inspire her passionate instincts, and a proper young lady would not desire a suitor who did. But at least she could let down her guard in his company. And she trusted him. Adam was anything but a born heartbreaker.

He was not anything like Lord Devon Boscastle.

"When are you going to give me the surprise you promised?" she said softly.

"By no later than tomorrow morning."

She sighed. "Not sooner?"

"I doubt it."

She lowered her gaze. "What are you waiting for?"

"I can't tell you, but"—he leaned into her, his gray eyes darkening—"I *can* tell you that you'll be surprised."

She had the most horrible urge to laugh. He was trying to be so serious. But . . . How unfair it was that she found herself suddenly making a comparison between his unassuming pleasantness and the chiseled masculinity of a certain rogue. The mere fact of noting the difference between the two men made her feel as if she were betraying Adam. Could he help it if he was a little on the dull side? Was he to be faulted because he did not make her heart race?

"Are you going to kiss me like the other libertines at the party?" she whispered.

He hesitated. It was obvious he didn't know she was joking.

"Just how many libertines have you kissed?"

She would have teased him a little more, heaven knew he could be far too somber, had a deep and disturbingly familiar voice not drifted down the hallway.

"We seem to have interrupted a little tête-a-tête, Mrs. Cranleigh. Can you imagine? What a sight to shame our innocent eyes. A pair of lovebirds stealing pecks in the corner. Whatever is the world coming to when the young branches of the aristocracy have twisted in this abhorrent direction?"

"Don't be such a naughty tease, Devon," his female companion scolded, although Jocelyn was quick to perceive that there was more amusement than censure in her voice. "You'll embarrass them."

He cleared his throat. "Oh, very well. Who the blazes are they, anyway?

Jocelyn took a deep breath and turned. She was perfectly aware by the glitter in his eye that

Devon had recognized her. Adam, to her regret, appeared to have absolutely no idea that he was being baited. He separated from her with such alacrity that he nearly fell over the brass telescope propped against the wall.

"Chiswick," Devon said in such a disparaging voice that Jocelyn felt compelled to spring to Adam's defense. "You're every bit as graceless now as you were in fencing school."

"He isn't graceless at all," she said as Adam rather ungracefully straightened from his undignified stumble into the telescope.

"No?"

Devon's all-too-perceptive gaze assessed Adam's guilty expression and awkward stance until it was all Jocelyn could do not to give him an elbow. Why now, of all times, did he have to retreat behind that blank submission? He had been a courageous enough officer during the war. Why did Devon Boscastle's offhanded jab have to turn him into this . . . this tower of helpless treacle?

Instantly, she castigated herself for the unkind analogy. Picturing the man she intended to marry as a portion of incapacitated pudding felt like an act of perfidy. But, really, shouldn't he speak up for himself? Why did he allow Devon to unsettle him?

"I'm sorry, Boscastle," Adam finally said in a fashionably cool voice that Jocelyn could have applauded. "I had no idea you'd reserved this hallway for your personal use."

She beamed at him, whispering, "Well done."

Devon lifted his magnificently sculpted shoulders in a shrug of insouciance. "That's quite all right, Chiswick." His gaze cut straight to Jocelyn for a brief but meaningful moment. "I've already had my use of the hallway for the evening. I suppose it's only fair to share."

She turned her head to answer Adam's questioning stare. "I believe I'm ready for that breath of fresh air you mentioned."

"What breath—"

She nudged him forward and swept down the hall, resisting the urge to acknowledge Devon's grinning countenance. Mrs. Cranleigh gave her a wan smile. Jocelyn smiled back, despite the fact that she knew the widow had a reputation for wickedness that Devon Boscastle would surely exploit during the course of the party.

It was several steps later before she became aware that Adam had not accompanied her. She pivoted, drawing a sharp breath at the scene unfolding behind her.

Devon had evidently sidestepped Adam and taken him by the arm; his dark profile was superimposed over Adam's in an attitude of unmistakable mischief.

"Adam?" she asked evenly. "Are you accompanying me, or must I walk alone?"

He didn't answer. He was gazing up at Devon as if he'd just been given the Ark of the Covenant. The faintly awestruck grin on his face was off-putting. As was the realization of how, well, how short and stocky he appeared when standing in Devon's shadow.

Or was Devon so tall and leanly muscled that other men simply shrank in comparison?

She edged a few inches closer to eavesdrop on their conversation. Then promptly wished she hadn't.

"Remember," Devon was saying in an authoritative voice. "Firm hand. As a cavalry officer, I can say with assurance that's the secret, the only way to deal with her type." And he smacked one of his own strong hands into the palm of the other to demonstrate his point. "Firm hand when you bridle her. After she comes to trust you, you have to mount her as often as possible until she's broken in."

"Firm hand," Adam repeated.

"And mount her often."

Devon raised his head to regard Jocelyn with a gaze of imperturbable self-possession. "Do forgive us. We got caught up discussing our host's young Arabian mare. Chiswick has confided in me that he's considering purchasing her. I thought I might offer a few tips on how to break her in."

Adam flashed him a look of gratitude. "You remember that Devon also served in the cavalry, don't you?"

Jocelyn paused several heartbeats before answering. "*Yes*. But I don't recall *you* expressing an interest in Alton's Arabian."

"Well, a man doesn't always wish to discuss such indelicate details with a lady." Devon straightened in a way that seemed to diminish Adam by a few more inches. "After all, most women would rather chat about their frocks than horseflesh."

"Oh, Jocelyn likes horses well enough," Adam said with unwitting guile. "She's quite an expert equestrienne, you know. One could ask her almost anything about . . . about . . . "

She coughed loudly to stop him before he was lured any deeper into Devon's game. She could not believe how easily he'd let himself be caught, and with that blue-eyed satyr standing in the background as if he hadn't instigated the whole thing. The most perplexing part was that she'd never seen Adam so nonplussed before. He usually kept his wits about him; in fact, one of his best qualities was his ability to stand calm while all his male friends behaved like fools.

Devon Boscastle was obviously a bad influence. Judging by that unholy twinkle in his eye, Jocelyn had indeed escaped a dreadful fate when he had not appeared at her table all those years ago.

Any woman who married Devon would never know a moment's peace. But, a truly unwelcome voice whispered in the back of her mind, wouldn't that woman also know pleasure—and be willing to pay the price?

She expelled a sigh as Adam finally walked up

beside her. It wasn't his fault that he'd been made to look foolish. Devon had become a master of impropriety under the tutelage of his older brothers. Still, she expected more of the man she was to marry.

"Why *did* you let him play you like that?" she asked in an undertone as the two of them fell in step.

"Gracious, I've no idea. You aren't angry at me, are you, Jocelyn?"

She spared him a sidelong glance. He *was* attractive. He cared for her sensibilities. He was neither a scoundrel nor a gambler. A young lady could do far worse, and she didn't exactly have suitors lined up asking for her hand.

"No, I'm not angry."

And as they turned the corner to walk between two marble statues of Venus and Vulcan, she glanced back involuntarily at the man they had abandoned.

Devon Boscastle.

The destiny she had escaped—and wasn't she fortunate? He was the one who deserved her anger. With a few careless remarks he had made Adam appear weak and even a little slow-witted. Which wasn't at all a fair assessment of his character.

Adam halted without warning. "How rude of me," he said, pivoting. "Would you and Mrs. Cranleigh like to join us for a walk, Boscastle? Jocelyn has announced a need for some air."

"Oh, for heaven's sake," she muttered. "Don't go encouraging him. Doesn't the devil stand in wait for an invitation?"

"I'm only being polite," Adam whispered. "He stood up for me at school a few times. Kept the bullies at bay, you know."

No, she hadn't known. She hadn't really been willing to attribute any good qualities to Devon, who sauntered past her at that moment with a faint smile. "That's quite all right, Chiswick. Mrs. Cranleigh and I plan to exercise some other options this evening."

"Just listen to him," Jocelyn muttered. "No, don't listen."

"Did you say something, Miss Lydbury?" Devon inquired.

"She's got something stuck in her throat," Adam replied rather lamely. "One of those violet pastilles the girls use to sweeten their breath."

Devon raised his left hand. "Remember, Chiswick. Firm hand. Show her who's the master."

"Yes. I will."

"And mount her often."

Adam flushed brick-red and glanced edgewise at Jocelyn with a sheepish grin. Clenching her teeth, she grasped his arm to propel him forward.

"Do you still wish to walk with me in the garden?" he asked without looking at her.

"What do you think, Adam?"

"I—"

A few minutes later, their walk forgotten, they joined their friends in the main salon for champagne and an impromptu game of charades. Jocelyn and Adam naturally chose each other for partners and ended up putting on a pantomime of the balcony scene from *Romeo and Juliet*.

Jocelyn climbed the gallery above the salon and stood at the railing while Adam beseeched her with silent gesticulations from below. Of course, everyone guessed which characters they were pantomiming, but it was fun and even romantic to watch the pair of them play their parts until Adam tripped over a footstool and made his audience laugh, including Jocelyn.

She knew he was the perfect man for her. A clumsy Romeo who respected her was worth more than a hundred unreliable rogues and their indecent offers. And she could only hope that friendship would be a strong enough foundation for the solid marriage upon which she had set her heart.

Let the Lily Cranleighs of London engage in love affairs that were bound to come to a bad end.

Jocelyn aspired to a peaceful life herself. Marriage. Family. Security. Self-worth. Escape from her father's constant deprecations and insufferable conceit. There was no place in her dreams for a rogue no matter how much she had once wished it to be otherwise.

Chapter Three

※

Devon rested his shoulder against the enormous marble sculpture of a lion-drawn chariot that dominated the upper gallery. It was a secluded spot. He could stare down at the activity in the main salon all he wanted without being seen. A grin deepened the faint grooves that bracketed his mouth. He could even laugh out loud if he felt like it. And there was quite a bit to laugh about, actually.

Chiswick had just tripped backward onto his tailbone, the most inelegant Romeo in the history of amateur theatrics. Jocelyn had rushed down the stairs to his rescue. Devon's gaze idly followed her graceful descent.

His brow arched in amusement.

She was reaching down to put right the footstool that Adam had overturned. Adam was reaching out for . . . Jocelyn's rear end. Devon snorted as the man below gave her bum a covert pat. Well, well. Was Jocelyn going to slap him, shove him back onto the floor?

Devon leaned his forearms across the black-iron balustrade to watch. What would she do?

Nothing.

He shook his head. Perhaps she hadn't even felt Adam's sneaky pat. Perhaps it had been only an almost-fondling. A pat of the air, and not of Jocelyn's roundly shaped rump. Perhaps, he mused, Adam had interpreted that ineffective gesture to be what Devon had meant by a firm hand.

You'll never ride her at that rate, he thought woefully. And for an instant he indulged his imagination in what it would take to pleasure the aloof Jocelyn in bed. He'd wager he could find a way to make her take notice.

But could he make her forgive him, *truly* forgive him? Only now did it come back to him that the main reason he had refused that long-ago invitation was because he'd disliked her father and resented the man's air of arrogant command. Devon hadn't known Jocelyn well enough to say whether he'd enjoy her company or not.

He wondered how she managed to stand her ground in the face of Sir Gideon's dictatorial self-assertion. The soldiers who'd served under him despised the man, which did not necessarily make him a poor leader. But there had been whispers of cruelty under Gideon's command, suppressed, of course, before they could be substantiated.

It shouldn't matter to Devon one way or the other. It didn't really. Jocelyn appeared to be able to hold her own.

And hold Devon's interest, dammit. Why now of all times did that Boscastle instinct to both seduce and protect have to emerge and threaten to spoil the decadent fun he had planned? If Jocelyn needed protection at all, it was probably from men like himself.

He was wild at heart and thought it was too late to change.

He of all the Boscastle siblings had suffered the most from their mother's death and their father's shifting moods. Drake had borne the brunt of Royden Boscastle's physical outbursts. Devon had learned to play peacemaker at an early age, and if it had not been for the overpowering support of his brothers and sisters, he could easily have drifted through life without anchor, without attachment.

His soul had wandered afar for so long he did not hold hope it could be redeemed.

"Spying on something interesting?"

He glanced off to his side at Lily ascending the staircase, answering her with a grin. "The unplanned performance within the scheduled performance is one of the evening's memorable moments." He allowed his gaze to travel over her silk-swathed figure. "At least so far. I'm open to private play."

Lily came to stand beside him at the balustrade.

"Why are you going out of your way to show Chiswick in a poor light? It's not like you. Or am I mistaken?"

His grin deepened. "I don't have anything against old Chinny. I'm only making mock of him to vex Jocelyn."

She raised her fan and, like a duelist, directed it at his shoulder. "Why? What has she done to offend you?"

He deflected the fan with a flick of his wrist. "I don't know. Nothing, really, although her family has let it be well known that I've offended them."

"Is this a story I would enjoy?"

"I was asked to dinner years ago by Sir Gideon Lydbury in an obvious invitation to a courtship. Not only did I have the bad grace to fail to appear, but I completely forgot to send either an excuse or apology afterward. In fact, I went away."

"She did not appeal to you?" Lily asked with a skeptical smile.

"Marriage didn't appeal to me," he replied. "Nor does it to this day."

He moved away from the balustrade and began to walk down the corridor that connected the two staircases. He didn't feel like discussing his private life with Lily when he had not been able to understand it himself.

"So the two of you share a past," she mused, strolling a few steps behind his tall shadow. "A secret, hmm?"

He halted to laugh in mild amusement. "I'm more interested in present pleasures, such as who will be sharing my bed this weekend, and I don't think I've made a secret of that."

She made a languid half-turn, torchlight gilding her voluptuous form. Her posture suggested a calm indifference to his confession.

But he knew better.

She glanced up at the tiger skin stretched across the wall. "Do you like hunting?" she asked in a curious voice.

"Only when the game is wild and a match for my skill," he answered wryly.

She traced a tapered fingertip across the edge of her ivory fan. "That sounds positively . . ."

"Yes?"

"Fascinating."

"Does it?" he murmured, his gaze hooded.

For a moment neither of them said anything. Devon allowed the silence to expand before he added, "I believe this is the first uninterrupted conversation we've had since we met."

Her mouth lifted at the corners, and he noticed the fine lines etched on her flawless skin. She was said to be selective in her choice of lovers, highly sought after as a mistress by many titled men; and, as rumor went, was a woman who lost all her inhibitions under the sheets. The fact that neither of them were liable to fall in love with the other made her even more attractive.

"The first time I saw you," she said, her tone

sultry and teasing, "was at a picnic. I asked our hostess for an introduction, but you mysteriously disappeared before it could be made. I was told only that you were Drake Boscastle's little brother, and that this fact alone should serve as my warning to pursue you at my peril."

"Then you should also have been warned that there's nothing little about me," he said with an engagingly honest smile.

Her lips parted. Her full breasts lifted beneath the bodice of her high-waisted gray silk gown. Before either of them could speak again, the thud of footsteps on the stairs spoiled the mood.

Devon exhaled in irritation, not only because he'd been interrupted at a provocative moment, but because the intruder was Jocelyn's older brother, Colonel Jason Lydbury. His thin lips curled into a faint sneer as he recognized Devon. He was a broad-chested, attractive man in military uniform who favored his bullish father in appearance.

And, apparently, in his dislike of Devon. God, the Lydbury family was even worse for holding grudges than the wild Boscastle brood.

"Well, isn't this a shock?" Jason said as he glanced from Devon to Lily. "A Boscastle brother cornering the prettiest lady at the party."

Devon's eyes darkened in warning.

Lily's gaze kindled with wicked humor. "If only I had thought to bring my aunt."

"She would most likely not be safe from

seduction either, madam," Jason said in a dry voice. He gave Devon a look of subdued disapproval. "You see, there appear to exist even among the aristocracy certain noblemen who do not think twice about giving a lady personal insult."

Ah, another reminder of how Devon had slighted Jason's sister. He released a sigh and offered Lily his arm. "It seems I have forgotten my manners again. May I escort you to the refreshment room?"

"Very well." She lowered her gaze in demure acceptance only to look up again in alarm as another woman hurriedly arose from the stairs to enter the hall. "Goodness," she murmured in resignation. "I believe the party has come to meet us."

This time the interloper was Jocelyn, her cheeks faintly pink, her eyes dark with an unreadable array of emotions. Except for the glance of naked reproach she threw Devon's way.

He grinned back at her. He didn't know why, but he seemed suddenly compelled to prove that her low opinion of him was well-deserved. Or to prove to himself that he was not only lethal to a young lady like her, but that he'd done her a great service by staying out of her life.

"Is there a matter of urgency?" Jason asked her, his mouth tight with censure.

Jocelyn cast a curious look at Lily. Devon could have sworn it was an age-old assessment of female rivalry, even though there was no comparison between them. Lily was a fleeting pleasure. Jocelyn was, well, too sweet and unsophisticated for him to spoil. "I was wondering if anyone had seen Lord Chiswick," she said.

"Why?" Devon asked, unable to resist teasing her. "Is his mother looking for him?"

Jocelyn refused to acknowledge the remark. "Adam and I were supposed to play Devil's bones upstairs. We were just together and then he disappeared."

"Oh, dicing." Lily straightened, her lush body brushing Devon's hip with a lingering pressure he knew was no accident. "How fun. I do love to play."

"So do I," he said very softly so that only she could hear him. "But at a private table. Name the time and place."

And then, he didn't know why he did it, but he glanced past her to where Jocelyn stood watching the exchange with an expression of barely veiled scorn in her wide brown eyes. She couldn't possibly have heard him, although by her look she appeared to have guessed he was not discussing throwing dice with Lily. It made him want to laugh.

Mrs. Cranleigh herself did not deign to respond to his remark. There was no need. Her acceptance had been understood the moment he'd laid eyes on her. He had only to wait for her to summon him. And he felt confident he would not be waiting long.

* * *

Sir Gabriel Boscastle, officer and self-confessed imperfect gentleman, arrived at the party during the late supper-dance. It was his first invitation to Lord Fernshaw's affair, although his more sought-after Boscastle cousins topped the guest list every year.

Alas, his dark nemesis Drake Boscastle would not be here for Gabriel to provoke. Drake and his governess bride apparently planned to enjoy their marriage bed for an indefinite period. Not that Gabriel blamed his cousin. Resent him, yes. But not having Drake to wheedle did take the fun out of bedevilment.

In light of Drake's retirement from the wicked life, however, Gabriel had no choice but to compete and sin with the remaining unmarried Boscastles. Oddly enough he was finally beginning to relish his role as the rival outsider. His entrée into the London world of his notorious family had unlocked endless avenues of entertainments previously denied him.

And he intended to enjoy them, one hedonistic pleasure at a time.

His demeanor detached, he allowed a maidservant to draw his black woolen coat off his shoulders. The lingering approval in her eyes assured him he would not have to spend the night alone. He gave her a beguiling smile that promised everything and nothing at the same time.

"Will that be all, sir?" she asked.

"For now."

As he strode from the vast entry hall, she stood clutching his coat while another maid hurried to her side to pepper her with questions about the party's latest handsome arrival.

"Two Boscastle men at the same time," one of them whispered, loud enough for him to hear. "It's too much for my heart to bear."

Gabriel laughed.

Certainly he had nothing against sleeping with a maid, but he had not driven all the way to Essex to tumble his host's servants. His sights were set on a rather more challenging goal: the seduction of Lily Cranleigh. The fair widow had made it known that she desired sex, and protection, but not within the bondage of marriage. Nor did she require wealth. Her late husband had left her material needs well-satisfied. She bestowed the same sexual legacy on her lovers.

Of course, the fact that Devon Boscastle was known to desire her only heightened her appeal in Gabriel's view. He might not have even been interested in bedding her had Devon not announced his intentions to make her his mistress. Gabriel sometimes thought he needed rivalry to survive.

He did not even bother to glance back to see if the maidservant had followed him; his gaze had sharpened on another woman's lusciously curved silhouette and spill of brown-gold hair. Not Lily, but definitely a possibility for the next few days.

This young lady had an inborn air of the unattainable that challenged him; he'd bet his miserable soul they'd never met. And who was the stiff-lipped behemoth of a man she kept stealing peeps at? God help him. It wasn't Chiswick, was it? The cavalry officer who looked like a veritable caveman, but who faithfully visited his grandmama every other Sunday.

"The widow is mine, by the way. How are you, Gabriel?"

He half-turned to acknowledge the deep-voiced greeting that drifted over his shoulder. He was not at all surprised to see that it had been issued by his cousin Devon Boscastle. Could it be that Drake's younger brother had picked up the gauntlet of friendly rivalry that had fallen between Gabriel and Drake? They insulted each other to no end. They competed for the same ladies. But God help the man who threatened a Boscastle.

He lifted his shoulders in a guileless shrug. "Have you staked a claim?" he asked innocently, knowing full well that he had. Everyone in London had been talking about Devon and Lily when he'd left.

"Ask her," Devon said, grinning.

A smile of arrogant self-assurance settled on his cleanly sculpted features; it occurred to Gabriel that Devon might be the youngest male in the immediate line, but he was every bit as full of the devil as his brothers.

Playful, mischievous Devon always ensnared in one scandal or another, known for his peace-making charm and sexual prowess. It really wouldn't be wise for a man to underestimate a rival. And Gabriel had learned early in his life to watch his back.

"She's mine," Devon added with a certainty that the rake in Gabriel could only admire. After all, he and Dev were blood relations, but—

"Do you care to wager whose bed the widow warms first?" he asked before he could stop the impulse.

Devon cut him a challenging glance that confirmed Gabriel's suspicions. For all his reputation as a youthful proponent of Eros, Devon appeared more than ready to carry on his brothers' infamy.

"I'm game if you wish to waste your bet." Devon gave him a friendly clap on the shoulder that would have sent a weaker man staggering.

Gabriel held his ground, laughing in genuine anticipation. He had nothing to lose and, despite himself, he had always liked Devon, a fact that would not in any way deter him from doing everything in his power to win their wager. "You're on."

Devon had just dismissed his valet for the evening when he spied the note that had been slipped under his bedroom door. He debated going out in the hall to catch the messenger, then decided against it. Secret notes passed between admirers were not an unusual occurrence at a sophisticated Society affair.

Pranks and impromptu little parties within the main house party were the primary reason most of the haut ton guests attended in the first place, although no one would ever admit it.

He had tactfully declined a handful of discreet offers over the course of the supper-dance. His last conversation with Lily had left him with no doubt that her capitulation was at hand. The fact that Gabriel desired her did not matter one way or the other.

And it wasn't as if either man were in love with her. Or that she loved either of them.

He'd thought, however, that she might withhold her surrender for at least another day. In Devon's experience, a slow prelude to sex usually made a lady's surrender all the more enjoyable. He was a man who liked to savor his lover's every sigh, and he valued friendship and trust as well as passion.

Still, he wasn't about to offend Mrs. Cranleigh by playing coy when the following week promised such unbridled pleasure.

And yet to his surprise it wasn't Lily's obvious charm that came to his mind. Another unbidden temptation stirred, refusing to be ignored. A woman whose wide brown eyes had regarded him with amused distrust. A woman he had let slip through his fingers years ago and, tonight, ironically, had made his fingers ache for the chance to touch her.

Jocelyn Lydbury did *not* belong at a party like this, he thought. Adam was a poor excuse for a protector. In fact, if he'd been doing a proper job of guarding her, he would never have left her alone for even a minute with a rogue like Devon.

Crossing the room, he bent to pick up the folded paper and to break open the still-soft seal. The carefully worded message confirmed his belief that the lady was even more impatient for a night of lovemaking than her coquetry at the party had let on.

My dear Devil,

We are both old enough to admit and yet young enough to act upon our desires. Despite my reputation, I am a private woman at heart. If your pursuit of my attention is more than a fleeting temptation, meet me tonight at a quarter past midnight in the east tower where we shall enjoy privacy to reveal our true intentions.

I trust that I have not misread your interest.

Will you wear your infamous domino for me?

L

The paper bore the rather overpowering scent of lilies, her namesake fragrance, but oddly not a perfume that she had ever worn in his company. It seemed a little unsubtle to drench an invitation in cologne when she'd been leading him on a chase for over a month.

He dropped the letter on the desk on his way to the oak armoire. Casually he removed his long-tailed evening jacket in favor of the domino—the highwayman's black hooded cloak and half-mask—that had rendered him one of London's favorite scandals. He wasn't sure whether Alton meant for a masquerade to be part of this year's entertainment, but Devon had brought the costume along in case.

He should have expected that Lily Cranleigh would find his short-lived career as a highwayman an aphrodisiac. She had made several references to his past in their conversations. Still, who would have thought that a single regrettable interlude could ignite so many fantasies in the hearts of women scattered throughout England, most of whom he'd never met?

He shook his head in amused resignation. So much for impressing the ladies with his subtle wit and well-earned reputation for sexual inventiveness. It hardly seemed fair that he should reap continued profits for committing a crime he would prefer to forget.

But the fact remained. His masked counterpart had brought many an aloof lady to her knees, which only went to prove that there really was no rest unto the wicked.

Or unto the Boscastles if one chose to recognize the difference.

Chapter Four

It seemed to take Jocelyn forever to wend her way through the lonely castle hallways, then up a steep staircase to reach the east tower. The sounds of revelry in the west wing grew faint; the piping notes of a flageolet echoed poignantly in the dark. When she had first received Adam's note a few hours earlier, she'd thought the notion of a midnight summons sounded romantic and adventurous.

Who would have guessed her proper suitor capable of such a passionate gesture?

Or that he'd make her venture such a long way to reach their rendezvous. Lord, she must have traveled a mile across the interior courtyards of the castle before beginning the strenuous climb up this stone staircase.

It went without saying that if a proposition to tryst in the tower had come from any of the other young men at the party, she wouldn't have been the least bit tempted to accept. No one had ever tendered her such a wicked offer before.

Which was what made his invitation to meet in secret all the more irresistible. To judge by his spidery handwriting, he was as nervous about an illicit encounter as she was. But Adam was both a brave officer and an honorable man, and he'd hinted that he intended to ask for her hand at the house party. Had she not been convinced that a marriage proposal was in the offing, she would have flung his invitation in his face. Though privately, Jocelyn was a little pleased that he was showing this reckless streak. Never once had she guessed that such a lively spark smoldered beneath his endearing predictability.

And he'd asked her to wear a mask to protect her from being identified on the way here, bless his upbringing as a gentleman. At least he'd chosen a spot where they were unlikely to be discovered by a wandering houseguest.

A very secluded spot.

A little too secluded for their first rendezvous.

But they were going to be married. It made a difference, she assured herself. All was well that ended well.

Suddenly she stood before the tall arched doorway of the tower. Anxiety had begun to diminish her sense of anticipation. What if she and Adam were caught? They'd be forced to rush into their marriage, and she would not be able to have the fairy-tale wedding of which she'd dreamed. It might not be the end of her life, but it certainly would be an embarrassment. She'd never done anything like this in her life.

Before she could change her mind about proceeding with the rendezvous, the door swung open and she found herself gazing into the room. Her first impression was of a dark-clad figure standing against a backdrop of even darker shadows. Scant moonlight filtered through the single leaded window.

"Be careful," warned a baritone voice that sounded familiar and yet strangely more masculine than Adam's—except on the infrequent occasions when he gave his impression of Wellington as a party favor.

She lifted her hand self-consciously to her mask. It was surprising to discover how attractive Adam appeared in the dark. The shadowy backdrop made him appear manly and a bit menacing, in an oddly appealing way. "It's as black as—"

An iron grip closed around her wrist and drew her effortlessly into the room. The door shut behind her with a heavy thud that reverberated in the silence. She half-stumbled, then felt herself steadied by that firm grasp again.

"This was a hell of a place to meet," he remarked drily, his mouth against her cheek. "There isn't even a bed to—"

"A bed?" she whispered.

His voice. It sounded, well, heavens above, no wonder his voice was so unexpectedly deep and muffled, he was wearing not only a mask but a handsome black hooded cloak that swathed him from head to mid-calf. And he must be wearing a new pair of boots that boosted his height. She had to admit she was secretly delighted by his daring getup. Adam didn't seem at all himself. Had the costume brought out his masculinity? His masterful side? A side that she had not dreamed existed?

She would never have guessed a disguise could make such a difference.

His big intrusive body walked her backward against the wall. She drew a deep breath as he demanded, "Am I going to have to take you prisoner? Or do you surrender yourself to me without a struggle?"

She giggled in disbelief. "*What?*"

"Do you want to pretend you're my hostage?" he asked in an amused whisper. "I didn't have enough notice to make preparations for your captivity." He turned his head as if assessing the dark. "I suppose there might be a tapestry tassel I could use to subdue you."

His voice. A shiver ran through her. Oh, dear God. When had Adam sounded so thrillingly wicked?

"Subdue? Your *hostage?*"

"It might be uncomfortable on this cold stone floor, but I can lay my cloak beneath you," he said gallantly, as if he'd participated in dozens of trysts before. "Would you like me to tie you by the wrists or by the ankles?"

His voice. Her throat closed. She wondered if this was the start of a swoon. Tie her . . . by the wrists or the ankles? She could not have heard him correctly. He had *not* asked such a question.

"Or both?" he offered rather politely. "Bondage is one of my favorite games, but I'm all for pleasing you."

"You did *not* just say you intend to bind me with a tassel," she said in a low-pitched voice.

"A tisket. A tassel. What does it matter? Just as long as we don't leave telltale marks on that lovely flesh. We don't want anyone at the party to guess what we were playing."

"Who are you?" she whispered, the words raw in her throat.

"You're not allowed to know my identity," he answered in a stage whisper. "Isn't that what you wanted? To be taken by a stranger?"

She shook her head, shivering again. She could not decide whether her befuddlement stemmed from shock or from the fact that his gloved fingers had set off in a wandering foray down her cheek to her shoulders, only to dip in the valley of her breasts and wickedly circle her nipple. A wave of faintness swept over her.

The hooks and eyes of her gown, which had taken the house maid a dedicated quarter-hour to fasten, sprang open as if by a wizard's touch. A breath of cold air mingled with the whispering touch of warm leather to caress her skin.

Half-naked, she thought. A man in masquerade had just loosened her gown and stroked her breasts. And her body had responded. Her nipples tightened into tingling points. Her voice unsteady, she said, "This game has gone too far."

"Then I'll play whatever game pleases you," he replied, his firm mouth stealing down her mouth to the tops of her breasts. "Do you want me to hold you up, or hold you down? I could have chosen a place better suited to passion, by the way. What made you want to meet me in the tower?"

That voice. It did not belong to Adam, muffled or not. Nor did the knowing touch that teased her breasts before sliding down her belly to the moist hollow below where she only touched herself when—

"You aren't Adam," she said; her bones seemed to dissolve the instant she spoke the words, even though somewhere deep inside she'd known it from the moment he'd taken her into his arms. No disguise could change a man from a gentleman to a devil.

He hesitated, irony vibrating in his low velvet voice. "And you're clearly not Lily Cranleigh, although I don't think I'll hold that against you."

"Lily?" she echoed faintly.

"I'm flattered, actually, that you went to all this

trouble to arrange a tryst. But if you desired me, angel, there wasn't any need for deception. I would have most likely come out of curiosity. Or to satisfy yours."

"I don't know what you're talking about," she whispered.

"Unless intrigue is the element that excites you," he added.

His eyes glinted as if to mock her through the slits of his mask. A gasp rose in her throat. The next thing she knew he was bending her backward, over his sinewy forearm in a position of subjugation. The steel-hard muscles of his thighs tightened and locked her to him. He angled his body closer until she felt his shaft thicken against her belly.

His hard mouth descended on hers in a deep, devastating kiss that would have silenced her had she been capable of putting two words together in a coherent sentence. Indeed, she was submerged in too many sensations to wage a defense. She wanted . . . wanted whatever his hands and mouth were doing. Gentle. Ruthless. Irresistible. A stranger and yet someone strangely known to her in the midnight shadows. He kissed her throat, her shoulders, then slid his mouth lower to suckle the tips of her breasts.

Oh, the pleasure. The sinful yet sweet pain that speared her belly and aroused a physical craving she ached to satisfy. She felt moisture seep from between her legs, warm, shameful, slick.

Somewhere in her mind she insisted he stop, but the plea was never voiced; she couldn't decide if she was submitting to his skill or was too stunned to mount a resistance.

There was little doubt that he knew how to take advantage of her indecision. His hard mouth swept back up her breasts to her throat, then to her lips for a kiss that arrested her thoughts. Not Adam. Not Adam, she told herself as he drew her down onto the floor—or had her bones collapsed? She only knew she was falling.

What in heaven's name was he doing? No, it wasn't a heavenly thing at all. It was earthly and burning-all-over wicked. Perhaps it would be better not to ask herself what he had in mind—his motives were flagrantly obvious even to one of her unimpeachable past.

"Come apart for me," he whispered. He blew his warm breath on her wet aching nipples and laid his cheek against her breast. "Give me everything you have."

Something inside her wanted to obey him. Some incautious part of her wanted to blame her breathless disequilibrium on the darkness that engulfed them. But even the darkness did not allow her to continue pretending that the strong body molded to hers belonged to the man she had come here to meet.

It was time to unmask the impostor who had taken his place.

* * *

Devon could not remember a time when he'd been as aroused by this sort of game. She was panting softly, gasping for breath as if she had never been kissed before. Now that he thought about it, there was an awkwardness in the way she moved against him that broke through his dark haze of desire. Or was she moving *away* from him?

He closed his eyes and summoned all his control. He'd heard that the widow liked sex hard, fast, and uninhibited. As a matter of personal preference, Devon enjoyed extended hours of nuance and foreplay; he was a tease who excelled at making his mate moan and quiver before completion. Naturally, he could adapt to please. He could play it Lily's way if that excited her.

Except that the woman quivering in his arms was not Lily Cranleigh, and he knew it.

Her scent. Her voice. He recognized her, and he didn't. Her genuine but passionate response to him did not in any way remind him of the sophisticated bed partner he had sought. Yet she had invited him here. Had she been afraid to sign the invitation with her own name? Had she feared her note might fall into the wrong hands? Or that he might not be amenable to a tryst if he knew her identity beforehand?

It didn't really matter. She was trembling deliciously in his arms. She had desired him enough to risk this rendezvous, and he knew how to handle the rest.

"Let's do away with our masks, shall we?" he murmured. "As a matter of fact, let's do away with the dress you're wearing."

"It's *you*," she said in a strangled voice.

"Of course it's me," he murmured.

Jocelyn did not need to ask his name. Mask or no mask, she knew.

Who in attendance at the house party was devious enough to lure her to the tower using a respectable gentleman's name? Who but a master of immorality and subtle persuasion would not only have dared, but succeeded?

"Devon Boscastle." She stared up into his beguiling face as he wrenched off his hood and removed his mask. His beautiful mouth quirked into a grin.

"Jocelyn." He added insult to injury by breaking into laughter. "It is *you*."

"Of course it's me," she said, straightening indignantly. "As if you hadn't lured me here."

"This is a pleasant shock," he said, and he meant it. "I had no idea you desired me, or that you were such a naughty girl at heart."

"I don't," she said quickly. "I'm not."

Devon studied her in bemusement, not certain whether he should continue their game or run for his life. Now that he'd gotten a taste of what he had blithely refused in the past, he wanted the pleasure of her, although not the inevitable repercussions that came with seducing a young lady of her inexperience. He'd thought she hadn't taken his offer earlier in the evening at all seriously. If he'd known, well, he would have insisted they meet in a better place.

But the look on her face warned him that she hadn't expected their tryst to go this far. As surprisingly desirable as he found her, he wasn't sure he appreciated being summoned to the tower under false pretenses himself. Of course, she could talk him into going further if she really tried. He wasn't a man to hold a grudge against a lady, especially one as tempting as she was.

Her voice broke into his reverie. "How could you be so arrogant and underhanded as to lure me here under false pretenses?"

He lifted his brow in surprise. "For what purpose would I lure you?"

"Don't make me say it, Devon. It's too embarrassing." She rubbed her forearms briskly. "I mean, a lady could hardly admit such thoughts aloud, and your actions have spoken quite clearly what I find impossible to describe."

He snorted. "But a lady can lure and be lured to the tower for a tryst?"

"Then you admit it," she said in triumph.

"I admit nothing of the sort. And do stop shivering in that disconcerting manner. If I were going to eat you up, I would have done so by now."

"I'm not shivering because I'm afraid of you," she retorted, lowering her hands. "It happens to be as cold as a crypt up here."

"Why are you here, anyway?" he asked, his voice sharp with reproach.

"Not for the purposes you intended, I assure you."

He looked at her for several moments, then started to laugh. "I thought you invited me to meet you."

She widened her eyes. "One of us has clearly come uncorked. Did you, or did you not, attempt to debauch me only a minute ago?"

"All right," he admitted easily. "I attempted to seduce you. May I point out, in my own defense, that you did not exactly wage the Battle of Armageddon to stop me?"

She opened her mouth to object, but all that emerged was a rather incoherent croak. She *hadn't* put up a fight. She would be a ninny-hammer to protest her participation after the fact.

"Well, I didn't know it was *you*," she said finally, and that, at least, was the irrefutable truth.

He shrugged, then proceeded to further confound her by stating, "I didn't know it was you, either."

"Let me assure you that I have never placed myself in such distressing circumstances before."

He gave her an infuriating smile. "Then what did you want?"

"What I wanted—what I want," she said, backing awkwardly to the door, "is to pretend that this never happened."

"I think that's a good idea."

"Thank you," she said.

"You're welcome."

"And good-bye. Again."

"Wait." He blew out a sigh and placed his large hand over hers before she could open the door. "Allow me."

"Allow you to what?" she asked suspiciously.

"To make certain it's safe for you to go."

"It certainly isn't safe for me to stay here with you," she said, moving out of his way. "It—"

"Hush a moment. I hear something."

She averted her face. What he most likely heard was the irregular thumping of her heart. What a devious man he was. What an unabashed blackguard. She crossed her arms tightly across her unhooked bodice as he made a pretense of pressing his ear to the oaken door. Henceforth, even the air he breathed must be regarded with suspicion.

"Dammit," he muttered.

She began the complicated business of rehooking the back of her gown, no small feat in the dark with neither a maid nor mirror to guide her hands.

To think she had been lured here in the hope of a proper marriage proposal. To think she had let him— No, that did *not* bear thinking about.

Adam would understandably regard this dalliance in deceit with horror should he learn of it. He might even take it upon himself to challenge

Devon to a duel. If Jocelyn did not do away with him first.

A possibility that was tempting her more by the moment.

The object of her homicidal musings straightened abruptly, his voice edged with a contagious disquietude. "I hear someone coming up the stairs."

"Well, bolt the door again," she said urgently.

And just as urgently he replied, "There isn't a bolt, in case you hadn't noticed."

She backed away from him in panic. "How could I have noticed? I was being held up by a highwayman. 'Tie me up or—'"

"Damnation," he muttered, his voice deep and unsettling.

"Don't stand there swearing," she whispered. "Do something helpful. Hide."

He flung her a frown of annoyance. "What a brilliant strategy. Do you have any suggestions as to where?"

"There has to be a cupboard, or a wardrobe in here." Her gaze settled on a low bulky trunk against the wall. "That's a chest over there. Come on."

They moved forward as one and bent simultaneously to pry open the brass-hinged lid, staring down dubiously into a space that would not have contained Devon's head and shoulders, let alone his lanky frame.

"Perhaps if you curled up into a little ball like a

hedgehog," she said, biting her lip. Of course, he'd be decapitated and dismembered in the process, but that was not her concern.

He dropped the lid in disgust. "Even if I could fit, you'd have to explain what you were doing alone in the tower. Did you tell anyone you were meeting me?"

Her voice rose. So, unfortunately, did the sound of approaching footsteps.

"How could I tell anyone I was meeting you when I did not know it myself? I was deceived into this tryst."

"That makes two of us, doesn't it?"

"What if it's Adam?" she asked, staring at the door in dread.

"Adam might be preferable to certain other parties that come to mind," he retorted.

"Oh, forgive me. Perhaps it's only Lily, the other woman you meant to seduce tonight. Did you invite her here, too?"

"I never invited anyone," he said curtly. "And we'll be damned lucky if it's either of them."

She swallowed. Her panic seemed to be escalating while he grew calmer, or perhaps he had already resigned himself to whatever would come. Perhaps to him this was an everyday occurrence.

"A footman, do you think?" she whispered. "Lord Fernshaw's footmen patrol the hallways at all hours during a party. I don't think any of his staff would dare interrupt a . . . whatever this is. Do you?"

He did not answer her. He was, in fact, preparing his defense against the inevitability of whatever unprecedented misfortune might come through the door. He couldn't put his finger on it, but his truest instincts, the deep-seated ones that had saved his backside more than once during battle, forewarned him that there were far more demonic forces at work than dutiful footmen.

"Please, Devon," Jocelyn said, seemingly sensing disaster, too. "Do something. I cannot be discovered in your company."

"I don't particularly wish to be discovered in yours."

"It takes two to tryst, you know."

"Just remember you said that."

"I'm not liable to forget anything about this night."

He strode past her to the window; the tall canted panes had been too slender to permit an escape even during Jacobean days, and they weren't about to widen now. He banged his fist on one of the leaded seams, but the glass did not shatter.

He turned and stared at her.

No matter how desirable she had proved to be a few minutes ago, this was the woman who would most likely deliver his coup de grâce, and some would say it was a belated and fitting stroke of fate.

Her. *Her.* Of all the women to end up with. For what purpose would she have played this trick on him? Had it been four years in the making? He'd flirted with her earlier, expressed his interest in her as a woman. Had she sent him the note to meet her but been afraid to sign her name?

If he'd known she'd wanted to see him alone, he wouldn't have refused, but he would have made sure it was in a place of his choosing.

Except she denied she'd wanted to meet him at all. And suddenly he wondered if her father had contrived to bring this about. Revenge. Entrapment.

"Here," he said roughly, and reached her in two swift strides to make haste of restoring the hooks she had not been able to reach at her back. He felt her tremble in reaction to his touch and swore inwardly. No matter the outcome of this situation, she as a woman would come out the worst.

She raised her face to his. "I *can't* be caught with you."

"It's too late," he said more dispassionately than he meant to, stepping in front of her. "You should have thought of that before you invited me to meet you here." He should have thought of it, for that matter. But then no one would care if he and Lily were caught in the act.

"I did not—"

The door opened. It wasn't a footman. It was far worse. Jocelyn's brother appeared before them, a candle in hand. He glanced from his sister's grave countenance to Devon, who strove to present himself as . . . as an innocent bystander?

He grimaced inwardly. As if such a stance were remotely possible, or even true. Whether Devon cared to admit it or not, he had known that those had not been Lily's overlarge, over-scented breasts he'd kissed with unforgivable ardor during what had suddenly begun to feel like a lifetime ago.

Another life. His past life. Well, there was nothing to be done for it.

"This," Jason announced when it seemed he had found the voice to underscore his look of shock, "is even worse than what I had imagined."

"Isn't it, though?" Devon asked.

Jason shook his head in bewilderment. "I had deceived myself into believing that even you were more principled than this, Devon. As for you, Jocelyn. I can only say that I have never felt such shame."

"Who told you where to find me?" she asked in a clipped voice.

"Never mind that. It's not something I wish to discuss with either of you."

"Why the bloody hell not?" Devon demanded. "I insist that you at least enlighten me, as I seem to be in the dark."

"You're not in a position to be insisting on anything," Jason said with disdain, then apparently reconsidered and reached into his vest pocket to produce, with dramatic flourish, the folded paper that bore a suspicious resemblance to the one Devon had received earlier in the evening.

"Voilà," Jason said in a tight voice.

"*Voilà* what?" Devon asked in annoyance.

"You wrote this invitation to your rendezvous, didn't you? I discovered it on my sister's dressing table."

"I didn't write anything," Devon replied, his voice unrepentant. "I was the one invited here, if the truth be told."

Jason stole a glance at his sister. "Jocelyn, perhaps you could explain this disturbing situation."

"Isn't it obvious?" She hazarded an indignant look in Devon's direction.

He would have laughed had he not had a sense of how this would end. He knew how it must look. The only thing obvious, unfortunately, was Jocelyn's vaguely tousled and all-too-tempting appearance.

And Devon's cloak. Lord love him, she was standing in the middle of it, and any attempt to retrieve it on his part would only serve to justify Jason's concerns—as justifiable as those concerns were. Even if Devon had not invited her to meet him, he'd have been perfectly willing to continue their encounter had they not been interrupted. She'd made him absolutely wild, out of his senses.

"I was misled into coming here," she said. She sounded so believable that Devon was grudgingly forced to concede that they had most likely both been deceived.

"It appears the two of us were misled," he said darkly.

She gave a huff of breath.

"All I know," she continued, "is that I was given to believe I was meeting Adam in the tower."

Devon rubbed his face. God, he'd been seducing her, and she'd thought he was Chiswick?

Jason acknowledged this statement with a cynical shrug. "Except that Adam is not here. He is, in fact, at this very distressing moment leading a search for you throughout the castle."

"And all I know," Devon interjected, feeling more compelled by the minute to defend himself, "was that I was led to believe I was meeting Mrs. Cranleigh."

"Who also is not present," Jason murmured, his brow creased in speculation. "Be that as it may, however, it does not explain why Jocelyn is standing upon your cloak, Boscastle. The male mind leaps to a rather unsavory conclusion."

There ensued a stretch of bleak silence that might have extended even longer had not a commotion arisen from behind the partially opened door.

Voices resounded from the tower stairs, voices babbling in concern, in excitement. A veritable Tower of Babel, Devon thought, and futilely wished for a large goblet of wine, preferably laced with some swift but gentle-acting poison, and a bench to collapse upon so that he could meet his demise in comfort.

But the Fates, whose benevolence Devon had taken for granted until this night, seemed to have withdrawn their favor, for one masculine voice predominated. Devon did not immediately identify it, although Jocelyn and her brother appeared to respond all too clearly. Their faces reflected a mutual horror that brought to his mind those friends who, during the war, had survived death and sworn that at the crucial moment, various scenes from their lives had passed before their eyes like the acts of a play.

Indeed, as the door was pushed fully open, Devon thought the tableau bore all the markings of a Shakespearean tragedy. Or comedy. Or both.

Sir Gideon Lydbury approached his daughter in utter silence. He was a handsome man, silver-haired, his trim body betraying little effects of his age. He did not raise his voice in anger. He did not curse, which Devon might have mistaken as an encouraging sign had he not sensed otherwise.

"I might have expected to find you involved, Boscastle."

Devon unflinchingly returned his stare. "Then I wish you had warned me in advance. I had no premonition of this myself."

"It was a misunderstanding," Jocelyn said. "We did not meet—"

Sir Gideon turned, his hand upraised to strike her, and something broke inside Devon. Discipline was one thing, and his own sire had certainly never spared Devon's back the rod. But to hit a woman in rage, well, it made him want to hit someone himself.

Unfortunately, that someone happened to be Jocelyn's father, who most likely thought his action merited. Suddenly it seemed irrelevant to Devon how he or Jocelyn had become ensnared in this situation. He might waver back and forth over believing her claim of complete innocence. Perhaps she was pulling a prank because— He couldn't think of a strong enough reason she would play this game unless she sought revenge for a past insult.

But a calculated vengeance of this nature after so many years seemed not only implausible but more underhanded than he could fairly attribute to her. Even if she had willfully befooled him, she was still a member of the weaker sex, and his natural instincts to defend her overwhelmed his less worthy proclivities.

"Don't touch her." He blocked the older man's hand with his right arm and raised his left to shield Jocelyn's face from the impending blow.

Not that she appreciated the gesture. She dealt his arm a good shove off to the side and swung around him to confront her father, although the quiver in her voice made him doubt that this was the first time she'd had to defend herself against abuse. Her brother, he noticed, did nothing to protect her.

"Would you punish me before others?" she asked, a question that prompted Devon to wonder how far her father's reputation for corporal punishment extended beyond disciplining soldiers. He waited for her to ask him to intervene.

Sir Gideon slowly lowered his hand, ignoring her to glare at Devon. "I interpret your action in thwarting me as not only an admission of guilt, but as one of accepting responsibility."

The strange glow of triumph in his eyes refreshed Devon's earlier suspicion that Gideon had set this trap. But . . . no, it still did not make sense. This whole plot reeked of a more personal reprisal.

He lifted his head and answered with austere resignation. "It was my fault. I deceived her into thinking there was to be a treasure hunt in the tower."

Jocelyn stared at him as if he'd taken leave of his senses. And he probably had. "A treasure hunt?"

"Kindly do not interrupt me, darling," Devon said without looking at her again. "I will not shirk whatever responsibility befalls me."

Sir Gideon nodded. "Then I will make the arrangements for your wedding."

Chapter Five

※ ❧

Jocelyn felt as if she had been turned to stone. Surely her legs would not move if she lifted them and attempted to escape. Her father, here. How? Why? When had he arrived? When had he ever deigned to attend a party not hosted by a political ally?

Who had masterminded this conspiracy?

Her thoughts came to a sudden halt as Adam walked into the tower and gazed upon her in wounded condemnation. Adam. Her Adam. Oh, the fool. Would he deny that he had sent her that note? Yes, if, as she had begun to realize, he had not sent it at all. Would he be quick-witted enough to defend her anyway, or would he allow her to suffer her disgrace alone?

Not exactly alone, she thought with a shiver, stealing a sidelong look at Devon, even if she could meet his gaze. She and that beautiful black-haired devil were embroiled in this together—whatever *this* might be. At least Devon had had the decency to stand up to her father's intimidation, although decency was not how she would have described Devon's actions of a few minutes earlier.

Or her own.

Her heart still clamored inside her breast from his shameless kisses. She understood too well now why young women dreamed of being a Boscastle bride. She knew why they went to ridiculous lengths to capture a moment of Devon's undivided attention in the park, or at parties. His fame as a libertine and superb lover seemed not to be exaggerated. She was afraid to think of what might have happened had her brother not arrived to save her from herself.

However, she'd never aspired to become a rakehell's lover. She'd meant to marry a respectable man, and that man was certainly not Devon, even if she'd wished for him long ago. Apparently, she wasn't alone in her consternation; he looked even more unhappy about being caught than she did.

Then how had this happened? Had this tryst been one of his wild wagers? Were his friends laughing themselves sick over how it had ended? And how *would* it end?

"Jocelyn," Adam said, shaking his head as if he had awakened from a dream, "I just don't understand. How did this come about?"

"I don't know," she said miserably, meeting his bewildered look. "I thought I was meeting you here."

"Meeting me? In the tower. Why would I invite you to this desolate spot?"

"I thought . . . I thought you were going to propose to me."

"In the tower? Good God."

It was evident that he would not find the wherewithal to rescue her from this disgrace. Nor could she lay all the blame at Devon Boscastle's door, as much as she might wish to. No one had forced her to come to the tower. No one had forced her to respond to Devon's kisses.

He told her father that he would marry her, but surely he would change his mind. In the heat of the moment he had defended her. By tomorrow he would have reconsidered.

She, as a woman, would never be able to escape the consequences.

And if she understood the cruel underpinnings of Society at all, those consequences would be the swift execution of her dreams.

Devon's face darkened as he discovered his cousin Gabriel standing outside the tower door, and with him one of Jocelyn's closest friends, Lady Winifred Waterstone. If he'd harbored any hopes for quiet settlement, he had to relinquish them. Witnesses would surely seal his fate.

He brushed around his cousin. "Your interference is not welcome, Gabriel."

Gabriel glanced up shrewdly at the tower door. "I came to help. It would seem as if you need it."

But Devon was in no mood to be moved by a show of concern. In fact, now that he was removed enough from the situation for reflection, he thought it unlikely that Jocelyn or her father had been involved in his entrapment. It crossed his mind, however, to attribute a conspiracy of this nature to a proven malfeasant such as his cousin. Had he not been warned by his brothers that Gabriel wasn't to be trusted?

"Please tell me that you did not arrange this tryst, Gabriel," he said slowly, searching his cousin's face. "Or that it was your idea of a joke."

Why else had Gabriel been so assured of making a conquest of Mrs. Cranleigh? His suspicions mounting, he remembered that it had been Gabriel who had taken Drake's governess-bride to a brothel before their marriage in the hope of stirring up mischief for no discernible purpose.

Gabriel shook his head again. "I came here to help, that's all."

"How did you know where to find me?"

"I followed Jocelyn's father. He and Adam were on a witch hunt when it seemed she had disappeared. All I knew was that your name was mentioned, and I could not locate you."

"And you know why now."

"You found the debutante more to your taste?" Gabriel hesitated. "I admit she's worth a second glance—"

Devon gave him a cynical smile. "More than a second glance, I'm afraid. Her life is ruined, Gabriel, whether I marry or abandon her."

"I am a Boscastle, too, Devon. Let me try to help—"

Devon glanced up. "We can discuss this later. This isn't the time."

What had been done had been done. Even if he had been tricked, no one had forced him to feel what he had felt when he'd held Jocelyn in his arms. No one had made his bones ache with desire and befuddled his brain so that for a few irrevocable moments nothing in the world had mattered but possessing her.

And now, for better or worse, he would.

It was, of course, impossible for Devon to sleep that night. He could either accept the hand that had been dealt him or seek to unmask whoever had contrived to dishonor him. He had no known enemies. He gave offense to few men unless it was deserved.

Which reminded him that he had been unfair in accusing Gabriel and owed his cousin an apology. He left his chamber, resolved to make amends.

Gabriel's room was located at the far end of the hallway above the castle's long window-lined gallery. As there was no footman in sight, he took the liberty of knocking quietly, then letting himself inside when there was no reply.

A beeswax candle burned low on the nightstand. With a wry smile he stood with his back to the wall and waited for the naked man and woman entwined on the bed to disentangle and dress.

The man did not bother. Rolling onto his side, he trained a pistol in Devon's direction and sprang nude from the side of the lush redhead who was still sprawled in a daze on the bed.

"Jesus God," Gabriel said in irritation. "I almost shot you, Devon."

Devon watched the woman's white bottom disappear over the other side of the bed. "Good evening, Lily. I hope I haven't caught you at an awkward moment."

She cursed from the floor and wrenched the silk coverlet out from under Gabriel's arse.

"Did I come at an inconvenient time?" Devon inquired in amusement.

Gabriel rose and strode without the least sign of inhibition to the dressing screen. His mouth set in a resigned smile, he gathered Lily's clothing into his hand and tossed it to her huddled form.

"Here, Lily. We wouldn't want you to catch a nasty cold."

She pulled on her gown and rose. "You're both bastards, you know. It's in the blood."

Devon lifted his brow, allowing her to squeeze around him. "It's a damned nuisance getting caught, darling."

The door closed with a decisive click, and he turned his attention back to Gabriel's shadowed form.

"You won the wager. Congratulations."

Gabriel lit a cigar and laughed. "I was about to win it just as you barged in."

Devon grinned. "Bad timing?"

"For both of us it would appear." Gabriel released a sigh. "Let me assure you again I had nothing to do with what happened tonight."

"I suppose you're going to deny that Lily was in your bed, too?" Devon asked drily.

"That's different. We had a wager. You and I both know that she and Jocelyn are different."

"I don't know Jocelyn at all, if you want to know the truth."

Gabriel shook his head in sympathy. "It's the Devil's luck what happened to you tonight. I'm not certain I'd have handled myself as well as you did."

Devon backed into the door. It was almost dawn. "I suppose it remains to be seen how well I'll deal with what comes next."

"I might be gone by morning if I were you."

He hesitated. "Perhaps I will be."

But he knew he wouldn't, and not merely for honor or because he'd given his word. Even now the memory of Jocelyn beat in his blood, sparked a heated anticipation inside him that defied reason. Sweet, slightly wicked. Soft brown eyes and a father who would not forgive her for what she had done.

He would not be gone in the morning. He was a man who faced whatever was thrown in his path.

Jocelyn awakened to the sound of pigeons gathered on her windowsill. She sat up and stared at the mask she had dropped on her dressing table. What was the point in hoping that last night had been a dream? She had not slept enough to even pretend to deceive herself. Her father's parting words had haunted her throughout the night.

"You will accept the consequences of your misconduct with grace and integrity."

He had left the estate before the other guests had even been alerted of his presence. His discretion notwithstanding, Jocelyn was fully aware what the topic of gossip would be at the breakfast tables, although perhaps by now Devon would have fled, and Jocelyn would be left alone to suffer the ensuing scandal.

She sank back onto the bed, wondering how long she could hide in this room before she would be forced to emerge. Perhaps an hour passed as she pondered her immediate future. Her stomach growled with hunger, and it was barely past dawn. Never having denied herself a single meal in her memory, it soon became obvious that she could not languish indefinitely. Sooner or later she would have to face Society.

And Devon.

A slow flush of heat washed over her body. How could she ever have known she could be rendered so helpless by a man's touch? Her first taste of passion.

The worst part wasn't that she had submitted to him so easily. The worst part was that she had wanted more. Ached deeply for a full awareness of what he had awakened.

And Devon had known. He lived and breathed seduction. He had a sorcerer's power when it came to pleasure.

And her father was forcing him to marry her.

It was still early even after she had washed and dressed. Many of the guests would stay abed until noon, sipping chocolate and answering correspondence. Even so, she could not forestall explaining how she and Devon had become engaged overnight when the entire ton knew her to be enamored of Adam.

She would have to face Adam's wounded indignity again. But there was nothing for it. She must simply steel herself to accept whatever the day would bring.

Prepared as she might be to defend herself against slander, she had not mustered enough courage to confront the man who had contributed to her ruination.

No sooner had she stepped outside her door than she saw him in the hall. The sight of her sinful lord prowling about took her aback. Though early in the morning, here he stood, freshly attired, too handsome to behold at this early hour. Ill prepared to hide her emotions, she said the first thing that came to mind.

"Are you returning from another assignation?" As if the mere thought did not turn her inside out. How could a woman of tender sensibilities marry a rogue who scoffed at the notion of fidelity and friendship?

"Are you on your way to one?" he teased, turning the tables on her.

"Most assuredly not."

His blue eyes kindled with unbridled mischief. "You went to one last night."

"So did you. And look where we are now."

"That is actually why I'm here," he said.

She drew back a step, her voice climbing an octave. "Oh?" She could swear he knew that she'd been thinking about him all morning. That he knew the sight of him made her body thrum and her thoughts tangle inside her head. He must be used to women melting under his charm. She wondered all of a sudden if he was going to ask her for help to break their engagement.

He lowered his head to hers. "I think we ought to come up with a plan on how best to handle what lies ahead."

She pressed herself back into the doorway. He had a subtle way of speaking that forced the breath from her lungs. If she married him, she would have to gain control of herself. She could not stop breathing every time he walked into the room.

"Are you asking me to come up with a solution to escape getting married?" she whispered.

He blinked in surprise. "If I abandoned you to disgrace," he said carefully, "I'd be labeled a cad and defiler of women. I've been labeled many things in my day, mind you, but nothing quite that bad."

"I'd be labeled even worse," she said under her breath, feeling a little ashamed of herself for accusing him of low motives. But then she'd only had her own family as an example of what love was, or was not. "What sort of plan did you mean?" she asked after a long pause.

He cleared his throat, his wicked smile coaxing a sigh out of her. "A plan to defend ourselves against what people are going to say about us."

"You mean the people at the party?"

"For a start." He leaned into the door frame, raising his arm above her head. His eyes were the blue of the sea during a storm. "Has your father ever threatened you with physical force before last night?" he asked unexpectedly.

Panic flared inside her. How could he possibly know? He couldn't know. No one knew. Her father's violent outbursts were a guarded family secret, infrequent enough so that months and months would pass with Jocelyn convincing herself they had never really happened.

"Why would you ask such a thing?" she asked with a puzzled laugh.

He stared into her eyes as if her evasive reply had not deceived him for one instant. She had never met anyone like him before, and she was too ashamed to answer truthfully. She prayed he would not press the issue and force her to lie because she couldn't tell him.

"I just wondered," he murmured. "He seemed so quick to lift his hand that I couldn't help noticing."

"And coming to my defense."

"I couldn't help that, either," he said pensively, his fingers brushing an errant curl from her cheek.

Now pleasure mingled with panic. He was so purely male and protective that she almost could not bear it. "I heard you and your cousin cross words last night," she said in a desperate bid to divert his attention. "Do you think he was the one who tricked us?"

He looked down at her with a smile that said he knew she had evaded his question. "I'm not sure it matters." He shifted at the hip, and she found herself suddenly fused to his hard, angular body. "Why don't you at least admit that you enjoyed what happened between us last night before we were caught?" he asked, running his fingers up her forearm to her throat.

"Because I didn't know it was you," she whispered, a fact that seemed to nullify whatever she may or may not have felt at the time. Or what she felt now. Tiny bursts of heat ignited low in her belly and sent throbs of warmth into the depths of her body.

She was vaguely aware that his other hand had settled around her waist, and that she had made no attempt whatsoever to dislodge it. Her surrender spoke for itself, as he surely knew. "Do you think Chinny could make you shiver when he kissed you?" he asked in a museful voice. "I did."

"I've already told you," she said, her voice so low and husky she did not recognize it. "I thought I was kissing—"

Before she could finish, he had opened her bedchamber door and swept her inside, pinning her against the wall. She closed her eyes. His kiss was brief but potent, a defiant challenge to her assertion that he did not make her shiver. He held her face between his hands and teased her lips open with his tongue, ravishing her mouth with a raw hunger that reached into some deep part of her she had never known existed.

A wicked thrill burst deep inside her belly. It seemed far worse to be kissing him in the daylight, in her bedroom, than it had last night when she had not realized who he was.

But she knew him now. She knew what desire was. The moment he touched her again, her will dissolved into warm darkness. She was giddy, flushed, and flustered when he broke their kiss, his lean face buried against her neck. His hand slid up the side of her dress to brush a tantalizing trail across her breasts. She felt herself responding with a shiver of anticipation, supported by his hard body, so devastated she couldn't bring herself to look at him.

Then suddenly he appeared to regain his composure, and he released her. They were standing once again outside the door. She realized in dazed resentment that he was half-smiling at her, managing to look wickedly appealing and indifferent at the same moment while it was all she could do not to fold at his feet.

"You didn't think it was Chinny then, did you?" he asked in an undertone.

"No," she said. "For one thing, Chinny would never—I mean, *Adam* would never have behaved so badly."

He brushed his knuckle across her kiss-swollen mouth and smiled. "Then he's a damned fool and will never know what he's missed."

She shook her head. She felt rather faint and in need of a meal. "Are you going down to breakfast?"

"It's probably not a good idea. I'm liable to throttle the first person who congratulates me on getting leg-shackled, or asks how I could have been so stupid as to get caught alone with a decent young lady."

She pursed her lips. What a shame he was a man who minced words. "Perhaps I shall take a tray in my room and spare myself that humiliation."

He rubbed the back of his neck. "It might be better if I faced everyone first."

"And said what?" she inquired hesitantly.

"I haven't decided yet. I suppose it depends on what is said to me first. Your father has already informed our host of our surprise engagement."

"Surprise hardly seems adequate to describe the unravelment of our lives," she said wryly.

The castle had begun to awaken. Servants bustled to and fro with pitchers of washing-water, lavender soap balls, and messages to be delivered to private rooms. The first of the sporting events was scheduled for the afternoon. As Jocelyn had long ago resigned herself to the fact that she had been endowed with a figure and constitution more suited to athletics than to Almacks, she anticipated leaving the party with at least one of Lord Fernshaw's generous prizes.

She had not, understandably, expected to lose the decent man she had hoped to marry with a reluctant rakehell standing in his stead.

Devon began to edge back down the hall, his gaze locked with hers. Evidently neither of them wished a repeat of the previous night's humili-ation, although it seemed unlikely that anyone would be scandalized to discover them together now, having already been caught. They were engaged, as incredulous as both parties found that fact to be.

"We shall have to walk through this trial with dignity," she murmured, retreating behind her door.

He bowed. The effect of this refined gesture was regrettably compromised by the unholy twinkle she detected in his eye when he straightened.

"Dignity," he said. "Now there's a novel con-cept. I shall have to give it a try."

Chapter Six

She practically collapsed upon her bed. Perhaps he would run away. Perhaps he would join the East India Company to escape her. Jocelyn would be mortified and rendered unmarriageable as a result. A rebellious part of her nature insisted that even that humiliation would be preferable to a husband who did not desire her. One who might flaunt a succession of demimondaines around London. There was no reason for her to assume that he would willingly forsake his former ways.

Still, whatever the future held for her and Devon, there remained the rest of the party to get through. Dignity was to be her lodestar. She resolved to steel her spine and conduct herself with as much dignity as possible. She would merely smile mysteriously and shrug when someone asked how she and Devon had fallen in love.

Love was supposed to be mysterious, wasn't it? Well, this affair fit the bill. It was a mystery how they had ended up in the tower together, not to mention how they'd manage if they did have to marry.

Still, she could always hope by some miracle that her family, the Boscastles, and Lord Fernshaw's guests might decide to dismiss the whole matter and go on with the party as if nothing untoward had happened.

It wasn't the least bit likely, though.

Captain Matthew Thurlew sat in a pew in the village church, his head bowed in a pose of pious contemplation. Unbeknownst to the country dolt of a parson, the Sunday morning sermon was an apt one, though the delivery was bone-numbingly overwinded.

"Babylon is fallen, fallen!"

Thurlew's mouth thinned in a pleased smirk. The thundering fool might well have shouted, "Boscastle is fallen, fallen!," for all who knew Lord Devon understood that a marriage of convenience would strike a fatal blow to his freedom.

He glanced askance at his fellow sinners, only three of whom had escaped Alton's Sunday breakfast to appease whatever sense of morality they pretended to possess. For an hour or so they could feign piety before returning to their sins.

It sickened him.

They did not represent the grandeur of the English aristocracy but rather the gross abuse of privilege and power.

While Lord Devon exercised his lordly prerogatives, Matthew's only brother languished in a Cornish prison awaiting trial for highway robbery. It was likely the boy would be transported if not hanged.

It was Matthew's conviction that Daniel had been led astray by none other than Lord Devon Boscastle; almost a year ago Boscastle, Daniel, and another friend had, as a prank, held up a carriage inside which they believed was a young courtesan they'd met earlier in the evening.

The carriage had belonged to a senior banker. A footman had been accidentally wounded. In Matthew's estimation Devon had walked away from the affair with a mere slap on the wrist.

The Boscastle name was a key that unlocked the doors of influence.

But Daniel Thurlew had been unable to resist the Temptor. He had fallen prey to a criminal life while his high-born friends went on their sinful way.

He closed his eyes once more in contemplation as the pastor, a devoted man, raised his voice.

"Babylon the great is fallen, is fallen . . . because she made all nations drink of the wine of the wrath of her fornication. . . . "

There was no formal announcement the following day of the unanticipated betrothal of Lord Devon Boscastle and Miss Jocelyn Lydbury. The official statement was to be given later that evening. Speculation, of course, ran rampant. A certain young lady claimed to have known all along that Devon and Jocelyn had been enjoying a torrid affair in secret. Supporting this suspicion, one or two older guests spoke of old gossip that concerned a broken dinner engagement years ago.

Lord Devon, it would appear, had not been interested in the notorious Mrs. Cranleigh at all. His attention to the widow had most likely been a screen to shield his true passion.

Now that the two unlikely lovebirds had been caught in the act by Jocelyn's indignant father, their ardor for each other had been revealed, to the delight of everyone at the party, from the youngest maid to the oldest matron.

Scandal, Boscastle style.

The guests might even have been content to settle for the story of a simple love match had it not been for the peculiar behavior of the two main players toward each other in the aftermath of their tryst.

They seemed to be ignoring each other.

Were they playing discreet?

Had they quarreled?

Was Devon avoiding Jocelyn out of respect for her, or was there a darker motive?

"They're probably embarrassed to have gotten caught," Lord Fernshaw's wife speculated over her breakfast toast and kippers. "I think it's terribly romantic. Four years, and they have desired each other."

Alton shook his head. "I don't think it's that

easy to embarrass a Boscastle." Or for one to wait four years to satisfy his desires, but that thought went unspoken.

The other Boscastles in attendance at the party refused to say a word on the matter. Sir Gabriel Boscastle, whose own reputation was anything but pristine, claimed to know nothing; it was no secret he'd led a rough life and had not always been close to the other Boscastles, but even so he remained loyal to the line.

No one was brave enough to gossip about Devon to Emma Boscastle for fear of a lethal tongue-lashing. Her ward, Charlotte Boscastle, had barely left her room since the scandal broke and therefore could not offer an opinion.

Lily Cranleigh appeared to be in a foul temper. Lord Chiswick looked bereft, and Lady Winifred Waterstone, Jocelyn's confidante, hesitated to talk about the matter at all.

It wasn't shocking that Devon had seduced a young lady at the party. But no one had expected him to get caught, and the question of the hour was whether he would wriggle out of the wedding trap. Unless, of course, he had walked into it on his own.

Fortune, not surprisingly, continued to frown upon Jocelyn that day. In fact, after an uncomfortable breakfast, during which she could barely eat, or even meet Devon's gaze across the table, fortune apparently decided that she had not suffered enough humiliation.

In keeping with tradition, Lord Fernshaw had decreed that his guests would partner up in pairs to participate in an energetic game of battledore and shuttlecock. By process of elimination only the best players would be deemed worthy of forming a team in the final competition.

It was a game at which Jocelyn excelled. She hoped to take home this year's grand prize for her skill, a splendid pair of minotaur bookends.

Unfortunately, she and Adam had been chosen as partners. Against Devon and Lily. At her distressed look, Alton took her aside to whisper, "We chose the names Friday afternoon, before you and Devon, well, before."

Yes, before.

She understood Alton's inability to express exactly what had come after. But she did know that suddenly she wasn't in a sporting mood; Adam looked utterly miserable, she could only hope she would not be forced to play at all because Devon had disappeared immediately after breakfast, and no one could say where he'd gone.

He strolled into view a few moments later. She did not even have to glance around to know that he had arrived. Conversations stopped, heads turned, and for all she knew the birds ceased their happy chirping. Female looks were slanted beneath wide-brimmed straw bonnets. The young men grinned and elbowed one another as if to celebrate the arrival of the sinful nobleman.

Of course, when Devon crossed the courtyard

and actually reached the lawn, conversations restarted like a dozen bubbling fountains.

No one dared to look at him directly, except for Jocelyn, who decided that it would not help the cause of dignity to ignore him.

His face seemed harder and more deeply shadowed than it had earlier in the day, although she could not say he appeared particularly concerned or even perturbed that life as he'd enjoyed it was to come to an unexpected end.

Or perhaps he did not intend to end his pleasurable existence, at all.

The competitors were allowed twenty minutes of practice with their partners. As Adam virtually ignored her, Jocelyn found herself swatting her shuttlecock to her dearest friend Winifred, who made no secret of her consternation at the recent turn of events.

"Why did you not let me know it was Devon you desired?" she whispered as they took their positions.

Jocelyn batted her cork into the air. "I was deceived into meeting him, and he claims it was Lily he meant to seduce."

Winifred lowered her battledore. "To s—"

"Ladies and gentlemen!" Lord Fernshaw shouted from his dais on the lawn. "Please join your partners. The competition has begun."

Jocelyn stood self-consciously at Adam's side as a group of young men, Devon in the fore, forged to the edge of the lawn. Stripped down to his shirtsleeves and black broadcloth trousers, he stood a good head above even the tallest guest; his lithe frame moved with a fluid elegance that made his companions seem as awkwardly jointed as wooden puppets.

"Are you ready to play?" Adam asked her stiffly, refusing to so much as look at her.

She glanced at his long-chinned profile in regret. "I'm ready. Adam—"

"Take your position, Jocelyn," he said, stepping around her. "This is hardly the place for trivial chitchat."

Chitchat.

Oh, he despised her.

He could not even bring himself to look at her. She marched forward, her arm upraised. What did she care for a stupid competition when her life was ruined? What did—

She found herself suddenly standing face-to-face with her opponent, Mrs. Lily Cranleigh. Dignity, she reminded herself. This was the time to show dignity. But then Lily let her racket drop to the ground, and when Devon went to retrieve it, she sent Jocelyn such a malicious look that dignity ceased to matter.

Lily laid her hand on his shoulder as he straightened.

The match began.

And all of a sudden Jocelyn could not control the force that seized hold of her. It blazed through all her genteel breeding. It consumed her so completely that it almost made her believe in supernatural possession of a person's soul.

One moment she was flying across the court-yard to keep aloft the cork-and-goose-feather shuttlecock that Adam had carelessly sent sailing over her head. The next she and Lily were running toward each other in a mad race to bat their separate shuttlecocks higher than the other.

From the corner of her eye she glimpsed a rather evil grin on Devon's face. Then she heard Lily mutter, "Don't you worry, Devon. I know how to take care of my competition. I'll show your little wallflower what's for."

She felt a fleeting moment of uncertainty. Was that a threat? Did the widow view her as her competitor for Devon's sexual favors?

Well, of course. She was a naïve little wigeon to think otherwise. Just because Devon was being forced to marry Jocelyn did not mean that he in any manner whatsoever meant to change his ways.

Or the widow to change hers, man-greedy trull that she was.

"I know how to take care of my competition, too," she muttered under her breath, the muscles in her shoulder tightening with anticipation.

"What?" Lily asked, her arm freezing.

Jocelyn's voice sounded so menacing and unladylike that Lily glanced at her in surprise. There followed the briefest instant when Jocelyn actually felt ashamed of herself. She almost took a step back as a courtesy.

But then one of the male guests laughed. And even if it wasn't Devon, she could imagine how amusing she and Lily must look to his jaundiced eye, one the woman he desired, the other one he did not, yet would have to marry, battling over a bit of feathered cork.

Suddenly she did not care. The whole of England could be watching, and she did not care. She was a woman obsessed with a single goal. She was a woman whose own brother had once told her that she could flatten him in a dead run faster than all of Boney's armies combined.

The two shuttlecocks spun upward toward the sun, hers and Lily's, competing for the same current of air, competing for a prize not acknowledged or even clearly defined.

"Mine," Lily muttered with one arm raised, the other crooked at the elbow to push Jocelyn away. "It's mine, you greedy guts."

Jocelyn's mouth tightened, and her vision blurred at the edges. The ladylike response would have been to retreat, to give Lily the chance to swat her shuttlecock first.

But she didn't. She couldn't. In fact, she couldn't even see properly to say exactly what she was doing.

"It's my cork," she said in a rather frightening voice.

Lily grunted. "The bloody hell it is. That is *my* shuttlecock."

"No, it isn't."

"Yes, it *is.*"

She stretched her arm toward the sun. And sprang into the air to swing her racket. Her elbow collided with Lily's large, heaving breasts. Her racket connected, in a loud solid whack, with Lily's perfect, uptilted nose.

Lily looked down as a thin trickle of blood spurted onto her upper lip. Her squeal of pain and outrage shattered the enrapt silence like a thunderbolt. "She attacked me! My God, I'm bleeding. Oh, my God! There's blood all over . . . everywhere. I'm fainting. I'm going—"

"By God," a young gentleman cried. "She's going to faint! Somebody catch her."

"It came at me like a meteor," she bellowed, amazingly vocal for a woman in a swoon.

A male guest pushed Jocelyn aside. "Don't fret, Mrs. Cranleigh."

"My nose! My nose! Am I disfigured?"

"I daresay the bump will go down in a few weeks," the gentleman consoled her.

"*Weeks?*" she shouted.

People were running all over the court. Servants with dampened napkins, unattached men who would kill for the chance to comfort the distraught and injured widow. Jocelyn stumbled backward and barely felt the masculine body that buffeted her before she was standing alone.

"Good God, Jocelyn," Adam muttered, pulling his own handkerchief from his vest pocket. "You didn't need to assault her. I understand this situation has got you all upset, but, *really.*"

"I didn't do it on purpose," she said, although no one paid her any attention. The entire focus of the players was on Mrs. Cranleigh's battered proboscis, and the understandable fuss she was making over her opponent's unladylike aggression.

"Oh, for pity's sake," Lady Winifred said as the widow slumped into the arms of the first two men to reach her. "One would think she'd been hit by a rifle not a racket."

A well-built, fair-haired man who bore an air of authority sauntered up behind Jocelyn, his handsome face wearing a grimace. "She's making enough of a damned racket, I know that."

"I feel awful," Jocelyn whispered.

"Not as bad as she does, I reckon," her brother Jason said as he shoved his way through the gathering. "What the devil did you do that for, Jocelyn? It was hardly sporting."

Winifred gave him a little push. "It was only a game. Everyone knows you can get hurt playing games."

The fair-haired arrival grunted. "Perhaps we can send her on a slow boat to Peking. I have one anchored in the harbor about to launch. A long sea voyage would give her time to heal."

"I think I'm the one who should take a boat to China." Jocelyn slipped back a few more steps. Then another, and another, until she was standing alone at the edge of the crowd.

A fat raindrop fell on her forehead. Why

couldn't it have rained an hour earlier so that the wretched game would never have been played?

How was she supposed to make amends for behavior unbecoming to anyone but an Amazon? What unearthly urge had possessed her?

She wheeled awkwardly, unable to listen to Lily's sobbing for another moment. Unfortunately, she could not make the undetected escape she'd hoped for. Devon stood directly in her path, his gaze averted. *Oh.* Now *he* was so embarrassed that he couldn't even look at her. And if he said anything about his lover's nose she might just hit him, too.

"Please let me pass," she said with all the composure she could summon.

"Wait a moment," he murmured, then bent to pick up something on the path.

"If you're going to make fun of me," she said to his down-bent head, "you can at least have the kindness not to do so to my face. I've taken about all the humiliation I can withstand."

"You've dealt your share of it, too," he said. "And I wasn't making fun of you." He straightened, his eyes dancing with unholy mirth. "Here. I was only going to give you this."

She stared down at his hand. Cupped in his broad palm was a goose-feathered shuttlecock. *Her* shuttlecock, to be precise, the one she had been certain Lily had stolen. The blood drained from her face, and she could not utter a word. To think she had battled in public over a cork, and it hadn't even been her cork.

"Well, never mind." He looked around appraisingly as if to reassure himself that no one was watching. Then he slipped the shuttlecock inside his long-tailed morning coat. "It will be our secret. It's the least I can do, considering."

"Considering?" she asked in hesitation.

"A husband and wife are meant to be on the same side, aren't they?" he said with mischief in his voice.

She swallowed hard. How could she possibly guard her heart against the man when he said things like that? she wondered wistfully.

"I wish someone had stopped me before I made a spectacle of myself."

"There wasn't time," he said, shaking his head. "You shot across the lawn like a bullet." He paused. "I've never seen anything like it. I was quite impressed by your initiative."

She held back a laugh. "Now you *are* making fun of me."

"God forbid. I am not. I would never mock a woman with an arm like yours."

She backed away from him. The other guests were approaching, Lily among them. "Perhaps you should comfort her," she said awkwardly.

He glanced around.

"It appears she's got enough company at the moment."

She nodded, half-turning to escape. "I really want to go to my room now."

"Wait a minute." He grasped her by the wrist.

"Devon—"

"I'll show you a detour if you don't want to meet anyone on the way."

She sighed. "After what I just did, I don't ever want to meet anyone . . . "

He pulled her behind a high wooden trellis overgrown with ivy. "This doesn't look like a detour," she said dubiously, her gaze lifting to his.

He grinned, whispering, "It isn't, but someone's coming."

There was barely enough room to hide, let alone place any distance between them. She stood peering out through the ivy, Devon at her back, his hand resting on her shoulder. His warm, strong hand, slowly turning her around to face him. His sultry gaze captured hers, enticed her with the promise of dark pleasure. She swallowed a moan. Then his arm locked around her waist and crushed her to his chest and heavily muscled thighs.

She closed her eyes, not fighting his embrace. If anything she arched as if she were inviting more, although of what she was not sure. His heart. His strength. All that he was.

She could still hear voices on the pathway beyond the trellis. She drew a breath, opened her eyes in hesitation. He smiled and tightened his hold, refusing to relinquish her, his eyes glittering with temptation.

The voices drew nearer, then dimmed. Temptation flared. She gave herself up to it.

Devon lowered his head to kiss her, and both the sky and the sinful blue of his eyes blurred as she parted her lips. Anticipation shivered down her spine.

His kiss seduced her. A dangerous languor took possession of her body, her mind. She was aware of his arousal, the thick column of muscle that pressed through her clothing like a brand. She stopped breathing, his mouth devouring hers. This moment alone existed. This man.

And then the voices penetrated her haze of pleasure. Two male guests were walking past the trellis. One of the voices sounded familiar. His gaze rueful, Devon lifted his head to listen.

"God, what a sight that was. She almost knocked Mrs. Cranleigh senseless. What did the woman ever do to her?"

"If your head wasn't in the punch bowl half the time, you'd know. Jocelyn is Boscastle's lover, and he got caught with the wallflower in the tower and has to wed her."

"He was caught by her father?"

"Sir Gideon himself. And all I can say is that Jocelyn must have inherited his violent streak. My uncle told me that he used to beat . . . "

Their voices faded. Jocelyn broke away from Devon, feeling sick inside. She could have corrected that gentleman at least on one point. There was actually quite a bit more that could be said on the subject of her father, but she hoped that it would never be said in her presence, or that Devon would hear it.

She edged around him.

He turned swiftly, staring at her in concern. "Jocelyn—"

"It's all right."

"Dammit—what about the detour?" he called after her.

She merely shook her head and turned blindly into the tall row of cypress trees that led to the castle. She was glad he didn't make everything worse by trying to follow her.

He watched her escape with the dignity of a royal princess—a princess surrounded by a court of ignominious subjects. He'd been fully prepared to either ignore or defend her against the hurtful remarks they'd overheard. But Jocelyn hadn't given him a chance to react one way or another.

And now that he thought about it, he wasn't sure what had caused her such obvious distress: the gossip about him and Lily or the reference to her father. She hadn't given him much of a hint.

Still, he'd seen the humiliation on her face before she had fled him, and the Boscastle in him had wanted to come to her defense. But could he defend her against the wounds of the past? The truth was that he'd been sickened himself to hear her being degraded. And he was at least partly to blame.

He heard Lily coming up the path, her soft laughter indicating that she had not been mortally wounded after all. As a gentleman, he should undoubtedly emerge from his hiding place and ask about her injury.

But he did not move. He couldn't when he could still see Jocelyn's slender figure weaving in and out of the trees. He wanted to run after her. He would have if he had known what to say to comfort her. He only knew that he hated to see her so distressed.

A little later that same afternoon, however, in an impromptu boxing match that started in the topiary garden, he "accidentally" knocked into the hedgerow the two men who had been discussing Jocelyn on the path. He then apologized profusely for the matching pair of black eyes that the two dazed gentlemen would wear by evening.

Of course, only an idiot would have believed it was an accident. But no one dared say a word, except for his older brother Grayson Boscastle, the fifth Marquess of Sedgecroft, who had taken it upon himself as the head of the family to guide his siblings away from sins he had once committed. In this instance, however, Grayson seemed to approve of Devon's pugilistic outburst.

"Good for you," Grayson said. "A man ought to defend the woman he intends to marry."

The woman he intends to marry. The mere thought gave Devon a piercing pain right between his temples. He strode out of the garden without a backward glance, his coat slung over his shoulder.

"May I assume by your morbid silence that what Emma has told me is true?" Grayson inquired, following at his heel. "You were caught in a compromising position with Sir Gideon's daughter, and you have agreed to marry her?"

Devon slowed as they reached the castle's inner courtyard. "It's true," he said distractedly.

Grayson exhaled through his teeth. "Well, I have to admit that this is a shock . . . and that the lady certainly knows how to aim her racket."

Devon grinned reluctantly. "She wasn't supposed to aim for her opponent's nose."

"How did it happen?" Grayson asked quietly. "How in the name of God did you let yourself get caught?"

He shook his head. "I don't know. I was led to believe I was meeting another woman."

"That wouldn't happen to be the same one whose nose is by now swollen like a sausage?"

"All I can tell you is that Jocelyn and I were apparently deceived into meeting each other."

"Do you have any idea by whom?"

"I thought at first it might have been Gabriel."

Grayson frowned. "A reasonable guess, considering he has been in competition with Drake for years. Yet while Gabriel has lived a hard life and enjoyed his little torments, he's still one of us."

"I know," Devon said.

"If we were dealing with any outraged papa other than Sir Gideon," Grayson said, "I would suggest a bribe—"

Devon held up his hand. "I did not go to the tower without an inherent understanding that a tryst, even one planned, carries a certain risk."

"It's the element of risk that makes a rendezvous irresistible," Grayson agreed.

"The problem with this line of reasoning, unfortunately, is that I assumed any risks incurred would be easy to rectify. I didn't know I was meeting Jocelyn."

"I am sorry, Devon," Grayson said. "At least she is not without a certain charm."

"Yes," he conceded. "It would have been nice, though, if we had been a little better acquainted before walking to the altar."

He stared up at the east castle tower, thinking how elegant and benign it appeared in the daylight. "Having been foolish enough to walk into a trap," he said quietly, "I have no choice but to accept responsibility, if only in outward appearance. Everyone assumes I will run away, but I'm perfectly willing to give her my name."

"And nothing more?" Grayson asked after a thoughtful pause.

"I don't know what I have to give," Devon said

with a self-deprecating smile. "She's probably not getting the best end of the bargain. And I suppose, well, a man can go about his private affairs after he marries, can't he?"

"Many men do," Grayson said, nodding.

"Have you not been tempted to stray?" Devon asked.

Grayson smiled. "It has never entered my mind even once. I find myself more than satisfied with Jane, both in our bed and in her company."

"Perhaps that is because you chose her."

"Yes, perhaps, although you must remember that our courtship was anything but smooth."

Devon resumed walking through the courtyard. He did not have to love Jocelyn or make her any promises in private that he did not intend to keep. He did not have to change his ways to accommodate their arrangement. They could come to a compromise.

Honor would be satisfied if nothing else.

Less than two hours later, Jocelyn's brother found Devon in the library with a group of other male guests and quietly informed him that he had received a message from Sir Gideon insisting that the wedding be performed within a week so as to discourage speculation.

Devon shrugged. Having resigned himself to the inevitable, the time and place did not seem to matter.

"He would prefer," Jason added, "that the ceremony take place in Lord Sedgecroft's London chapel for the sake of privacy. If Lord Sedgecroft agrees, that is."

Grayson glanced at his brother. "That is suitable to me, Devon. Do you object?"

Devon smiled wryly. "No." And strangely enough it was true.

Chapter Seven

✿ ✿

Jocelyn's father had also requested that the engagement be announced later that night at the party in front of witnesses. Although he would not be present himself, he had asked his son Jason to serve as his proxy. It was obvious he thought a public pledge would bind Devon to his daughter.

And a hollow pledge it would appear to be.

It seemed unlikely, in fact, that Devon would visit the salon merely to please Sir Gideon, especially in light of the fact that his friends were upstairs laying odds on how many hours he'd last before he made his escape. He had been absent at dinner, leaving Jocelyn to make excuses for him that no one believed.

"Perhaps he just needs time to accustom himself to the idea," Winifred said in a consoling whisper as the two women walked the winding corridor to the salon.

"Perhaps he needed time to pack his clothes," Jocelyn replied with a reluctant smile. She picked up the skirt of her pale-pink-and-gold gown and stared ahead at the small crowd already standing at the doors of the salon. The glittering light from the chandelier inside threw a glow of brilliance on the expectant faces.

She knew immediately that Devon was not among the gathering of guests.

Perhaps he would not appear at their betrothal announcement. Perhaps the past would repeat itself.

She would stand like a wooden soldier while her peers toasted her engagement to a man who had ruined her and was now making his feelings about marrying her apparent to everyone.

Her brother shook his head in an apparent conflux of sympathy and resentment. He said nothing because there really was not much to say. Devon's absence was painfully eloquent.

Adam stared at her in burning silence except for an occasional loud sigh that only played on Jocelyn's already strained nerves. No matter how badly he felt, she was aware that he had made no more mention of offering for her hand. It was for the best. He would never trust her again after what she'd done. She wasn't sure that she could trust herself.

Lily did not show, either, but then the bride-to-be had practically attacked her with a battledore and the widow had taken to her bed with a cold compress. Swollen nose notwithstanding, Mrs. Cranleigh's lack of enthusiasm for this announce-

ment would be understood, even if those attending the party had hoped to witness another
conflict between the two women in competition
for Devon's heart.

After almost two hours dragged by, the guests
grew noticeably restless. How disappointing that
the drama everyone had anticipated would not
come to pass. Had Lord Devon fallen out of love
with Jocelyn? Had he loved her to begin with?
His failure to share this moment with her
suggested he had not.

Grayson sneaked off to Devon's room a half-
dozen times to fetch him, only to return with a
terse smile and a wan joke about this being
another of the pranks his brother was known to
play.

Gabriel offered to search the gardens for his
missing cousin. Emma quietly assured Jocelyn
that Devon would do his duty, but that punc-
tuality had never been his strong point.

"What is Devon's strong point?" Grayson heard
Gabriel inquire of Emma over his wine goblet.

She smiled, but her worried gaze strayed to the
doorway. "His charm."

"Then I should like to see him charm his way
out of this coil," Gabriel muttered.

Grayson stole a surreptitious glance around the
salon. A coil, indeed. Jocelyn was slumping in a
chair with a stony expression on her pretty face
that said she didn't give a damn whether his

brother had fallen out of love with her or fallen off the face of the earth. Which it appeared he had—he sat up suddenly, recalling how Devon had reacted to past crises. Had he not plunged into a tailspin when their mother and youngest brother had died? Had he not gone off on his horse to ride for hours on end?

A young wilding himself, Grayson had not particularly paid attention to the woes of his siblings as he was growing up. Now, as the family patriarch, he found himself having to offer guidance when he had only begun to grasp the meaning of his own existence . . . the mere existence of his wife and son.

"Excuse me again," he murmured to the assembly in general. "I shall return with my brother or I shall not come back at all."

Three minutes later he was striding across the unfamiliar estate to the paddock and stable. His brother was cantering down the slope in the misty moonlight while Grayson waited, trying not to lose his temper. He understood Devon's passion for horses, but he didn't understand his taciturn behavior.

"Where the hell have you been?" he demanded as Devon finally reined in alongside him, his angular face detached. "Your betrothal was to be announced hours ago."

"Didn't you make excuses for me?" Devon asked, dismounting.

Grayson folded his arms across his chest. Devon loomed even taller than he, and suddenly Grayson wondered how well anyone knew the dark young devil, or what he would do in Devon's place.

"Everyone is in the salon waiting for you. I did not know how to explain—"

Devon pulled off one of his black riding gloves. "I went to get her a betrothal gift."

Grayson threw up his hands. "It'll have to be one hell of a gift for her to forgive you for this."

Devon broke into a grin. "It is. At least I think so."

Grayson narrowed his gaze. "Jewels?"

"Would you expect less of a Boscastle?" His blue eyes dancing, Devon drew a bulky blue velvet pouch from his coat pocket. "You and Drake are the ones who taught me the power of a bauble on the female heart."

"What sort of bauble are we discussing?"

Devon laughed. "A diamond tiara."

"A— You're not bloody serious. Where in Essex would you find a diamond tiara?"

"Inside the mansion of one of our doting aunts."

"You rode all the way to Aunt Catherine of Arrogant's house to ask for her tiara?"

"I did."

"The tiara she swore to wear at her own funeral?"

"Well, I didn't say it was easy."

Grayson shook his head in admiration. "You're the only devil I know who could coax the old battleax to part with her diamonds. What possessed you to think of it in the first place?"

Devon glanced away. He couldn't lie to his brother, but he wasn't about to confess the truth, either. He only understood that Jocelyn had been hurt today, and his instincts had told him, well, he wasn't sure his instincts had told him to go hunting for a tiara in the middle of nowhere, but that's what he had done.

And he felt rather pleased with himself that he'd succeeded.

"Chloe always used to say that every young lady should have a diamond tiara," he said, as if that were enough of an explanation.

Grayson lowered his gaze.

"Aunt Catherine didn't happen to have another tiara on hand, did she?"

Devon hesitated. "Why?"

"For Chloe," Grayson said in a subdued voice.

Devon swallowed. Chloe was their vivacious raven-haired sister who had married Dominic Breckland, Viscount Stratfield, the previous summer. She and Devon had always been close friends, although he had not seen her recently. "It isn't her birthday," he said, frowning. "Why would you want to take her a present?"

"It seems she has lost the child she was carrying. I came to the party, actually, to tell you, but it appeared you had enough problems of your own."

"Is she all right?" he asked in concern.

"I believe so, although she's not in the best of spirits."

Devon shook his head. "I had no idea she was expecting."

"Neither did I," Grayson replied, clearly as distressed as Devon felt at the news. "She's with Jane now at the country house. We were all supposed to return to London together. If you and Jocelyn do end up marrying at my house, it might take Chloe's mind off her own troubles."

"I'm not certain that getting married will make my troubles go away," Devon said without thinking.

Grayson grinned as a groom walked toward them to take the lathered stallion. "After witnessing what damage your bride-to-be can inflict with a battledore, I'm not prepared to disagree."

One or two of the older guests had already retired for the evening. Even Lord Fernshaw appeared to accept that Devon would not put in so much as a perfunctory appearance; tactfully he made the suggestion that the party be moved to the conservatory for a soothing moonlight musicale. Perhaps, he told his wife, a violin concerto would ease the evening's disappointment.

Jocelyn rose from her high-backed chair. She could not tolerate another minute of this mortifying nonsense.

"It's past midnight." She was painfully aware that several of the more considerate guests had been waiting for her to concede defeat.

Lady Cordelia Fernshaw, Alton's young wife, took her by the hand. "Well, I'm famished. We shall have a midnight collation in the conservatory. Alton's dying to show off his skills on the violin. I advise everyone to bring some lamb's wool, and pray do not reveal to my husband that I was the one who suggested it."

Jocelyn smiled at her in wry gratitude. It was no secret that the midnight collation had been meant to celebrate her engagement to Devon.

"I'm ravenous myself," she said. Surprisingly, it was true. There was a strange freedom to be found in being rejected in front of one's friends. She had survived.

As if on cue Alton and Gabriel Boscastle stepped forward to offer her their arms. Jocelyn would have laughed at their gallantry if she hadn't simply wished to make a quiet exit. Adam had shrunk away from her in an apparent effort to distance himself from her continued disgrace. Her brother stood with a helpless look on his face.

Quite unwillingly she found herself walking with her hand tucked into the crook of Gabriel Boscastle's arm. The man was a scandal unto himself. But beggars, she supposed, could not be choosers.

"Keep your head high even if you wish you were dead," he said in a deep voice.

She laughed. "I believe my heart is still beating. I don't wish I were dead, but your cousin . . . "

He glanced down at her. She saw a resemblance to Devon in his face, but his was a harder, more careworn countenance. "I know of ways to revive the spirits of a lady who has taken a great fall."

She halted, her brow lifting at this remark.

"Perhaps I should walk alone, after all," she murmured.

"Relax, Jocelyn. I only meant to remind you that there are other options available if my cousin fails in his obligation."

She studied his rugged face. He was beyond bold. "Are you implying that I become—"

"My mistress?" He smiled down at her with unabashed amusement. "Are you interested?"

"I'm too stunned to answer that question," she replied, tempted to laugh at his audacity. "I cannot believe you would even suggest such an arrangement when I am involved with your own cousin."

He laughed. "Perhaps the fact that Devon is my cousin has something to do with my suggestion."

"Do you wish to use me as a weapon?"

"A weapon? No. You're a prize to be won, not a weapon." He paused. "As a matter of fact, I find I'm rather fond of my cousins."

She glanced up suddenly.

A deep hush had descended over the salon.

Jocelyn shivered in awareness before she even

turned to discern the cause. "I will walk by myself, Sir Gabriel," she said carefully.

"No, you won't," a baritone voice said from behind her. "Thank you for keeping an eye on her, Gabriel. How good to know that I can count on your decency in my absence."

Her pulse quickened as she turned to stare up into Devon's dark, saturnine face. Despite his offer, she realized that he was not looking at her at all; he and Gabriel seemed to be engaged in a silent clash of wills that sent a shiver down her arms.

It seemed quite clear that their rivalry had not flared up merely because Gabriel had been caught at her side, although she was not entirely sure from whence stemmed this discord. Did it concern Lily Cranleigh? Winifred had informed her of the wager between the two men.

She felt a little like a princess caught in the warring fire of two great dragons. But then Gabriel shrugged and stepped away with a low, amused laugh. The dark tension eased from Devon's face.

The dangerous impulses that had charged the air suddenly diffused. What did Devon expect when he'd all but abandoned her, anyway?

"I do have an excuse," he said with the briefest glance at her brother. "Whether it is good enough or not to merit a pardon will be for Jocelyn to decide."

She slanted him a cynical look as he raised his

hand to hold before her a blue velvet pouch. The party guests closed in a circle around them, curiosity overwhelming the courtesy of allowing him to gain a private exoneration. She was curious herself.

"What is it?" she asked, biting the inside of her cheek.

Devon's voice was velvet nonchalance. "A bauble to beg your pardon."

"A what?" she asked.

From the corner of her eye she noticed his brother Grayson standing at the door. He raised his brow at Devon. "Don't be modest, Dev. That is a most *expensive* bauble."

"Am I going to see it to decide for myself?" Jocelyn asked drily.

Devon grinned. "Of course. Hold out your hands."

She pursed her lips in suspicion, then obeyed. He emptied the contents of the pouch into her gloved palms. There was a collective gasp of awe from the guests crowded around them.

Jocelyn stared at Devon, not in a mood to be impressed. Why would he think her a woman to be bought with baubles? she wondered.

She had never been impressed much with trinkets in the past. Why would she start now?

But that question came before she looked down at her hand to discover the devil's temptation glittering in the form of the most exquisite diamond tiara she had ever had the joy to behold. Its delicate stones radiated fire from every facet set upon a beautifully wrought gold band. In truth, his gift did make her feel like a princess. A disgraced one, but a princess nonetheless.

"How did you know I have always wanted my own tiara?" she asked before she could stop herself.

He shrugged. She glanced up and suddenly noticed the tiny drops of mist that shimmered in his hair. Her gaze descended. There was a smudge of mud on the top of his left boot.

How on earth had he contrived to purchase a tiara of this quality in the sleepy Essex countryside? True, the Boscastles wielded both power and persuasive charm that people could not resist, but . . .

No man of her acquaintance had ever fought a duel over Jocelyn, or lavished her with such shocking extravagance. No one had singled her out before or paid her this much attention. She was not quite sure how to react, or what Devon expected her to say.

She stared directly into his eyes. His unwavering gaze increased her heartbeat and for a breathless moment she thought he might see something inside her she could not perceive herself. She had convinced herself he would not show up tonight. She had certainly not expected a present like this.

"How did you find this in so brief a period?"

"Is it to your liking?" he asked as if his very existence hinged on her answer.

Artful rogue. She would be stamped petulant by posterity if she denied him her appreciation. And, indeed, the act, no matter what motives had inspired it, did stir her gratitude. Truthfully, she was overwhelmed.

"It's the most beautiful thing I have ever owned."

He broke into a grin at her response. She could have sworn she heard his brother Grayson sigh in relief. And if only for tonight she wanted to believe that their marriage was not merely the end result of a masquerade, but something more.

Chapter Eight

❧ ❦

Devon remained at her side while her brother announced the betrothal of his sister to one of London's most eligible noblemen. The hopeful debutantes present whispered that their hearts were broken over the loss of their blue-eyed scoundrel. Devon's assorted group of male friends appeared subdued by the official announcement. He ignored both camps and concentrated on paying attention to Jocelyn. It was an easier duty than he'd expected.

It certainly did not hurt her cause that she'd responded to him so passionately when they'd met in the tower. Remembering the soft pleasure of her body sent a keen desire knifing down his spine. And he wanted more. The smile that curved his finely molded mouth as congratulations broke out around him came more easily than he expected.

He turned to place his arm around her waist. "Perhaps you should kiss me to celebrate our betrothal."

"Not in front of everyone," she said faintly.

But he kissed her anyway. His hard warm hand slid up her shoulder to her nape, and his fingers tightened there as he slanted his mouth over hers and kissed her as if there was not another person in the world.

He'd meant it to be only a symbolic embrace, nothing more. But then he felt her hand press against his chest. He heard the deep sigh that escaped her, and an unfamiliar ache took hold of his heart.

"There." He withdrew without warning, his hand drifting down her back.

She lifted her dark gaze to his. Something fierce stirred inside him. Unbridled desire, the duty to protect—those he understood. What puzzled him was the undefinable emotion that he felt when he was with her.

He drew his hand to his side. She smiled but did not move, murmuring, "I suppose you think you just proved something by that display."

And he had.

She could not deceive him, although he silently applauded her ability to dissemble. He recognized a woman's desire when he'd aroused it; he'd felt the sexual heat that ignited between them. His blood warmed in anticipation of what other fires he might awaken in her luscious body.

"It was a kiss to seal our betrothal," he said, exhaling in satisfaction. "No one even looks the least bit shocked."

"As you say," she retorted, sweeping ahead of

him to the doors of the salon for their celebration supper.

Devon followed her with a reluctant smile, pausing at the door to glance at his brother. "Did I redeem myself to your satisfaction?"

Grayson gazed at Jocelyn's receding figure. "It's not my satisfaction that you need seek, although it seems to me she's already—"

Devon glanced up at the soft cry that came from Lady Winifred. She was standing behind Jocelyn at the end of the candlelit corridor outside the salon. At first he could see no reason why both women seemed to be frozen in their tracks.

Then he gazed down the hall in the direction of Jocelyn's gaze, and what he saw brought his blood to a sudden boil. Propped up between two enormous stone urns loomed a mahogany coffin in which was laid Devon's infamous black velvet domino and below it a wreath of dead weeds and dried flowers. An old skull served as the head.

Nailed to the base of the coffin was a crude placard in the shape of a gravestone that read:

Lord Devon Boscastle
Better off Dead than Wed.

He strode to Jocelyn's side, his jaw tightening in uncontrolled fury. He caught a glint of pain in her gaze that was quickly masked before she gave a low stilted laugh. "I have nothing to do with this," he said, turning her in the opposite direction.

"But it's true, isn't it?" she asked softly.

He allowed his sister Emma to brush around him to grasp Jocelyn's arm. "It's just a silly prank," Emma said in a clipped voice. "You are not to let it upset you."

Jocelyn nodded slowly. "Of course not."

He ground his jaw. "I don't find it at all amusing."

Jocelyn smiled wanly, shaking her head at the small crowd gathering to witness her reaction to this unprecedented insult. "I only want to know where the bridal coffin is, and if I could please select the gown for my demise. I do not have a domino of my own."

His dark gaze swept the faces of those around them. "If I do find out who did this, I vow that coffin will be put into service."

She touched his arm. "Let's go to supper, Devon. There was no true harm done, and nobody's going to confess with you threatening to commit murder."

He stood, his anger escalating as she walked past the hideous coffin, Emma and Winifred like guardian angels at her side. He knew she was only trying to be reasonable, and if someone wanted to play a joke on him, he could take it. Pranks were one thing at a party, but that didn't mean she deserved to be the target of someone's malicious sense of humor.

"I bloody well mean to know who did this," he said, swiveling to stare at the remaining guests who had not been able to tear themselves away from the grim surprise. The ladies had been thoughtfully whisked through a side door by Lord Fernshaw's servants.

His gaze narrowed on the dark unsmiling face of his cousin.

"It wasn't me," Gabriel said quickly. "Trust me, I have far better ways to spend my time."

Devon shook his head. "So I noticed in the salon."

"I wasn't aware you were so possessive," Gabriel said carefully. "I was only holding your place."

Devon's mouth thinned. He was perfectly aware Gabriel was not capable of this sort of cruelty, but he'd be damned if he knew who was.

"Gentlemen," Grayson said, laying a firm hand on the shoulder of each man. "Let us not give the ton any more reason to talk. If you have this much energy to expend, save it for Alton's tournament. Or better yet, join Jocelyn at supper."

Gabriel glanced at Devon and nodded. "Friends, cousin?"

Devon nodded his head in apology. "Help me get that damned coffin outside before anyone else comes upon it."

Gabriel nodded. "I can do one better. Why don't I pay a visit to the village undertaker and ask if he's sold any coffins lately?"

* * *

Jocelyn was amazed at the attention she was paid at the supper table. Scalawags and unattached men who would never have dared approach a young lady of her stainless character before paid her court. Flattering toasts were made in her honor. At one point she even toasted herself and the empty coffin, ending her eulogy to Devon with the promise that she would "resurrect him on their wedding night."

Adam shook his head at her uncharacteristic display of spirit, slouching in his chair. It was obvious his opinion of her was lowering by the hour. Her brother smiled blankly. A few kinder guests whispered that the sight of the coffin had been too much for Miss Lydbury to bear. She was coming undone from the strain.

"I think you've drunk more than your share of claret," Winifred whispered in her ear on the pretext of dropping her fork.

Jocelyn bent down under the table to whisper back, "Why? Didn't you get to drink your share?"

"One of us should remain sober, don't you think?" Winifred whispered reproachfully.

Jocelyn nodded in agreement. "Good idea. I shall concern myself with drinking, and you, Winifred dear, shall do the thinking."

"He gave you a diamond tiara, Jocelyn."

She reached up to steady the gold circlet that threatened to slip over one eye. "It's beautiful, isn't it? He's beautiful, too. But somebody thinks that by marrying me his life will end."

Lady Winifred frowned as an unrestrained chorus of male laughter broke out around the table. "I never thought to see the day when you would be brought to . . . to . . . "

"You're turning into an old prude," Jocelyn said, lifting her head.

"You have broken Adam's heart," Winifred said in distress.

"What was Miss Lydbury looking for under the table?" one of her newfound admirers called from his chair in a cheerful voice.

Winifred gave Jocelyn a wry glance. "Her dignity. It seems to have disappeared."

The young man laughed harder. "Well, in that case, let dignity be lost. It's a damned nuisance, anyway." He rose from the table to approach Jocelyn's chair. "Or should we look for it together?"

She giggled, and if she'd had her wits about her she would have sensed the spellbinding silence that fell over the table before she did. A disturbingly familiar hand covered hers and firmly removed the glass she was holding. Devon had returned from his grim duty of having his coffin taken from the castle.

"Don't tell me you've been toasting our betrothal without me, darling," he said, resting his chin against her nape. "I thought I'd been forgiven for being late."

She angled her head to glance up at him. It didn't seem fair that three glasses of claret had not rendered her any less immune to his presence. Her heart still quickened as his gaze traveled over her. That awful tightness in her throat still made it difficult to breathe. And she still remembered all too vividly the brand of his sinful mouth on her bare breasts. The thought of the liberties she'd allowed him brought heated blood to her face.

"Fancy me," she murmured. "Look who's back from the dead."

His smile held a hard edge that made her squirm in her seat. "Someone is going to wish for death, I promise you."

"It was only meant as a joke, wasn't it?" she queried slowly.

He looked into her eyes. "Were you amused?"

"In a macabre sense," she admitted. "It would have been more amusing if I didn't feel personally responsible for putting you in the grave."

He nudged aside the avid-eyed baronet who was sitting at her left side and swung his lanky frame into the empty chair. "Do I look dead to you?" he asked quietly, his brow arching.

She drew her breath. "No, Devon. Not in the least."

He claimed her wrist and drew her from the chair. "We have not danced together yet."

"Please, not tonight."

He cast her an appraising look as he led her onto the dance floor. "Yes, tonight. You will *not* show anyone that you care what is thought of you."

She was surprised to find herself able to move through the figures of the set. Surprised that his calm words gave her courage. How many times had she danced and flirted with young men in the hope of a proposal? Of love? This man did not love her at all, and she wasn't decided what she felt for him. The only relief was that he seemed easy to confide in, a surprise considering the deception that had brought them together. Desire and confidence. Was it enough upon which to build a marriage?

She realized suddenly that he was staring at her, studying her face as if this were the first time they'd met. He wasn't smiling, either, and the dark spark of sensuality in his eyes sent little shocks through her body.

How handsome he was. Those wicked blue eyes, his chiseled bones, the strong clefted chin. The beauty of an archangel. How easy it would be to fall hopelessly in love with him.

"I'm sorry for what just happened," he said, his hand on her shoulder, urging her a little closer.

It seemed unfair that his touch could make everything seem tolerable. She made no attempt to move away. In fact, she felt as if she were magnetized to his hard, powerful body. Drawn to him and stripped completely of her defenses.

"Your friends are placing bets on whether you will even meet me at the altar," she said, stealing another look at his face.

"Those are not my friends."

But would he meet her? she wondered.

He glanced past her to the door. Jocelyn wondered if she would see Lily Cranleigh standing behind her if she turned around. She gazed resolutely at Devon instead.

The dance ended. She retreated, her gaze moving unwillingly across the room to the door. If Lily had been waiting for him, she was not now. And whatever Devon might have felt for Mrs. Cranleigh, whom everyone knew he had pursued, he did not leave Jocelyn's side until the sky began to lighten and the weary guests sought their beds in anticipation of what scandals the next day might bring.

It was overcast the following morning. Jocelyn tarried in her room until breakfast was over. Then, when she thought the coast was clear, she sneaked downstairs and went for a bracing walk alone around the wooded estate.

Some of the guests had gone back to bed, despite the disturbance of hammers banging and men shouting from the clearing where the annual tournament would be held three days hence, on Thursday. Tents with fluttering banners and gold-tasseled valances were being erected around the jousting arena. From the slope where she stood hiding she could see several men practicing on horseback.

She did not spy Devon's tall figure among those practicing, although she could hardly miss his cousin Gabriel thundering across the lawn on a muscular black steed.

He reined in and waved at her, proving that she was not well-hidden in the least.

She pretended not to see him and climbed down the slope to return to the castle, then stopped. A man appeared to be skulking in the great hornbeam grove she had cut through to avoid bumping into anyone she knew. There was absolutely no way to escape walking by him. She took a breath and barreled on.

Her heart sank when he turned toward her. "Adam," she said, finding it suddenly difficult to swallow. "Are you on your way to practice for the tournament?"

"If I participate, I shall most likely direct my lance at Devon Boscastle's black heart," he said bluntly.

"I see."

"Do you?"

"I think so," she said softly.

"Well, I bloody well don't."

She didn't, either, not really. None of it made sense. And she would never, ever admit this to Adam, but marrying Devon Boscastle was not anywhere near as distressing as it should be. As a matter of fact, it was the most wonderful thing that had ever happened to her. The only wonderful thing.

She glanced around. No one at the jousting arena could see them, although she couldn't be sure about the view from the castle windows. She had dreaded the inevitable moment when she would face Adam alone, but at the very least she owed him one final conversation. A conversation that she apparently was meant to carry herself.

He examined her in frowning silence for such a long time that she began to hum and edge away. He looked as if he had not slept in days. His face seemed a bit pale, and the size of his chin more pronounced. She did not blame him for hating her, but she wished he'd at least understand that none of this was her doing.

"Adam," she began in hesitation, "I—"

"That same night that you met Devon in the tower," he interrupted in a strangled voice, "I had just asked your father for your hand. I wanted to surprise you." He paused as if to let his confession sink in. "But, blast it," he said, his voice rising, "you went and surprised us all to hell, didn't you?"

"You don't understand."

He shook his head. "I wanted it to be proper and respectful. I'd no idea you were a woman who would let herself be seduced by a man like Boscastle."

"I thought I was meeting you," she exclaimed.

He regarded her with a chastising scowl. "Why would I do anything as reckless as to invite you to tryst in the tower? There are mice in places like that, you know."

"I thought you might have wanted to propose to me in a romantic setting."

"Mice are not in the least bit romantic." He

examined her with a rather pained expression. "I wanted to tell you in private that I'm prepared to call out Boscastle for what he's done to you."

"Are you serious?" she asked, aghast. "You've never fought a duel before. He has." At least she'd heard rumors to that effect. One only had to see the two men together to realize that Adam could never best Devon on a dueling field.

"I'm well aware of that," he said crossly. "And I don't particularly want to challenge him, but I feel as if I've been horribly wronged."

"So does he."

"Not by me, he hasn't. Surely you don't believe all that nonsense about someone sending you a note in my name, and that Devon just happened to be invited, too. He's a known rake, Jocelyn. He's always entangled in one affair or another."

"I think I do believe him," she said, only realizing it now herself. "He's—" She looked up suddenly. "He's coming. Dear heaven, that's him coming through the trees toward us now." And she didn't know why she should feel this sudden sense of panic intermingled with anticipation, but she did.

Adam's eyes widened in alarm. "Don't stand so close to me."

"There's a virtual chasm between us," she said under her breath and forced herself not to jump back as if they had indeed done something wrong.

Not that she or Adam had any reason to feel guilty, unless one took into account the fact that they had been discussing killing Devon. By the cynical glance he gave them, he might have overheard the incriminating part of the conversation.

"Well, look at this," he said, stopping short as if he were completely taken by surprise. "If it isn't my bride-to-be. And Chiswick. Together. Should I leave the two of you alone to lament what might have been?"

Jocelyn pursed her lips. "I'll do my lamenting in private, thank you. I was just leaving."

"So was I," Adam said stiffly.

"Well, don't let me chase you off," Devon said. "Carry on with your conversation. I believe I heard mention of my name in connection with a duel. Is there something I should know? People can get killed during duels, you know."

Adam turned such a waxen shade of white that Jocelyn thought he might swoon. She had no choice but to come to his rescue. "We were only discussing who would be challenging whom in this year's tournament."

Devon stretched his arms into the air, drawing her gaze to the lean, tapering lines of his torso. "Ah, yes, the tournament. I'm looking forward to a good fight this year for some odd reason. I hope whoever challenges me is prepared to be pounded into the ground."

He looked capable of it, too, she thought ruefully. Fit. Virile. Muscular. A young male at the peak of his prowess. "Did you come here to tell Adam how well you felt?" she asked pointedly.

He flexed his shoulders again and smiled. "Would you care to practice against me, Adam?"

She wasn't sure, because she didn't dare look in his direction, but she thought Adam might have swayed on his feet.

"Fernshaw's said to be offering a spectacular prize this year," Devon added as an afterthought. "I've heard it's a fine piece of horseflesh."

Adam had regained his color if not his confidence. "If it's all the same to you, I shall practice later in the afternoon."

Devon gave a careless shrug, then glanced up at the darkening sky. "It doesn't matter to me, although it does look as if it's going to thunder." He dropped his gaze and looked directly at Jocelyn. "Perhaps you ought to return to the castle before it starts to rain. Unless, of course, you and Chinny are not finished with your conversation."

She shook her head. She couldn't think of anything else to say without making the situation worse. "I believe we're finished."

Devon cut a sharp glance at Adam. "Are *you* finished, Chinny?"

Adam squared his shoulders, his chin jutting forward. "Completely."

"Then why don't you go away?" Devon asked quietly.

And that was the moment when Jocelyn realized that for all his playful charm, there was far more to Devon Boscastle than he let on. If he wasn't the archfiend himself, he had to be one of his favorite sons, and no matter how he acted the insouciant, there was little that escaped his perception.

Chapter Nine

❧ ❧

Devon strode toward the clearing on the out-skirts of the castle where the tournament would be held. Carpenters hammered away at makeshift stands for the spectators. A few of the bolder ladies had already gathered to watch the young male guests practice their swordplay and riding skills behind the wooden barrier erected for tilting.

Lily sat in a green silk dress and cloak on a bale of straw. She turned her face away when she spotted Devon and stared absorbedly at Gabriel galloping across the field. Devon couldn't tell whether the swelling on her nose had gone down or not. He was too preoccupied with his own thoughts to care one way or the other.

He'd found her bare-arsed under the covers with his cousin, and while he couldn't honestly say he'd been surprised, it hadn't occurred to him at the time to assess the size of her nose. He didn't care whether he lost a bet or not, either; she wasn't worth his trouble.

What bothered him at the moment was the conversation he'd just overheard between Jocelyn and Adam. The pair of innocents had been completely unaware that he'd been listening to them behind the trees before circling back onto the proper path.

At first he'd thought their encounter was amusing. But something in the furtive tone of their conversation had provoked him, and it was still provoking him now. It wasn't that Adam had been considering challenging him to a duel— Devon understood male honor. What irritated him was that Jocelyn had tried to soothe the paperskull.

Perhaps he should have encouraged Adam to elope with her. It would have solved all of Devon's problems. He could even have pretended to be heartbroken in the wake of their elopement. Well, perhaps that would be taking a reaction too far. No one would believe a woman had broken his heart.

But he had to admit if only to himself that he wasn't wholly unaffected by her, either. No one had forced him to gallop off into the hills to beg his elderly aunt for her prized tiara. Or to stay at Jocelyn's side almost the entire night. To his surprise he had not wanted to leave her.

True, he was being coerced into this marriage, but he wouldn't need any prompting to take her

to his bed. He wanted her more every time he saw
her. In fact, it had become a challenge to subdue
his sexual response to her allure. Considering her
inexperience, he would take special care to seduce
her.

Hell, he wasn't fooling himself. He was dying to
bed her, and when the time came he'd be damned
lucky if he could resist her for the few moments it
would take them to undress. He knew she didn't
do it on purpose, but in a subtle but disconcerting
way, she beguiled him.

Why else had he spent the last hour or so ex-
ploring the castle grounds in the hope of finding
her? And while he was nonchalantly trying to
pretend he wasn't searching for her, she had been
alone with Adam.

He stopped and swore aloud. The way the pair
of them had jumped apart when he revealed his
presence had not only annoyed him, it had made
him feel like some dark villain in a fairy tale who
had stolen a princess from her true love.

Devon had never played a villainous part in
anyone's life before. But who knew? Perhaps he
possessed an untapped talent for evil. He certainly
did not feel the least bit heroic at the moment.

"Devon!"

He half-turned at the shout, not moving a
muscle as Gabriel slowed his cantering horse to a
walk. In Devon's current mood he was liable to
clobber his swaggering cousin.

"You're late to the practice, Sleeping Beauty,"

Gabriel said, casting a glance at Lily. "Come on. I have need of a target."

Devon hooked one arm over the ring. "I'm amazed you have the strength to even rise this morning, let alone sit on a horse," he said with a droll smile.

Gabriel flashed him a rude grin. "My stamina is remarkable."

"We shall find out how remarkable it is during the tournament," Devon retorted, grinning back at him. "Funny, I had no idea Fernshaw was allowing peasants to participate in this year's pageant. Haven't you been assigned to dung-sweeping?"

"Do you want me to sweep you up?"

Devon laughed. "Who are you jousting against, anyway?"

Gabriel dismounted and tossed his reins to one of the grooms. "Perhaps you should pay more attention to your competition."

"Why?" Devon had not only served as a cavalry officer, but had won every joust he'd ever fought in Fernshaw's tournaments. "No one has ever beat me."

"Perhaps your luck has changed."

"Perhaps it isn't luck." Devon vaulted over the railing, suddenly in the mood for the physical outlet his cousin had tauntingly offered.

"I must confess one thing," Gabriel said, walking beside him. "It was not by invitation that Lily came to my room last night. I know you and I had made a bet, but I decided that you did not need to have your loss of freedom thrown in your face. Apparently, she desired me all on her own."

Devon laughed again. "If that was an apology, it's already forgotten."

Gabriel shook his head. "I wasn't apologizing. I only told you so that when I vanquish you tomorrow, you will understand that it has nothing to do with a woman."

"Gabriel, when I knock your arrogant head off your shoulders, you can rest assured that Lily will be the last thing on my mind."

Gabriel waited several moments before responding. "What if it had been Jocelyn in my bed?"

Devon aimed a mock swing at his head. "You really do want to be taken down a peg, don't you?"

"If anyone bests me, Devon, let it be you."

Devon smiled reluctantly.

Gabriel lowered his voice. "I found out last night that the coffin had been stolen, not sold."

"I'd expected as much."

"And," Gabriel continued, "if anyone in the castle knows who's behind it, they're keeping it a secret."

"Now isn't this a sight to warm the cockles of my cold heart?" a voice drawled behind them. "Dare we hope this chill in the air between the two cousins portends bloodshed? It's about time."

Devon glanced around. Captain Thurlew and a group of his friends strolled across the lists bearing broomsticks and blunted lances on their shoulders. "What the devil are the broomsticks for?" Devon demanded in amusement. "To sweep opponents off the field?"

"Don't you know?" Gabriel asked with a grin. "We're jousting the first event with broomsticks. Fernshaw is afraid the amateur guests might hurt themselves."

"In that case"—Devon snatched one of the brooms out from under Thurlew's arm—"you ought to start practicing. *En garde.*"

Gabriel ducked, then caught the broomstick that his groom had procured and thrown him. "That's more like it," he said, laughing, and swung at Devon's torso.

Devon sidestepped with agile grace and dealt his own blow, catching Gabriel on the thigh. Gabriel merely grinned.

"That's getting a little too close to home. Do you mind keeping your broomstick away from my stones?"

"My apologies," Devon said, laughing. "I didn't know that you had any."

"Ask Lily."

"No, thanks."

A crowd had gathered. Devon noted that Lily had risen to her feet, presumably hoping for a violent display. Adam stood a few feet behind her, but Jocelyn was not in his company. Had she taken his advice to return to the castle? Had she and Adam made an arrangement to meet in secret later—

"Hell." A dull thud across his elbow brought his attention back to his battle with Gabriel.

"Sorry," Gabriel said with an insincere shrug. "I do hope that wasn't your sword arm. But perhaps you ought to pay more attention to what an amateur can do."

Come storm or sunshine, Lord Alton Fernshaw's annual tournament would be held.

By dawn the last shred of fairy mist had evaporated from the jousting grounds. The wooden seats overflowed with sleepy but excited spectators eager to witness chivalry relived. Or, if chivalry failed, as it often did in such circumstances, one could secretly hope to witness a genuine fight break out among the competitors.

This year, owing to the unanticipated scandal that surrounded two of Society's most charismatic gentlemen, there seemed to be a decent chance that these bloodthirsty expectations would be met.

To this end, bets had been privately placed on a personal battle between the two Boscastle cousins. Gabriel was nursing a thick lip from his practice with Devon the previous day, a defect that only made him more attractive to his female admirers. Devon wore a distracted expression so unlike his usual devil-may-care countenance that his smitten followers ached to offer him comfort.

Those wagering on Devon did so on the basis of his calvary skills and daring temperament. He was young, tough, and wild at heart. Gabriel seemed a little stronger, rougher around the edges. His supporters claimed that as a Boscastle outcast, he had nothing to lose.

The true question of the day, however, was which lady had fueled this rivalry?

The previously untarnished Miss Lydbury, or the disreputable but desirable Lily Cranleigh?

Would both women appear?

Wagers were being placed on this matter also, with Lily taking the lead, and a few gamblers remarking that Jocelyn had not been seen at the practices.

Jocelyn would not have missed the spectacle for anything; she had renewed her resolve to accept her fate. After all, she had come to Alton's party in the hope of a marriage proposal. Never mind that Devon Boscastle was a far cry from the respectable husband she'd had in mind. Sometimes the best-laid plans held a few surprises.

She and Lady Winifred took their seats while minstrels wandered about reciting poetry and serenading the damsels in the stands with the timeless love songs of thirteenth-century troubadours.

All those who attended came in costume. Jocelyn wore a bliaud, an overtunic of flowing violet silk with a gold-linked girdle that hung low on her hips.

After much fanfare Lord Fernshaw appeared and strode to his canopied dais.

The jousting rules were announced, the participants reminded that all weapons had been blunted in the friendly spirit of the tournament. The knight of honor severed the cords to the lists, and a herald shouted, *"Laissez-aller!"*

The tournament had begun.

It promised to be an entertaining event.

The grand prize to be awarded the winner of this year's tournament was an Andalusian blood stallion.

There wasn't a combatant on the field who did not covet the horse for his own stable. Or to merely ride on Rotten Row to impress the ladies of London.

Resplendent in his knightly attire, Devon Boscastle easily cut the most impressive figure of the day as he crossed the arena astride his spirited destrier. Beneath a peacock-blue satin jupon he wore a silver-mesh hauberk, and his blue eyes glistened with diabolical intent through the visor of his steel helmet. He commanded his horse with a masterful ease that sent flutters through more than one lady in the audience.

Jocelyn watched him enter the arena, then looked away, her heart thundering unaccountably. If he acknowledged Lily instead of her, she would probably challenge him to a joust herself. It seemed a logical leap in madness from attacking one's rival with a battledore. She knew he hadn't liked finding her with Adam. But Adam was as com- fortable as an old chair; Devon wasn't comfortable at all. He made her feel breathless, awkward, and painfully naïve.

"Jocelyn," Winifred whispered.

"Do not tell me he is making a spectacle of himself in front of that woman again."

"No. But he *is* making a spectacle of himself in front of *you*. A quite handsome one, I have to say."

"Don't tease me. I'm not in the mood."

"*Jocelyn.*" Winifred gave her a sharp elbow in the side, then stared pointedly in the arena.

Jocelyn turned her head. Directly below them Devon sat elegantly astride his dancing charger, a handsome sight even if she hated to admit it.

"A favor from you, fairest of all ladies, to carry with me into battle," he called playfully, one gauntleted hand extended in supplication.

She swallowed, telling herself she would *not* melt into a puddle over a pretty gesture. "What am I supposed to give him?" she whispered to Winifred.

"A shoe?"

"My shoe?"

"Well, then, a garter."

"I am *not* giving him a garter."

"Everyone here thinks you've given him far more than that."

Jocelyn blushed, then untied the silk belt attached to the gold-linked girdle that was a rather uncomfortable part of her costume. She tossed it into the air. Devon caught it on the tip of his lance and made a show of kissing it before he prompted his horse into a bow to salute her.

"What a chivalrous act," Winifred exclaimed, clapping her hands.

Jocelyn tried not to smile. "What an actor, you mean."

"Well, if that's an act, I should like to be in his play. Oh, goodness, is that Sir Gabriel he's fighting?"

The other combatant had just entered the arena on a massive gray warhorse. A black-plumed heaume concealed his face, but he sat in the embroidered saddle with an arrogance that made him easy to identify. He rode over to the stands to ask a favor of Lily Cranleigh, who lifted her knee and threw him her garter without any hesitation at all.

But Devon had paid *her* the honor, and even though she told herself it was probably nothing more than a token tribute, she felt pleased all the same. It might only be for show. He might no more be her champion at heart than she was a princess, diamond tiara notwithstanding.

She realized she'd captured him by default. For all she knew, or didn't want to know, he was still competing for Lily's attention behind closed doors. But if he could pretend in public to be a devoted fiancé, then it really only seemed right that she should do the same. The odd thing was how easy it was for her to pretend devotion to the rogue.

* * *

Devon urged his destrier into an easy gait as the cords were severed. He and his cousin cantered toward each other in a swirling veil of dirt kicked up by flying hooves. Gabriel was an impressive figure, the bastard, on his thundering gray horse.

But Devon had been born a horseman. His lanky, angular build lent itself more to agility and speed than his cousin's rugged strength.

He carried a heavy blunted lance in his left hand and aimed for the center of Gabriel's oncoming shield. If he struck with ample force, he would unhorse but hopefully not injure him.

His aim struck true.

Unfortunately, Gabriel sat firm on the saddle like the bravehearted guttersnipe he was, his padded shield absorbing the blow.

"Come on, cousin," Gabriel taunted as he wheeled his horse around for the next course. "Don't take your loss to heart. All the girls know Lord Devon would rather excel in the bedroom than on the battlefield."

Devon backed up his destrier with a skill that came as second nature. He could ride circles around Gabriel in his sleep. "I haven't heard any tales of your bravery fighting battles."

"That's because the men I fought are dead and cannot talk," Gabriel shouted over his shoulder. "It's only a game, isn't it?"

It *was* only a game, but Devon didn't give a damn. He'd lost sight of that fact the moment he'd looked up and sighted Jocelyn. He wouldn't exactly impress her if he lost. His eyes narrowed in concentration as he and Gabriel reentered the arena in an easy canter that belied their rivalry.

Game or not, he was going to win.

But this time . . . *this* time . . .

He rode firmly entrenched in the saddle, positioning his arm while Gabriel's horse thundered toward him. His concentration paid off. A few moments after his lance struck a shattering blow to Gabriel's shield, his cousin was jolted out of the saddle and hurled backward to the ground. The victory scored the winning *atteint*.

The spectators roared in approval. Someone tossed an ivy wreath into the arena. The heralds trumpeted, announcing Lord Devon to be winner. He had only two more events to win.

He stared down at his cousin in amusement. "That ought to take care of your gloating for a day or two."

Gabriel rolled onto his feet and wrenched off his helmet. "You ought to be grateful."

"Grateful?" Devon snorted. Rivulets of sweat were running down the sides of his nose band. "What for?"

Gabriel grinned. "Because I let you win so that you would not be disgraced in front of your fiancée."

Devon threw back his head and laughed. "Now I've heard everything."

Gabriel pretended to look hurt. "I sacrifice my pride, and you laugh at me?"

"Do you know what I think, Gabriel? I think you're a poor loser. There isn't a sacrificing bone in your body."

Gabriel didn't deny it, either.

Devon rode straight to the stands, dismounted, and bowed low to Jocelyn. She gazed down at him for several seconds as if she weren't sure what to say.

He did know that for some inexplicable reason he'd felt compelled to beat his cousin, and presumably it had been more a matter of male pride than of wanting to win a fine horse. Jocelyn, however, did not appear to look like a woman overly impressed by his tourneying skills.

Gabriel strode up behind him and slapped him on the shoulder, murmuring, "I'd make the most of this if I were you. Ask her to kiss your lance."

"I'll give you something to kiss."

Jocelyn rose from the cushioned bench. Devon could feel his cousin's attention drawn immediately to her willowy form, and fresh annoyance flared through his fatigue. She cleared her throat. Lady Fernshaw was standing beside her, prompting her what to say. "Lord Devon," she began awkwardly, "your bravery has been—"

Has been what? he wondered irritably. A waste of time? His gaze drifted from her face to her figure again. That medieval costume molded to her body as if to caress her every curve. It made him want to take her somewhere private and undress her. Strange that a few seconds ago he'd been aching all over and surly. Now he still ached, but it was a deeper, more familiar discontent. The discontent of raw desire.

He shook his head and tried to focus on what she was saying rather than on what he'd like to do with her when they were alone. Suddenly he realized she'd stopped speaking and was staring past him into the arena. Was Gabriel mocking him behind his back?

He swung around, his helmet under his arm. But Gabriel wasn't looking at Jocelyn at all now. In fact, he was watching one of Lord Fernshaw's footmen, dressed as a medieval squire, hurry toward the stands.

"I bring a personal challenge for single combat for Lord Devon," the footmen shouted, holding his side.

"Who sent you?" Devon demanded wearily of the out-of-breath messenger.

"Lord Chiswick, did, my lord."

"Chinny?" Gabriel asked with a snort of disbelief. "Chinny wants to fight *you*?"

"He has asked for hand-to-hand combat," the footman added in a dubious voice as he gazed up at Devon's towering figure.

Devon groaned. "All I want to do is to remove this ridiculous costume."

Gabriel stroked his jaw. "You could always refuse."

Devon raised his shield and rolled his shoulders as was his habit when he went into battle. "And then I'd appear to be a bully *and* a coward."

"It's complicated, isn't it?" Gabriel murmured. "If it were me, I'd go ahead and fight him. She's watching, you know."

"Yes," Devon said drily.

"I've seen the way you look at her," Gabriel added thoughtfully.

"I've seen the way you look at her, too."

"But I'm not marrying her. If you crush Chinny, she might be afraid to take a brute into her bed."

Devon had to snort at that. "Don't worry about how I'll fare in bed. I haven't had a complaint yet."

Of course he hadn't been married yet, either, nor had he dealt with the complexities of a permanent arrangement. He had confidence in his skills as a lover, but as to love itself? He'd always wondered why a sane man would subject himself to such prolonged torture.

And yet he went ahead and accepted the challenge. To do otherwise went against his competitive Boscastle spirit. He would not demean himself by turning away from a fight.

Three minutes later he stood facing his shorter, somber-faced challenger. He felt his resolve crumble. He couldn't harm Chinny. It would be akin to kicking an annoying pup that kept biting at one's ankle.

After all, Adam had a right to be offended. Devon *had* stolen Jocelyn out of his arms, never mind that he hadn't meant to. Adam had his honor to maintain, too.

"I don't want to hurt you, Adam," he said in an undertone, barely glancing at the squire who brought them their blunted swords.

Adam thrust out his enormous chin. "Well, I bloody want to kill you."

"No, you don't." Devon would have laughed if poor Chinny didn't look so determined. "We're old friends. This is supposed to be *friendly* swordplay."

"Everything is play to you and your damned brothers, Boscastle. War, women. *My* woman, or at least she was."

Devon swung his sword into an arc. "I didn't know you were capable of such passion, Chinny."

He saw Adam's gaze travel past him to the stands and resisted the urge to turn around. He could only imagine what Jocelyn was hoping—that her barbarian of a fiancé would not injure her heroic defender. Devon decided he was going to surprise them both.

He would be a gentleman and throw the match so that Chiswick appeared to be a hero. It really *was* play. It—

The solid whack of Adam's broadsword across

his shoulders jarred him to attention. He ground his jaw and straightened.

It had been a low, unchivalrous blow, but what bothered Devon more than the realization that Adam had taken advantage of his fairness was the realization of pain. He'd been whacked a good one. Unfortunately for him, it hurt. Unfortunately for Chiswick, it also unleashed Devon's temper.

He took a breath, feinted, and swung his sword so that the flat of the blade caught Adam under his wrist and sent his sword flying to the ground. The blunt point of his blade passed through Adam's padded chest shield to his heart. "Sorry, old friend," he muttered, swallowing at the look of injured pride that crossed the other man's face.

Adam nodded. "Think nothing of it. I'd never have made it through school without you defending me against the bullies. I owed you, Boscastle."

The herald trumpeted his victory. Devon lowered his sword and shook his head in regret. "Now we've both made idiots of ourselves. I don't think anyone was impressed."

Adam straightened. "Perhaps, but at least I feel I did my duty. In fact, I feel better about this whole thing all around."

"Then that makes one of us," Devon said with an unwilling glance at the spectators in the stands.

God only knew what Jocelyn had made of this

show. He would half-expect a lady of her sheltered background to be carried off in a faint. Or to weep openly because he had brought down her defender. He might have spared himself the trouble of wondering.

She was gone when he found her spot on the bench. He couldn't even be sure she'd witnessed him give Adam a thrashing. Whatever she'd felt about the tournament would have to wait for a private explanation. Perhaps she would be able to make more sense of his behavior than he could.

Chapter Ten

Jocelyn stood watching from her door into the hall until at last she spied Devon returning to his room. From a glance she perceived that he looked to be in a forbidding mood, not at all his usual self. She decided to give him time to restore his temper before she approached him in private.

She thought it possible that he and Gabriel had been warring today over a certain widow. But the fact remained that he had fought for her today. She understood that it had only been a mock battle, and mockery seemed to describe the marriage that loomed before her. But all the same Devon had taken a stand and fought without hesitation. It seemed to be the Boscastle way.

She had never been much of a fighter herself, but then she'd had little to fight for. It was easy for a shy young woman to find herself shoved into a corner. Her mother had been a quiet mouse who had never dared to gainsay anyone. Her father had believed it his duty to squelch what determination dared break through his only daughter's obedient demeanor.

For better or worse that determination was breaking through now, and Jocelyn did not have an inkling how to stop it. Apparently she was not the obedient young lady she had believed herself to be.

Emboldened by the behavior of her reluctant champion, she decided for the first time in her life that she would fight for what she wanted.

And she wanted to be Devon Boscastle's wife, although not just in name, because that meant nothing. She wanted to become the wife of his heart so completely that it mattered not whether women like Lily Cranleigh even existed. And surely, if he could be prompted to battle a friend on Jocelyn's behalf today, couldn't he be made to love her? She suspected this conclusion did not derive from a rational progress in thought, but neither was it entirely beyond the realm of human reason.

The immediate problem, however, was that she possessed no idea whatsoever of how to bring a challenging man like Devon to heel. He was an uncouth male animal who'd lived as he pleased until he'd gotten caught trysting with her.

A pair of chattering maidservants bustled past her door, lugging heavy buckets of hot water down the hall. Both entered Devon's room, but only one exited, her shoulders drooping in disappointment.

Suddenly Jocelyn found herself walking down the hall, only to hesitate outside his door. She could not simply barge into his bedchamber, engaged to the man or not. And then she reminded herself that a woman like Lily Cranleigh would have no such reservations. Besides, there was a maidservant within.

She knocked.

Devon opened one eye to see the chattering maidservant studying the broadsword he'd used to defeat Adam at the tournament. "Be careful touching that, poppet."

"Goodness, I didn't know blades came that big nowadays," the cheeky maidservant announced as she glanced saucily at Devon's naked figure. "Present company excluded."

He laughed. "You may leave now, you impudent wench."

"Observant is all."

He closed his eyes. "I'd wager there's quite a lot to observe at a party like this."

She knelt at the side of the tub to soap his shoulder. "You aren't half-joking. Secret meetings with someone else's spouse. Romps up and down the stairs, on the stairs—"

"I don't suppose you've heard who might have sent me an invitation to tryst in the tower?"

"No one knows," she said somberly. "And that's the truth."

"And the coffin?" He reached up to firmly remove her hand from his body. "I'll manage on my own, thank you."

She stood with a deep sigh. "Some people thought it was Sir Gabriel who brought the coffin to the castle. Isn't that why you gave him a thrashing today?"

He frowned. "We thrashed each other, and I can only hope that he's as sore as I am at this moment. He did not, however, have anything to do with that coffin."

"Gives a girl the chills, a thing like that."

Devon ground his jaw, remembering the pain in Jocelyn's eyes when she had been confronted by that grim effigy, and how she had endured the rest of the evening with grace.

But then perhaps she was not unaccustomed to enduring at all. Growing up with Sir Gideon could not have been pleasant for a young woman whose natural inclinations would have most likely aroused his disapproval.

And if Devon learned that Jocelyn had endured anything unpleasant in her past, he would take it upon himself to erase whatever dark memories might haunt her. Once they were married, Sir Gideon would be welcome in her life only when or if she desired to see him.

He shook his head. He didn't know what the hell had come over him.

One moment he was planning to ravish her; the next he was assuming the role of her protector.

Well, he couldn't deny his Boscastle heritage. He'd witnessed his brothers suffer the same bittersweet torment. He just hadn't realized it was his turn to suffer.

The maidservant's impish voice ended his musings. "I could wash you all over, if you like," she offered. "I'd have to use the towel, though. The cloth isn't large enough for a man your—"

She glanced around as the door gave a hesitant creak. Devon heard, but did not bestir a muscle. If the intruder proved to be his cousin Gabriel, hoping to even the score by barging in when Devon was naked, he was going to drown the bastard in the bathwater.

The maidservant edged away from the tub, noticeably silent.

Devon kept his eyes closed as he became attuned to the other presence in the room; the intruder was definitely not Gabriel, he thought in amusement. His blood stirred as he heard the evocative swish of silk drawing closer to the bath.

"Well, come on, girl," he said impatiently, smiling to himself. "Go ahead and wash me then. The water won't stay warm forever, and my muscles are tied in knots."

He heard the door close quietly, and he assumed that the maidservant had slipped outside. His chest tightened in pleasant surprise as he felt the hesitant touch of another woman's hand on his shoulder, then across the tight muscles of his chest. With arousing delicacy she soaped his well-muscled bicep.

Refined, gently questing fingers. He inhaled in anticipation and pretended not to notice the difference. His body noticed, though, with a rampant erection that broke the surface of the bathwater and tested his skills at playacting.

"Lovely," he murmured, reaching up to grasp his silent attendant's elbow, "but would you mind washing me a bit lower?"

He opened his eyes at her soft gasp and grinned. Jocelyn threw the cloth down on his throbbing penis and rocked back onto her heels. "You are the devil incarnate, Devon Boscastle."

"Jocelyn!" he exclaimed in mock surprise. "It's *you*. Isn't this a surprise? You're the last woman in the world I would expect to find washing my private parts. Is that what you came here for?"

Jocelyn had decided upon entering Devon's bedchamber that it was time to take the bull by the horns. She received quite a shock, however, when she discovered how big her bull was, and that she had caught him unclothed but, thankfully, not in an actual indiscretion with the girl who was attending him.

The maidservant standing at the tub had glanced up at her with a startled look. Jocelyn put her finger to her lips to shush her.

The girl grinned in understanding, silently offering Jocelyn the soap ball. Devon himself appeared to be relaxing in his bath with his eyes closed. She stared for an unguarded moment at his naked form, or what she could see of it. Her skin tingled with illicit pleasure at the beauty she beheld.

His thick black hair curled wetly against his strong nape. The deeply engraved muscles of his bare shoulders shone with moisture as did the steel-hard plane of his chest. Clutching the soap, she ventured a step closer to the bath only to drop the washcloth on his turgid organ, which he'd unabashedly asked her to wash when it was obvious that he'd known it was her all the time.

Was that what she'd come here for, indeed.

He surged up suddenly like a sea deity during a storm, sending wavelets everywhere as he shook water off his long, hard body.

And stepped in front of her before she could retreat to the door. The devil lurked in the grin he gave her. He blinked, his astonishment a blatant mockery. "By God, you gave me a turn," he exclaimed. "I didn't hear you come in. Did you knock?"

He took three steps and threw the bolt on the door, water dripping from his thick rod onto his tautly muscled thighs. She spun blindly, throwing him the towel laid across a stool. When enough time had elapsed for him to remember modesty and cover his nakedness, she glanced at his reflection in the looking glass.

He was still disconcertingly in nature's garb, modesty apparently not one of his priorities. The towel hung over his neck. It might have been a handkerchief for all it covered the broad contours of his chest and sculptured flanks. And that flagrant part of his lower body that protruded from a dark apex of hair . . . it defied description, although the adjective well-favored came to mind before she closed her eyes.

"Please put something on," she said in a faint voice.

"Give us a minute. I wasn't expecting company."

She opened her eyes and frowned. "You *had* company."

"She works here, darling." He toweled himself off with exasperating slowness. Jocelyn stole a peek at his lean tight buttocks as he bent to dry off his feet. Her throat closed at the sight.

"Don't mind me," she said under her breath.

He came up behind her, bare-chested, his hips snugly encased in . . . in nothing. He was still nude, his damp body a breath from hers. "Excuse me."

"I should think so," she murmured, her blood thrumming alarmingly.

He smiled at her in the mirror. "Do you mind?"

"Do I mind what?" she asked, swallowing drily.

"If I reach under your leg."

Her eyes flew to his. "Why on earth—"

"You're standing on my shirt."

She exhaled and quickly stepped aside for him to retrieve his shirt. He didn't put it on, though. Instead, he slipped his arms around her shoulders and turned her toward him. Her head swam at the chiseled magnificence of his male body. She felt a sudden need to recline on a sofa with a strong vinaigrette.

"Jocelyn?" he asked in all his undraped amusement. "I'm sorry for teasing you. I couldn't help myself. But I have to ask, what are you doing in my room?"

It was a fair question. She wondered the same thing herself before she finally recovered her wits. She had come to thank him for championing her today at the tournament, although she most certainly had not envisioned expressing her gratitude with him standing there in the raw.

"I wanted to—" She made the mistake of looking at his mouth. Those firm sensual lips that had given her her first taste of sin. And made her ache to sample more. "On second thought, what I meant to say can wait. At least until you are in a decent state."

"What is it you wanted?" he queried softly, tracing his long fingers down her shoulder with shivering gentleness.

"This may come as a shock to you, but I'm not in the habit of conducting conversations with the other party in the nude."

"I could undress you if you feel at a disadvantage." He bent his head to bite a most sensitive spot on her neck. His tongue instantly soothed the pleasant sting she felt.

She moaned, her breasts suddenly swollen inside the bodice of her gown. "I meant that *you* should dress, you demon, as you are well aware."

"Why? I've nothing to be ashamed of. This is my room and I'm not about to pretend I am a monk."

She shivered as his teeth nipped a wanton trail down her shoulder. "I doubt anyone would mistake you for a holy man, Devon Boscastle."

He raised his head and smiled. "You didn't come here to save me, did you?"

She decided she would not let either his virility or licentious charm put her at a disadvantage. She had braved this visit to have her say, and nothing, not a promiscuous maidservant nor her husband-to-be's utter absence of inhibitions, not to mention apparel, would distract her from that duty. If she was not going to marry the man, she would have to be able to resist him. Of course, resisting him and discouraging his behavior were two different matters.

"I came here to express my appreciation for what you did today."

He walked her backward with the loose-hipped stride of a master horseman. "I like the sound of that."

"Well, I can't say I like that look in your eye."

"What look would that be?"

She wasn't sure if he lowered her to the bed, or if she simply collapsed from an attack of over-stimulated nerves. All she knew was that she was sinking quite helplessly under the weight of his hard male body and that her breasts, perhaps the heart that raced wildly beneath them, lay crushed to his strong wet chest.

Yet when he kissed her, it seemed somehow natural, perhaps even imperative, that she submit. The imprisoning power of his position wrung the resistance from her bones. He slid his tongue deeply into her mouth and groaned as she lifted her arms to his neck.

"I came here to say . . . that no one has ever championed me before," she whispered. "I was moved by the honor you paid me today."

"I find myself rather moved at the moment, too, but I couldn't say that it has anything to do with honor."

She narrowed her eyes. "I was talking about what you did at the tournament."

"You mean when I walloped Chinny?" he asked with a grin.

"I don't mean that I enjoyed seeing him beaten, but I was grateful that you stood up for me."

"I could stand up for you now if you'll let me."

"*Devon.*"

"How grateful are you?"

"Grateful enough that I disregarded convention and came to your room."

"And you wish to reward my valor?"

She hesitated. "I'm not going to ask what you mean."

"I'd have flattened him if I'd known it would please you."

"That isn't exactly what pleased me."

"Why don't we find out what does please you?"

She swallowed at the dark seduction in his eyes. "I don't think I should answer that question, either."

"I don't think you need to," he said softly, showing her why with another deep, greedy kiss that left her head reeling and her body wanting more.

He ground his hips against her belly so that his rock-hard arousal rubbed the tender mound above her clenched thighs. Shocked, she twisted to dislodge his weight; he merely flexed his back and oh-so-slowly rotated his hips, his muscular body holding her immobile.

She moistened her lips, struggled for breath. "This is—"

"What a man and a wife do," he whispered thickly.

"Except that we have not exchanged vows yet."

"What do a few days matter?" he asked quietly.

She couldn't help laughing. "This from a man who swore he would never make the walk to the altar?"

"If I'm making the walk, I'll damn well enjoy what comes after."

She was losing the battle, not to control him as much as herself. How could she have known a man's body could evoke in her such unadulter-ated enjoyment? And need. Heaven help her, the friction of his overlarge organ had her woman's place weeping with need. She felt her nether folds near flooded with warm fluid at his rhythmic stimulation.

She clutched at his shoulders in a desperate bid to distract him. "Aren't you expected to be recognized at the feast in a short while?" she asked, her back arching involuntarily, her breasts feeling ripe and tender.

He laughed low. "I've a mind to feast on something else tonight. Something succulent and sweet."

She had little time to ponder that shameful if surprisingly arousing statement, for suddenly he had untied her bodice and exposed her breasts to his hungry scrutiny.

His eyes danced wickedly while his fingers pinched one tender nipple into a hard peak. "It did please you to watch me fight for you," he said amusedly, lowering his mouth to her aching breast.

"I thought you behaved bravely and, yes, it pleased me to watch you," she whispered. "I realize you practiced great restraint in what you did, or rather did not do, to Adam at the tournament."

"I'm practicing more restraint now, believe me."

"Devon, for heaven's sake," she said in an unsteady voice. "How would we explain this if we were caught again? You're lying naked atop me."

"At least you can't say I've deceived you with a disguise this time," he said wryly.

"Don't you think you should get dressed for the banquet?"

"I'd rather undress you."

"It would appear you almost have."

"Then I might as well finish."

Convinced he meant what he said, she turned onto her side to slide off the bed, but somehow the movement placed her in an unexpectantly stimulating position of sexual vulnerability with his knee thrust between her thighs. His strong arm shot out to encircle her ribs; his hand cupped the breasts he had unbound from her bodice.

"To hell with the banquet." He exhaled against her neck. "What is this annoying contraption that binds your waist?"

"It's called a girdle," she heard herself reply. "And it wouldn't have been a bad idea if I'd asked for the ancient chastity belt that accompanies the costume."

His free hand stroked down her side and slipped between her legs to casually part her plump nether folds. As she caught her breath, he whispered, "I daresay if I can get in and out of mail armor, I can unfasten whatever garment you wear."

And as proof of this dubious skill, he unfastened the gold-linked girdle and drew the thin skirt of her bliaud up around her hips, leaving her throbbing sex open to his pleasure.

She made one final attempt to rise only to find herself flush against his body.

"That's better," he said quietly, playing with the damp curls above her cleft.

"Devon . . . "

His warm breath teased her ear. The dominant warmth of his hard-muscled body stole over her senses. She felt herself soften, ache, her sex pulsing unbearably. She bit her lip to stifle a groan.

He whispered, "That's even better. Spread your legs for me a little more."

"What . . . what for?"

"This."

She gasped as he gently pressed one long finger between her dewy pink lips. Her muscles gripped him, her belly tightened, and if she had not been lying on the bed, she would have folded bonelessly to the floor.

"You're so very wet," he said, his mouth still pressed to her ear. "And tight as a bud." He slipped another finger into her aching passage and groaned his approval.

She opened her mouth and cried softly as he thrust his fingers even deeper, probing until he reached a part of her body that resisted the invasion.

"Sweet Jocelyn," he murmured. "I'll try to be gentle when the time comes."

When the time comes. And what was this? she wondered in bewilderment.

Her muscles tightened around his fingers, and she might have sobbed aloud had he not turned her swiftly and his mouth captured hers in another lustful kiss. He pulled her tighter to his body. His fingers quickened between the drenched folds of her woman's place, bringing her to a climax so intense that it seemed her heart would cease to beat.

Dazed, she buried her face in his shoulder and listened to the rapid pounding of his heart. Whatever wondrous devastation he had inflicted on her had not left him wholly unaffected. His breathing was uneven. His large hand stroked her in idle pleasure. She quivered again in his arms. And smiled inwardly at the thought of moments like this to come. She'd never guessed, but now that she'd been introduced to Devon's world, she had to experience more.

"Perhaps I should fight more battles as your champion," he mused, his voice drowsy with desire. "I—"

An abrupt knock on the door interrupted him. "May I come in, Devon?" a loud male voice asked. "It's me, Adam. I should very much like a man-to-man."

"As in combat?" Devon murmured, a scowl settling on his brow. "Jesus, I should have killed him when I had the chance."

Jocelyn raised her head in horror. Her body felt heavy and weighed down with . . . Devon. "He can't find us like this. Make him go away," she whispered, springing up at the waist.

Devon swore under his breath and threw his arms

across her midriff to arrest her flight. His blue eyes burned with frustration. "Go away," he ground out. "You've caught me bare-arsed in the bath."

"Are you in any pain?" Adam asked in concern.

Devon sighed and looked down in unabashed lust at the woman lying beside him. "Bloody agony. You aren't helping, by the way."

"I didn't mean to lose my temper today," Adam explained awkwardly. "I didn't even mean to challenge you if the truth be told."

Jocelyn reached covertly to pull down her tunic, but Devon caught her hand and laced his fingers in hers. "Don't move," he ordered her in a low voice. "No one is coming into this room."

"You can't even move?" Adam asked in alarm. "I must not know my own strength. Is it your back that pains you?"

"Somewhere in the vicinity," Devon answered wryly. "More a little muscle stiffness than anything else."

"Should I try to stretch it out?" Adam asked in hesitation.

Devon sat up, his face dark with irritation. "Is that what you came to ask?"

"Er, no," Adam replied. "As a matter of fact, I was possessed of the idea that it would be a good show of chivalry if all three of us appeared at the feast as friends. Having fought each other earlier in the day, that is."

Devon leaned down to kiss Jocelyn while drawing her dress back around those parts of her body he had stimulated and satisfied with such consummate skill. "All three of us?" he inquired absently, motioning her to sit forward so he could relace her bodice. "I assume that the third-party you refer to is Jocelyn?"

Poor unsuspecting Adam. He sounded completely disconcerted as he replied, "No. I meant that you, me, and Gabriel should muster a show of unity much like the Three Musketeers, if you will."

"I *won't*," Devon muttered darkly, then raised his voice. "Hell's bloody bells—did you say Gabriel?"

"He's standing right here beside me, if you can believe it."

Devon grunted. "What a coincidence. Don't tell me he just so happened to be strolling by my room the same time as you?"

"How did you guess?" Adam said in surprise, then hesitated. "I don't suppose you know where Jocelyn might have gone?"

Gabriel cleared his throat. "Adam is afraid that our fighting today might have frightened her off. She's gone missing again."

Devon leaned back on his elbows and smiled.

"Do you think we should seek her out?" Adam asked in an anxious tone.

"Would you be so kind?" Devon replied, placing his hand upon Jocelyn's knee. "I am quite worn out from the thrashing you gave me."

"I understand," Adam said with such gravity

that Devon could only shake his head in amused chagrin. "You must be incapacitated. I put up quite a fight, didn't I?"

"I can only hope to recover," Devon replied quietly. "I have rarely fought such a challenging battle before."

"If I do find Jocelyn before you, shall I give her a message?" Adam asked after an awkward pause.

Devon hesitated, his expression so perplexed that Jocelyn feared he was about to give her away. Instead, he leaned forward and brushed her lips with a kiss that hinted of banked sensuality.

"I think I should best deliver my message in person, Adam," he murmured.

"But you harbor no hard feelings?" Adam inquired again in a feverish voice.

To which Devon wickedly answered in an undertone that only Jocelyn could hear, "What say you to that question? Are my feelings hard or not?"

Twenty minutes later he had dressed in formal evening attire and stood guard in the hallway so that Jocelyn could sneak back up the stairs to her own room. She escaped just in time.

The castle was beginning to fill again as guests returned to their chambers to change out of their medieval attire for the sumptuous banquet in the great hall. Servants hastened to deliver clean water for washing, freshly pressed clothes, and scented billets-doux.

Lord Fernshaw's feast marked the final event of the house party. Guests were known to stay up until the small hours and doze fitfully on the journey back to London. It was a night to flirt, to dine, to dance, to say farewell to a lover, to arrange future assignations.

And to contemplate the future.

Devon sat at the massive banquet table and sipped his wine, laughing at the jibes and ribald toasts that his presence had inspired. None of the taunts, however, touched upon his betrothal. No one at the party would openly offend Jocelyn after today. He had not only made his loyalty clear, he had proven that he would fight to defend her.

But if anyone had told him a week ago that he would leave this party engaged to be married, he would have denounced that person as a liar and trounced him on the spot.

Married.

To Jocelyn Lydbury.

The young lady whose dinner invitation he'd ignored four years ago, and look at him now. That neglected offer had come back manifold in the form of a whirlwind marriage. Lord help him. It would have been easier all the way around if he'd attended the original meal.

As it turned out, he'd be eating dinner with her for the rest of his life.

He watched her with unwilling interest, reminding himself that his country wallflower's composed demeanor concealed quite a passionate nature. Her soft, willowy body heated his blood; the warmth and subtle charm she revealed each time they met proved perhaps even more attractive. He wondered how he was supposed to sleep beside her every night and pretend indifference to his needs.

It wasn't possible. Nor did he intend to deny himself the pleasure of their wedding bed. But as for what else either of them could expect after they exchanged vows, he could not predict.

Their eyes met. He raised his goblet to her and drank deeply, swallowing a laugh at her faintly reproachful frown.

Yet when another toast was made in his honor, hers was the first goblet lifted in the air.

It was as if the sheer meanness of social criticism had forced them into an alliance. Complain of their plight as they may to each other, they seemed to have made an unspoken pact to put on a good show in front of their peers.

The cruel-minded or merely curious who waited to see a crack in the veneer of the scandalous couple quit the table that night disappointed. For all his appearance of negligent noblesse, Devon's backbone had been forged of Boscastle steel—and strengthened by his father's cane. The cavalry had made a man of him. His sisters had made sure he knew how to treat a lady in public.

Let him and Jocelyn battle out their arrangement in the privacy of their bedchamber when the time came. There was no reason for anyone to know by his behavior his true feelings.

Nor did he have full knowledge of them himself, to be quite honest.

As for Jocelyn, well, her quiet, English country charm stood her in good stead. She smiled, said little, and gave second thought to those who wondered how long it would be before her Boscastle strayed.

All in all, the majority of guests agreed that Devon and Jocelyn not only made a handsome couple, but that the unfoldment of their secret romance had elevated Alton's annual house party to the status of the best affair they had ever attended.

Chapter Eleven

They were to be married in the private chapel of Grayson Boscastle's Park Lane residence the morning following their return to London. Emma Boscastle had promised to handle all the arrangements. Even so, Jocelyn had been on pins and needles from the moment the viscountess's carriage set upon the Epping Road, Devon riding behind with Gabriel and Grayson.

The ladies arrived in London twenty minutes before their gentleman guardians, and from that moment on there wasn't time to worry about much of anything. Jocelyn was absorbed into the passionate heart of the Boscastle family.

In fact, she and Devon spent only a few minutes alone on the stairs of Grayson's mansion the night of their arrival, and even then they were headed in opposite directions.

He was running upstairs to look for one of his unruly cousins who'd been firing spitballs at the servants. She was coming down from a hurried fitting with Lady Jane's seamstress to alter the wedding gown she was to wear the next day.

The house was full of Boscastles who'd rushed to London for the surprise wedding and the night-before supper to celebrate the event. With so many relatives reunited, it was practically impossible to carry on any sort of conversation without being interrupted in a heartwarming if exhausting way.

"Well, this is a surprise," Jocelyn said, her heart giving that pleasant but painful leap it did whenever she saw him. Handsome, seductive Devon Boscastle. How was it possible he would be hers? "I thought you might have run away on the way here."

"Sorry to let you down," he teased, grinning at her. "It's a hellish thing to discover that one has honor at a time like this. I thought you might have run away, too," he added ruefully.

"I've never run away from anything in my life," she said steadily.

"Neither have I." His blue eyes twinkled with mischief.

She nodded, suddenly not knowing what to say. He was marrying her, and he didn't want to. "Well, then, here we are, although one of us could still run away before morning."

But neither of them had.

When she'd awakened the next day, the very first thing she heard was his deep voice from the floor below. He and his brothers were laughing loudly. They were, she was discovering, a family quite unrestrained and prone to frequent laughter. She could only hope that his good spirits would continue and that they would have cause to laugh together often in the future. She'd never had much reason to laugh in her own home. It had been agony to watch her mother caught in such an unhappy marriage.

And now . . . She bit her lip. She didn't want to be caught in an unhappy marriage, and she didn't want Devon to feel caught, either.

It was a day a woman was supposed to enjoy. A bride was meant to be the center of attention, to feel beautiful, and cherished. She dressed with Grayson's wife assisting her, and then Grayson walked her down the aisle to give her away because at the last moment her father and brother had decided not to come.

She wasn't as nervous as she thought she'd be. She drifted through the ceremony with a curious feeling of detachment, as if she were in a theater box watching two actors pretending to take their vows.

Who was that raven-haired stranger who towered over his unassuming bride? It was all overwhelming. The dark beauty of the Boscastle family—all of them brimming with some vital essence that stirred her very soul—made her feel as if she'd been asleep until this very moment.

"Well," Devon murmured, coughing into his gloved fist, "we both appear to be here."

"Yes." She hid an unwilling grin.

"Your father and brother . . . ?"

She shook her head, forbidding herself to show she cared. It was a relief, if the truth be told, that her father had refused to appear. There would be no whisper of unpleasantness to mar her wedding day. "Not coming."

"Ah." A muscle tightened in his cheek. "I don't suppose they'll be missed in this mob." For an uncomfortable moment she was afraid he would probe more deeply. She had no explanation, not for him or for herself. She had yet to understand why her father had been as uncaring, as cruel as he'd been. She told herself that Devon was not like him at all.

To her relief, her delight, he merely said, "You look very pretty today, by the way. More than pretty."

The dark gleam in his eye made her believe he meant it. "Thank you," she murmured. "And you look quite handsome." But then he always did. "Did you sleep well?" she asked.

"Nary a wink. Did you?"

"Less than a wink." She drew a breath and gripped her small bouquet of white snowdrops.

"Are we planning to attend the reception together?" he asked as if he couldn't think of anything else to say.

"Isn't it tradition?"

"I . . . I don't attend many weddings, but I'd guess we're obligated to attend."

Obligated. What a heavy, somber word.

"Unless you don't want to attend," he added.

She stared straight ahead. She doubted that anyone watching them could guess their whispered conversation consisted not of prenuptial banter and underlying declarations of love as much as it did the practical concessions of two military generals forced together to declare a truce. They were little more than a pair of strangers standing at the altar.

"It occurs to me that one of us could still run away at any time after the wedding," she said thoughtfully.

"Only if one of us has not conceived a child," he replied imperturbably.

She glanced up at him in astonishment. "What did you just say?"

He shrugged, a mischievous smile lurking in his eyes. "Well, it's to be expected."

"What else is to be expected?" she whispered after a moment.

He looked at a loss. "If I am ever unfaithful to you, I promise you will not hear of it, and I will be discreet."

She fumed for another moment. "If you are unfaithful you *will* hear from me, and you'll most likely be dead, not discreet."

He looked down at her with one brow lifted. "Have we not agreed that this was to be a marriage in name only?"

"I don't recall that either of us had much chance to agree on anything."

He turned his attention back to the altar,

nodding as if in appraisal. "What on earth possessed me to ever believe you were shy?"

"I don't recall you ever paid me enough notice to perceive *what* I was."

"I shall have to pay notice now," he mused.

"What kind of notice?" she whispered.

"You know," he murmured, his voice wicked. "The kind of notice that a lady likes."

Her fingers curled inside her white kidskin gloves. A loveless marriage of convenience to a man who took a mistress when it pleased him might have been acceptable in her mother's eyes. Certainly more than one wife turned a blind eye on her husband's philanderings. Perhaps if Jocelyn had married into a conventional family she would have resigned herself to accept that untempting fate.

But one of the admirable, albeit scandalous, traits of the Boscastles was their stubborn refusal to swim with the tide.

Neither would she, even if she had not quite figured out how to swim at all.

The minister stood before them, his book open, and there was a rustle of noise from behind them as everyone settled down expectantly.

"You could probably still catch a ship to India if you hurried to the wharves," she said under her breath.

"Probably." He took her hand in a firm grasp. "But it's not a pleasant voyage."

"Do you think the voyage before us will be any smoother?"

"I don't know. I've never taken it."

I don't want to love him, she thought. I can't. I won't. I refuse.

And then the minister gave her an encouraging smile and she answered that she would. At least it was her voice that replied. And it was her heart that quickened as Devon's lips touched hers and set off a fierce tremor of longing that seemed to start at the base of her spine. She could only hope that no one noticed how her lips parted on an involuntary gasp when he kissed her.

He noticed, her husband. His strong hand pressed the small of her back. His perceptive eyes sparkled in brief acknowledgment before the demands of convention forced them apart. Well, perhaps it was not so much convention as the Boscastle family en masse.

She was so warmly welcomed into the clan that it almost made up for the fact that her father and brother had chosen not to attend.

There was little time to regret their absence, as Devon, her husband, had said.

She was summarily kissed, embraced, pinched once by a middle-aged uncle full of amorous mischief, hugged by sticky-faced cherubs, and swept into a general gala of mayhem and heartfelt wishes for happiness.

So began her first day as a Boscastle bride, a

day of pleasant confusion and warm acceptance, of silent yearning and uncertainty.

But her wedding night—she'd sipped just enough wine to give her false courage when Devon whispered that it was time for them to go home. Home. A place she had never seen. Her husband. A man to whom she had committed herself today. It remained to be proven how seriously he had taken his vows. It was always different for a woman, wasn't it? But he had shown himself to be a man of honor, and passion.

He swept her up into his arms in the hallway of his house and bore her with apparent ease up the stairs. "My servants are in a snit. No one forewarned them I was bringing home a wife."

She laced her arms around his neck. He smelled deliciously of soap, starch, and champagne, and he had stood at her side today before God and man. "No one warned you, either," she whispered, burying her face in the hollow of his shoulder so that he could not see her smile.

He carried her up the stairs to his room and laid her across his bed. The last time he'd left this house he had not thought to return with a permanent resident. Perhaps he had not thought at all.

But he couldn't help noticing how natural it seemed to see Jocelyn reclining on his four-poster. Their four-poster now, he amended silently. It was going to take him a long time to get used to having a wife.

And yet she had a way of warming a room. Not to mention what she did to his body temperature. In truth, he'd found himself looking forward to their sexual union since their last encounter in the castle. She had beguiled him with her response, and having been fool enough to fall into a trap, he did not intend to waste time in self-pity.

He knew of better ways to spend his time.

He turned to pull off his waistcoat and paused as he heard her rise from the bed. A moment later he felt her gentle white hands slide around his waist to the buttons of his shirt. He drew a breath and waited. She had pleasantly surprised him at each turn.

"May I help?" she asked, already at work on the task of undressing him.

He went still, his cock hardening at her eagerness to participate. This was a far but welcome cry from the woman who'd refused to talk to him when he was nude from his bath. "Be my guest," he murmured, drawing her hand to the waistband of his tight black pantaloons. "But don't stop at the shirt."

She wavered for an instant, then obeyed, her breathing noticeably uneven as she unbuttoned, then rather inexpertly tugged his trousers over his lean hips to the floor. Her gaze flickered to his rigid erection and lifted swiftly to his face. Her lips parted, moist, inviting. He noted the blush that tinted her creamy skin.

"Now undress yourself for me," he instructed her with a smile.

She hesitated before backing toward the dressing screen. He stepped over his discarded clothing and caught her elbow. "No, not behind there. I've a wish to see what my wife looks like."

He walked to the bed and waited.

She lowered her eyes and slowly peeled off her ivory-gauze wedding dress, then unlaced her chemise and short corset. Her breasts sprang free, the nipples puckering at his unabashed perusal. "You may leave on your garters and stockings," he said. "Take off your slippers and come to me."

"Shy at giving orders, aren't you?" she queried under her breath.

"I won't be at all shy when it comes to giving you what you need," he replied, his heated gaze scrutinizing her with raw sensuality. "Come here and let me show you."

She stared at him, her blood pulsing thickly through her limbs.

"I can wait all night," he murmured. "After all, we're married. I can wait . . . forever."

He lay stretched across the bed on his elbow, his pose languid, his body's response to her naked vulnerability revealing he was nowhere near as detached as his voice portrayed. Hard as steel. Her husband. He had a license to be licentious, and she had promised only hours ago to obey him.

She walked slowly to the bed, her breasts tightening, her body tingling in anticipation. "And now?" she asked softly, meeting his gaze.

He uncurled his long body and sat with his powerful thighs splayed. "What you are going to do," he murmured, his eyes smoldering with lust, "is to learn about love."

Her gaze widened. "At your feet?"

"Or at yours," he said, his broad shoulders lifting in an imperious shrug. "I have no objection to taking turns. I enjoy any number of positions. So will you, I'm sure."

The flagrant pleasure he implied made Jocelyn wonder how long she would be able to withstand his scrutiny before she lost the ability to stand at all. It was a question she would not be forced to answer. He reached out without warning and gripped the soft globes of her bottom, drawing her beneath him onto the bed with a single-mindedness that put an abrupt end to her dilemma.

Once again he gave her little chance to retain even a modicum of modesty. Ever so slowly he trailed his fingertips across her face, tracing the vein that pulsed in her temple, the contours of her cheekbone and jaw. She sighed with pleasure, seduced by his touch. Warm and strong, the power subdued; this was the way a man's hands should feel when he touched a woman.

"Close your eyes, Jocelyn," he instructed her in a languid voice.

She did, craving more. His fingers drifted down

her throat to her shoulder. She waited for him to stroke her breasts, the rest of her body. She gave a little moan of impatience.

He laughed quietly before capturing her mouth in a kiss. "I know what you want."

"And?"

His breath shuddered against hers. "I want it even more than you."

She opened her eyes. The desire on his face sent a bolt of electricity down her spine. Made her breasts swell and her sex moisten in anticipation. Her hips shifted, and he smiled a devil's smile.

As if it were the most natural act in the world, and perhaps to him it was, he slipped his fingers between her thighs and petted the pouting lips of her cleft.

"Drenched," he murmured in satisfaction. And pressed his glistening fingers to his lips. "Delectable. I don't have to do anything to arouse you."

She ground her teeth to suppress a groan, but could not control the shudder of desire that went through her. He was a highly sexed man, experienced in the erotic arts, and unapologetic of the fact; she should not be surprised that he knew instinctively how to disarm her. The tender recesses of her body throbbed in anticipation of the pleasure he promised.

"Jocelyn," he said hoarsely, allowing his iron-hard body to settle against hers. "How you tremble so. I could make you come without any effort at all."

She lifted her head. "I hope I shall be able to say the same to you one day."

"You might be closer than you realize. Until then, it would appear that I have you under my thumb."

To prove his wicked claim had merit, he stroked his callused knuckles teasingly across the tips of her breasts until she was almost panting, desperate for release. He caressed the curve of her belly, plucked shamelessly at her pubic hair and the tender bud it concealed until she conceded he was her master and that she would do anything for the pleasure he withheld.

He bent to kiss her softly on the lips, whispering, "How are you enjoying your lesson so far?"

She turned her face into the pillow. "My teacher is the cruelest of taskmasters."

"But a diligent student does not complain of her practice."

Well versed in the ways of lust, he teased her without mercy and exploited every sign of vulnerability that she revealed to him. She could not resist his devouring kisses, could not keep herself from responding to the touch of his strong hands over her body. She spread her thighs without inhibition and thrust out her breasts to invite his seduction, wondering if she would shock him by obeying what her body told her to do, knowing by his deep-throated growl of encouragement that she had not.

He was beautiful, aroused, and dedicated to arousing her.

He was the type of man whose magnetic charm she had assiduously resisted since her coming out. How she had looked down with scorn at other women who had fallen under a rogue's spell. Now she was married to one and should not expect an ounce of sympathy from either family or friends. Indeed, there were women of her close acquaintance who would envy her fate.

She was the wife of a sinful man, one of the wicked, warm-blooded Boscastle brothers. She glanced up at his shadowed face and felt her heart tighten at the dark eroticism in his gaze.

"I want to know everything," she whispered.

For an instant she thought she had displeased him; he did not react for so long a time that she wondered whether a woman should not admit her desires so freely while a man recognized no such restriction.

Then he rose up over her with a fierce look that stopped her breath. Before she understood that she had caused this loss of control, he had positioned her legs over his wide shoulders, grasped her bottom, and began rubbing his thick erection between the plump folds of her passage.

Her body rose to meet his in uncurbed eagerness. He ran one hand down her belly to the hollow between her thighs and deftly pinched the sensitive pearl of flesh above her sex. Her nerves tightened at the raw sensation, and she could sense him smiling down at her, although she had squeezed her eyes shut, embarrassed by the pleasure that flooded through her.

"I believe you'll teach me a few things of your own before we're done," he murmured.

Her breath rushed out; he bent his head and kissed her, capturing her soft cry, plunging his tongue deep inside her mouth as he eased his swollen penis into her damp sheath. She was startled at the stinging pain. The pressure that stretched her until she thought she would be split asunder. To her relief her body seemed capable of accommodating his size. The pain receded to a burning friction that was not altogether unpleasant. Some part of her seemed eager to accept the invasion.

He took advantage of her breathless discontent and pierced her on the next thrust, impaling her with such force that she froze beneath him, her hands gripping him in protest. She should not have been surprised at the discomfort, considering he had forced his large organ into so tight a space. But how a single act could feel at once carnal, shocking, and so necessary to her being she could not say.

It mattered not. This was an act of nature's design. She was his wife, and her woman's body welcomed him, moved against him with an instinct she could not deny. Her muscles clenched him, contracted, coaxed him even deeper. He thrust so forcefully she felt the impact all the way to her spine.

She lost herself in her husband. Her mind swam, her muscles coiled, her hips lifted, and still she ached, wanted more. More. His movements quickened. Her frustration grew.

She thought he must understand how she suffered. He groaned and arched his back, pressing her yet deeper into the bed. Her heels dug into his thrusting buttocks. He pumped harder, faster, and the world dissolved as he, too, convulsed, his body covering hers.

She broke into pieces, could not breathe. She was afraid to move. Afraid to open her eyes again for fear she would not see returned what she felt. Moments passed before he rolled onto his back with his arm across her quivering belly, and a peace sweeter than anything she had ever known stole over her, quieting the doubts and questions that clamored in the back of her mind.

A wife well-pleased on her wedding night. His reputation as a lover has not been exaggerated, although even to a woman as inexperienced as she had been until now, it was obvious that she had given him pleasure in return.

He lay in the untidy bed and watched breaking shafts of sunlight play upon the curve of his wife's shoulder. His wife. He said the word in silence and discovered it unfamiliar but not as displeasing as he'd anticipated.

Indeed, nothing about her had displeased him.

She was completely unlike the demi-reps who'd

indulged his wicked desires and come back for more. Not that he had never played with debutantes. He had.

But with the innocents it had been a different game. There had been rules to follow, consequences to consider. A man could end up getting married.

He reached out to caress the sun-heated spot on her shoulder. Was this the guileless young girl he'd avoided four years ago? Who was this warm-blooded woman who had become a temptress, his wife?

She was dangerous, whoever she was. Delectable, at turns shy and bold, not afraid to give herself to him completely.

The next thing he knew they would have a child. After last night's lovemaking, after years of care to prevent such an occurrence, he would be a fool not to acknowledge the possibility. He could not imagine it. He was not vainglorious enough, however, to be misled into thinking that nature would be interrupted for his lack of vision.

She shifted onto her side with a sigh. The counterpane creased against her ribs, revealing the contours of one creamy breast. He could see the damning imprints of love bites on her neck.

He swallowed hard and looked away, his mouth suddenly dry with desire.

Rarely in the past had he lingered in the early hours with a lover. The dawn offered more dangerous intimacies than the dark. He had given her his name. He had fulfilled his duty. No one could ask more of a man who had never even considered settling down. He'd thought he had time to pay off a few old debts, pursue more worthless pleasures before he came to this.

But the decision had been taken out of his hands, and he found himself sharing not only his bed, but his life, with an unassuming woman who had proven last night the truth of the old adage that looks could deceive.

He rose from her side and dressed quietly so that he would be gone before she awakened. He thought it likely that she would sleep a few more hours . . . and that it really would be a shame if she expected any more from him than he had tendered.

Everyone knew he was a rake, who answered only to himself, and just because he had a sense of honor did not mean he had a heart.

Chapter Twelve

❧   ☙

It was an hour or so after her husband had abandoned their wedding bed that Jocelyn awakened with the covers drawn around her bare form, and a pillow plumped beneath her head. There was no note under that pillow from her vanished spouse. No directions as to what was expected of her that day.

She dressed without ringing for a maid, if one was even employed to attend to such needs. She thought perhaps that Devon might be waiting for her belowstairs, but silence answered her as she called his name from the upper hallway.

Was she mistress of a house in which she knew neither the various chambers it contained nor the names of those servants who kept those chambers in order?

She had no idea what to do with herself. She would simply have to conduct a room-by-room search for the servants whom Devon had mentioned were in a snit over his unexpected marriage.

She wondered whether she would have to win their loyalty.

The question was answered to her satisfaction only a few minutes later when, as she was descending the stairs, she heard a persistent knocking at the door.

She stopped, debating how to proceed, when a tall man in the knee breeches of a butler came hurrying forth toward the door. Somewhere behind him a woman's voice whispered frantically, "Hurry up before it awakens her. God help us if that's one of his lordship's trollops again. I've been chasing them off all morning."

"I am hurrying, Mrs. Hadley," he retorted. "But if it is the trollops, I shall thank you to handle them. I do not consider getting rid of wanton women my responsibility."

Trollops? Jocelyn thought in horror. The housekeeper had been chasing them off all morning? How many of them were there? And what did they want?

"It's them," the butler muttered as he opened the door.

Jocelyn sank down upon the stairs to listen. From what she could hear from her hiding place, three young ladies had come to call at the house, not one of them properly chaperoned or behaving as if they obeyed any rules of etiquette whatsoever. All of them expressed disbelief, if not open hostility, that their favorite wicked friend had been forced into a union with an unremarkable

woman no one had considered a worthy con-
tender for the role of his wife.

It would appear that fast young women were
entirely too at ease calling upon her husband,
Jocelyn concluded, a habit she vowed would
come to a swift end. But not, naturally, until she
listened from the staircase landing to their spate
of spiteful remarks. The butler who had admitted
them into the hall stood in bewilderment and
insisted that his master was not home. The
women ranted on.

"We have come after hearing the most ghastly
rumor about Lord Devon over breakfast—"

"Is it true that he has married Jocelyn Lydbury?"

The butler backed into the hallstand. "Perhaps
you can call at a later—"

"I've never heard of her," one young lady said
with a sniff.

"I have," said the other. "And I can state with
authority that she resembles nothing so much as
one of those horses her father breeds."

"Then maybe," another lady offered waspishly,
"Devon has married her for the ride."

"He was tricked into marrying her."

"She attacked Lily Cranleigh with a battledore."

"Which is no less than that woman deserved," a
heavyset woman in a white apron announced
from the end of the hall. "And I shall ask you
now to take your leave so that your cackling will
not disturb the mistress. Lord Devon left express

orders she was to be allowed to rest after their first night home. He said she was fair worn out, and I've no doubt you understand what that means."

Whether the trollops understood or not, Jocelyn took that as her cue to descend the stairs, deriving no small delight from the shock that crossed the three faces below. "I am awake now, Mrs. Hadley. Pray, who is at the door? Beggar women again? Do they not know to call at the back?"

Mrs. Hadley, whose morals had been mightily offended by the company with whom Lord Devon had too frequently associated, threw open the front door with a flourish. "They're the trollops, ma'am, and I for one shall be most glad to see the last of their kind in this house."

"As will I," Jocelyn agreed, deducing from this bold announcement that she had gained her first ally in the war she fully intended to win for her husband's affection.

Although he would have sworn it was not deliberate, Devon set out to do his damnedest to prove to himself that he had retained control over his life. He spent the next week following his usual pattern of behavior, attending races and Gentleman Jackson's boxing rooms in Bond Street by day, his club by night, although he always ended up in bed with his wife.

He desired her above and beyond what he would have ever deemed possible. On those instances when Jocelyn remarked upon his absence, he suggested she invite her friends to visit or to accompany her shopping. He reminded himself that he had not chosen to marry, and if his wife complained of how he lived his life, he had not promised to change.

This he perceived to be not a cruelty but a fact of which he had warned her before they took their vows. He was not unkind to her.

He was, however, by birth restless, never content to remain in one place overlong, or with one woman for that matter, although he had not desired another since taking Jocelyn to his bed. He did not wish to contemplate what this might mean.

He had yet to uncover the identity of the person who had conspired against him, and, to this end, had asked his older brother Drake to meet him for a private discussion of the matter early one afternoon. Perhaps he needed the more detached perspective of one who was not personally involved. Drake was secretive, cynical, and suspicious by nature.

He found his brother waiting for him in the ground-floor library, perusing the disorderly rows of books that lined the ceiling-high shelves. They had talked only briefly during the wedding reception. Devon had known it would only be a matter of time before Drake would appear demanding to know the complete story of his brother's whirlwind romance.

Drake pivoted, his blue eyes narrowed in cynical amusement. "And you swore that you would rather be buried alive than wed. Is Jocelyn a benevolent undertaker?"

"It would appear that she and I were caught in a trap not of our making."

"Really?"

Devon seated himself in one of two chairs that flanked the fireplace. "I expect Grayson has explained the entire scandal, and Emma has added her disapproving version. There is no secret as to how it happened; the mystery that remains is who tricked us."

"Not the lady herself?" Drake usually stood a little on the skeptical side, his own temperament several shades darker and moodier than his other siblings.

"I thought at first it was Gabriel."

Drake nodded. "I recall that he escorted my wife to a brothel under the pretense of helping her when she was distressed."

"He finds it amusing to bedevil us," Devon mused. "But for what possible purpose?"

"Perhaps to prove that even an outcast can wield power over us. There was bad blood between our families in the past." Drake studied him in subdued silence. "You aren't convinced."

"Not at all," Devon confessed. "Either he's a very decent liar, or I am deceived."

"We shall have to find out. But like you, I do not think Gabriel is our suspect."

Devon shook his head. "I think I should handle

this myself. Pray God, don't let's get the Elders involved."

Drake glanced away, his wry smile bespeaking his agreement. The Elders were, in chronological order, their formidable siblings Grayson, Heath, and Emma.

Until his recent marriage Drake had tended to stand alone, or at least on middle ground when it came to family affairs. Chloe, Devon, and their deceased brother Brandon comprised the younger set of Boscastles. These three Boscastle offshoots usually banded together against their older sibs.

The six of them, however, never hesitated to join forces against the world.

"You have not considered that Jocelyn's father could have set a trap for you, have you?" Drake asked guardedly.

Devon frowned. "I doubt it." Although Sir Gideon *had* seemed interested in Devon as a potential suitor. "Well, that's possible, too."

"But unlikely," Drake said. "If such a ploy had failed, Jocelyn would have been utterly ruined. Perhaps your wife knows more than she is inclined to reveal."

"It wasn't Jocelyn," Devon said in a careful voice. "I've wondered, though . . . is the gossip about Sir Gideon's violent tendencies true?"

"Toward his troops? I've every reason to believe it. Unless you mean—" Drake lowered his voice, "with his family?" he asked in distaste. "Are you implying that he mistreated your wife?"

Devon swallowed, hesitant to voice what he suspected. "He's never to come to my house. Never. She has not mentioned him once since we married."

"Then let the past and all its pain be buried," Drake said quietly.

Devon exhaled. It was a relief to share his unsavory suspicion, although it sickened him to accept that it could be true. Hurting a daughter, a sister, a wife—any woman at all—was unthinkable to a Boscastle male.

Drake cleared his throat. This revelation had shaken them both. "Back to the matter of who deceived you at the party. You have no enemies that I have ever noticed. In fact, you claim more friends than most men of my acquaintance. Few of them, unfortunately, are worth tuppence."

Drake had hit upon the truth with his observations, although Devon did not realize it then. Confronting the person who had baited him would not change anything, of course, but it would give him a chance to avenge himself for the ignominy that had changed the course of his life.

Chapter Thirteen

❧ ❧

Her husband's attempts in the following days to resume his former activities had not escaped Jocelyn's notice, even if at night he sought her bed. She could not ask for a more passionate lover. But come the morning, she was well aware that he had withheld his heart. Apparently, his indifference had not eluded the attention of his sister Chloe, either. Recovering from her recent miscarriage, the vibrant young viscountess had taken it upon herself to support Jocelyn in light of her husband's neglect. Jocelyn had few true friends in London and consoled herself by spending Devon's money on new furnishings and guarding the door against the trollops. Mrs. Hadley, the housekeeper, proved helpful in both regards.

In between these endeavors, however, Chloe had escorted Jocelyn on several shopping excursions, a visit to the museum and a Parisian perfumery, as well as to a breakfast party that went on into the evening.

Today Chloe insisted they go to the park. Jocelyn had at first refused, suddenly realizing that all these efforts to fill her empty hours only made her more aware of her emptiness—and the fact that Devon's inattention was obvious to even his family.

"I really do not feel like walking in the park today, Chloe, but it is kind of you to ask."

Chloe, being a Boscastle through and through, had insisted. "You *will* go, Jocelyn, and you will flirt and show everyone that—"

"That I do not care if my husband neglects me?" she asked with a rueful smile. "But I do care. I care too much about him, and I don't care who knows it."

"Then you will come?"

She sighed. "Yes, but only because you will pester me incessantly until I do."

Devon arrived at the park at the fashionable hour with his boisterous friends, a little surprised to find his wife and Chloe walking together with several young men who had admired his sister before her marriage and, apparently, still did.

He leaned up against a tree and watched his wife in silence, waiting for her to notice him. It was Chloe, however, who spotted him first and detached herself from her faithful flock to approach him.

"Well, he honors us with his presence."

He smiled faintly. "How do you feel?"

"Well enough." But she glanced away after she answered him, and he knew better than to pursue the subject of the child she had lost.

"Was it your idea to bring Jocelyn here?" he asked after a long pause.

"Yes," she said brightly. "And I am happy to see how well she fits into Society. In fact, she's become quite the flirt, hasn't she?"

"Jocelyn?"

"Haven't you noticed, Devon? She is not the little wallflower everyone used to ignore. I lose one of my followers every time I take her out."

Devon looked up and feigned a casual glance in Jocelyn's direction; the truth was, he hadn't taken his eyes off her since he had arrived. He knew damn well Chloe was given to exaggeration and was trying to make him feel guilty for his inattention to Jocelyn, but . . .

Who the devil was she talking to? He had seen her walking to the edge of the water a moment ago by herself, and now there was a man at her side.

This broad-shouldered gallant fellow who was gazing down at her so enraptly was no one he knew, was he? He watched her tilt her head back and laugh. Her companion leaned into her as if he were enamored of the very air she breathed.

He glanced away, his mouth tightening in displeasure. He bloody well knew seduction when he saw it, but he had not expected to see it practiced on . . . his wife. Not with him standing here watching, although he didn't think he'd be any happier if the two of them were carrying on behind closed doors.

"Are you going to ignore her forever?" his sister asked softly from her position on the other side of the tree.

"She appears to be attracting enough attention," he replied in a deceptively uninvolved voice.

"But not yours."

"Let's leave the lectures to Grayson and Emma," he said with a beguiling grin. "You and I are on the same side, remember?"

She hesitated, her concern obvious in her eyes. She and Devon had been each other's champions against their overwhelming siblings all throughout childhood. And Devon knew, despite her insistence otherwise, that losing her child had rendered her emotions more tender than ever.

She sighed. "I am not going to lecture you. If you don't mind her taking a lover, why should I?"

He frowned and watched her saunter away to rejoin her friends. Did he *mind* Jocelyn taking a lover? Hadn't she just met this fool who was pursuing her? Hadn't she spent every night in Devon's bed? He hadn't given her any cause to seek another man's affections, had he?

He'd just lost sight of Jocelyn; he knew she couldn't have vanished into the air, and that she wouldn't let herself be led astray by a stranger . . . even if she had been lured to a midnight tryst with *him*.

He shook his head, realizing how ridiculous this had become. A man secretly observing his wife in a scenario that he had played too often in the past and working himself into a stew over it, too. He wondered how she would react.

He waited for her to walk away from her admirer. There. She'd taken a step aside. The blasted fool followed her. He frowned. Did she just give the Lothario an elbow, or a whispered encouragement?

Did she realize that her husband was standing only a few steps away? Her admirer seemed to have no inkling.

And surely she had not worn such clinging gowns before he'd married her. Where was her pelisse, anyway? Had she, or someone else, that jackanapes, slipped it off her white shoulders? He knew from practice how effective, how easy it was to unfasten a woman's cloak. How delectable it was to feather shivering kisses down her throat to her breasts.

He straightened his shoulders. He also knew how Jocelyn had moaned in delight when he'd taken tender bites of her plump breasts the night before. He couldn't imagine another man touching her. He wouldn't stand for it.

She glanced up, and he knew then she was perfectly aware that he could see her. In fact, if she had been any other woman of his acquaintance, he would have suspected she wanted to provoke his jealousy.

Was he jealous? No. Yes. Dammit, *yes*. He was burning up from head to toe. But it was, he reassured himself, an understandable sense of possessiveness that did not carry any deep implications. Just because he disliked other men playing up to the woman he'd been forced to marry didn't mean . . . it didn't mean anything.

He wouldn't *let* it mean anything. No one could make him feel what he refused to feel. And he felt nothing of any enduring nature. Nothing at least that was going to change him from a heartless rakehell into a devoted husband. Then he looked up again at Jocelyn and that man, and the unexpected twist of emotion that tightened his heart made a mockery of his self-deception.

Fight it as he would, he'd already begun to change.

Chapter Fourteen

❦ ❦

"I have not been in London long," the rather handsome gentleman was explaining to Jocelyn, who had only smiled at him in the first place because he had the innocuous, friendly look of one of her country cousins.

But it was becoming evident even to a lady as unschooled as she in the amorous arts that he meant to become far friendlier than she would allow. Common sense warned her that the wolves had come to investigate, to prey upon whatever weakness she might reveal.

Well, she had her own wolf to tame, and why was Devon leaving her to defend herself? She knew he'd been watching her, although she had not known he was planning to come to the park. It had sent a shock of pleasure down her spine to discover him leaning in the concealing shade of a tree, studying her in unnerving silence.

Still, as long as he was in view, she felt assured she could keep this forward gentleman at bay.

She raised her brow at the brush of a gloved hand across her shoulder.

"I understand," he said, "that your husband runs with a very fast and entertaining set."

She edged away. "I can't vouch for his friends," she replied. "You see, I've actually never met—"

He smiled, walking his fingers up her forearm to her wrist. "I don't care about your husband's friends."

Jocelyn stared down at his hand as if it were some annoying insect that had dropped out of a tree. She realized it was fashionable to flirt, for she had already observed that her sister-in-law Chloe was a natural at the game. Indeed, Chloe seemed capable of teasing the gentlemen who admired her and accepting all their careless compliments without giving either invitation or offense in return.

"I am on fire," her admirer announced with almost frightening passion.

Jocelyn studied him for several moments. "Would you like me to push you in the lake to quelch your flames?"

He closed his eyes. "Wit and beauty in one woman. I fall to my knees and die."

"Then do us both a favor." She pulled her hand free from his unwelcome grasp. "Die at someone else's feet. I already have a reputation for putting men in coffins."

It appeared, however, that this headstrong

gentleman took her rejection as a challenge. With an alarming absence of propriety he pursued her around the bench she had hoped would place distance between them. "Do behave yourself," she muttered. "My husband is watching. He shall call you out if you persist in your nonsense."

"Your husband isn't watching," he said in a devilishly sly voice. "He's gone off with his friends. Don't be such a doorknob, darling. The whole world knows that your marriage was arranged, and that in these unhappy situations, one is forced to find one's pleasure . . . elsewhere."

She whirled, infuriated because she resented being thought a lightskirt, because what he said about her marriage was true, but more because Devon had apparently sauntered off and left her at the mercy of a complete lackwit. Gabriel was suddenly standing under the tree where her husband had been.

"What I am forced to do," she said, plucking the hand he had laid once again on her person, "is to summon my husband to rid me of your unwelcome presence."

His thin lips lifted in a knowing smirk. "You'll become a most lonely lady if you await his attention. I'll wager that in a sennight you'll be seeking me or another out to ease your longing. Everyone knows your marriage is no love match."

"And everyone also knows," said a deep

mocking voice from the direction of the path, "that a gentleman who forces his attention on a lady has planted one foot in his own grave."

Jocelyn glanced around in relief even though she knew her dark rescuer was not Devon but his cousin Sir Gabriel.

Not her husband, who had disappeared at the very moment she needed him the most.

Still, in the light of Devon's disinclination to shield her from this unsavory encounter, she was grateful for Gabriel's intervention. It gave her the respite she needed to manage a graceful escape.

She wheeled, looked up, and found herself standing directly in front of her husband. At least it appeared to be Devon, although he did not sound like or resemble the indifferent devil she had come to know and desire. This low-voiced man exuded an unfriendly aggression that forced her to step back in self-defense. He did not even glance at her.

Gabriel was strolling up behind him.

Her husband's voice frosted the air with a forbidding chill. "Chloe has been waiting for your return, Jocelyn. And, you, sir." He stepped around her to confront the man who stood before him in white-faced apprehension. "I don't believe I've ever had the displeasure of making your acquaintance. Kindly give me the name of the man I wish to kill."

Devon was not a man easily provoked to anger. Yet suddenly he found himself confronting a man whose countenance he did not recognize but whom he had an unreasonable urge to murder.

A firm voice spoke behind him. "Do you want me to stay or to take the ladies away?"

Devon did not turn around to acknowledge his cousin. "Take them home. I demand retribution from this person who dared put his hands on my wife."

Jocelyn looked up at him in alarm. "It was nothing."

"It wasn't nothing. I saw him." Devon advanced on the other man, who by this point could no longer maintain his mask of bravado. "He touched you. I saw him with my own eyes. Damn him. He touched you."

"I merely brushed a leaf off her shoulder," the gallant stammered. "I meant no offense to either you or your wife."

A muscle tightened in Devon's cheek. "You bloody mushroom. I'll brush your goddamned head off your—"

"Not here." Gabriel forced himself between the two men, his voice urgent. "You were in enough trouble last year over a certain coaching incident that I recall."

"This is different," Devon said between his teeth. "I thought you were going to leave."

"Please, Devon," Chloe said, arriving to take Jocelyn's arm. "There are children in the park. And your friends, well, everyone can hear you."

The shaken gallant drew a silk handkerchief

from his pocket to dab across his forehead. "Will you not accept my apology? I mistook the lady's kindness for something else."

Devon cast an involuntary glance in Jocelyn's direction. He barely noticed that his friends had drawn near. "Why would you presume to seek her out at all?"

The man shook his head in bewilderment. "I'm not sure myself. I'd heard a rumor that she was—"

Devon's gaze darkened. "She was what?"

"Only that she was unaccustomed to London ways, as I . . . I am," he concluded somewhat lamely.

Devon gave him a murderous look. "Then perhaps you ought to return to your place of origin until you learn more of London ways yourself, one of which is that a man does not take liberties with the wife of another."

"With your permission, my lord, I . . . I think I will."

Jocelyn could not decide how best to break the tense silence that befell the small gathering as her offensive admirer executed an escape between a pair of governesses and her young charges.

Gabriel was staring down at the ground, his expression unreadable.

Devon stood with his arms folded across his chest, his eyes still smoldering with anger.

"Well," Chloe said with an uncertain attempt at a laugh, "this has proved to be an eventful walk. It seems we can't leave your lovely wife alone," she teased, one arm still protecting Jocelyn, the other extended to Devon. "I am quite impressed at your self-restraint. And good sense."

"Well done, Devon," Gabriel said, nodding in approval. "I hope you didn't resent my interference."

Devon merely shook his head.

Chloe gave him a worried look. "Why don't we—"

Devon pivoted and strode away before she could finish, Jocelyn gazing after him in concern. How on earth had a casual afternoon ended so unpleasantly? She wished she'd given that obnoxious man a good shove into the lake when she'd felt like it. Surely Devon didn't think she'd given him any encouragement?

"Don't fret, Jocelyn," Chloe said, her tone lighthearted, her eyes denoting a darker emotion. "Devon shall have to accept your appeal to other men, and this tiny scandal will be forgotten by tomorrow."

Devon leaned against the billiard table in his library, struggling to understand his behavior today. He'd left the park without any explanation, half-hoping he would run into that presumptuous upstart again and could purge himself of the anger he'd reluctantly suppressed.

What had the bastard claimed as his defense?

That he'd heard a rumor about Jocelyn. That she was unaccustomed to London ways.

And that feeble rationale had given another man leave to approach her?

He wouldn't stand for it. He didn't care if it had only been a harmless flirtation. He would not tolerate it.

How many times had he laughed at his friends who'd dueled when jealousy had gotten the better of them? Why had he thought himself above emotional entanglements? For several terrifying minutes today, reason had been unable to penetrate his rage. He'd thought he'd escaped the curse of his passionate Boscastle lineage, but it had only been lying dormant inside him all along, waiting for the right moment, the right woman, to emerge.

He picked up his cue and stretched at the waist to take a shot. From his peripheral vision he saw a figure in light-green silk slip into the room, her hair catching glints of candlelight.

"You're brave to beard the lion in his den," he said without turning around.

"Is the lion a danger to me?" Jocelyn asked in her soft, enticing voice.

He sank the ball into the center pocket and straightened, his gaze drifting over her. "Not to you, ever." He paused. "Was there anything on your shoulder today?"

She smiled reluctantly. "Only his hand."

He threw the queue down with a clatter and cursed. "I should have beaten the bloody guts out of him when I wanted to. Why did everyone try to stop me?"

"We were in the middle of the park, Devon."

"I don't care," he exclaimed. "No man is going to touch my—"

She walked slowly toward him. He felt heat ignite in the marrow of his bones, a heat that made him forget what he'd been about to say. He braced his hip against the table, waiting. He told himself that he could resist her if he felt like it.

Then she inquired in a silken voice that tore his intentions to shreds, "Will you come upstairs with me?" And he knew he could not resist her at all.

She had been determined to learn more about her husband. Yet moment by moment it seemed she discovered something unknown about herself while Devon remained a perplexing mystery.

She was not so unworldly as to imagine that either sexual pleasure or an arranged union equaled love. She knew there was at least as much decency in Devon as indecency.

She had learned it was far easier to incite a man's lust than his undying love, even if he incited both inside her.

She could not say exactly what occupied his time away from her. Perhaps she did not want to know. But when he came to her bed, he was hers, and she was determined that soon he would not want to leave.

She had decided upon leaving the park today that there was more hope for her marriage than she'd first realized. True, her father had insisted that Devon do the honorable thing. But his card of influence had been played.

The rest was up to her.

Perhaps it would be helpful to view her situation as a military operation. She could either bring her husband around to her camp or forge out blindly to battle him on his turf. And most likely lose.

A strategy was not only desirable but essential.

She wondered what weapons she could employ. She counted Chloe and Mrs. Hadley as her allies thus far. One could not undertake a war of this nature unarmed or lacking support and hope to win.

Of course, it did not take her long to decide what weapons she should use. She had only to follow her instincts.

Still, instincts or not, she was a little unsure of herself, that night in their chamber, when he removed his silk-lined coat, vest, and heavy muslin shirt. She stared at his beautifully sculptured back as he turned to lock the door.

She backed into the window, aching to offer herself to him. She decided that she would memorize the ridges of muscle interspersed with small white scars on his torso as long ago she had learned the winter constellation. Her gaze followed the sprinkling of dark hair that tapered from his flat belly into the pantaloons he had begun to unfasten.

He glanced up in that devilish way he had, the way that disrupted such basic functions of speech, thought, and the mere ability to breathe.

"What are you looking at, Jocelyn?"

She couldn't admit she'd lost all cognition so she swung her gaze to the window and answered, "The stars."

"The what?" he asked in amusement.

"I used to study the constellations from my window in the country," she said, glancing at him over her shoulder.

He pushed down his pantaloons and linen drawers to stand nude before her. "Perhaps we'll study something else tonight."

A cascade of chills started at the nape of her neck and spread through her body. How could she pretend to hide her own hunger for him when he had only to disrobe to immobilize her with such a damnable pang of desire?

How immodest, she thought suddenly, were the demands made upon a married woman. Still, those demands should be met. Her husband had certain needs, and he was a masterpiece of a man. And . . . she had invited him to come upstairs.

"Which constellation were you contemplating, anyway?" he asked in a pensive voice.

She said the first thing that popped into her mind. "Taurus?"

"The bull?" he asked with a laugh.

She pretended to peer out the window again. Of course, being a cloudy night the stars were completely obscured. "Perhaps Orion."

A shock of blue-black hair fell across his cheekbone as he laughed again. "The Hunter? Can you really see it from the window?"

"Well, I . . . I thought I did a moment ago."

He came up behind her, wrapping his arms around her waist. "I don't see a damned star in the sky myself, but who knows? Perhaps if we lie in bed together long enough, we'll see a meteor shower."

Chapter Fifteen

꧁ ꧂

Devon resisted the urge to linger in bed after making love to his wife. She was drowsy and replete, curled sweetly against his own satisfied body. Satisfied?

Siren, he thought, kissing her shoulder. Sorceress. And the dying remnants of his former life fought to reassert themselves.

He rolled out of bed and quietly donned his clothes, sneaking with his boots toward the door.

Somehow it felt safer walking the misty streets of London and taking the risk of whatever physical dangers came his way than remaining at Jocelyn's side. He debated stopping off to see one of his brothers. But he wasn't in the mood to be teased about his marriage, or to answer the well-meaning questions his sisters-in-law would ask about his wife.

Before he knew it, he had reached his club, assuming that the familiar male haven would take his mind off all things that threatened his basic sense of survival.

He entered the candlelit sanctuary and waited for the usual diversions to tempt him. Yet instead of stopping he merely nodded at the three men who slouched indolently in armchairs around a circular table. One was Captain Matthew Thurlew, the elder brother of his old friend Daniel. The other was Lord Burnham, an earl's son; the third a known rakehell. They were engaged in a graphic discussion of a certain Cyprian's sexual agility.

Their aura of world-weary discontent made him feel as if he were staring at his own distorted reflection in a distant mirror.

"God, it's Boscastle," Thurlew muttered, brightening. "Let there be sin."

"Are you betting tonight, Devon?" Burnham asked, his eyes half-closed.

"He's on honeymoon, you dolt," Thurlew retorted.

"Well, he won't be the first devil to spend his honeymoon at the hazard table."

The hazard table. Gabriel liked to gamble. Suddenly Devon knew he had found the distraction he sought. He had unfinished business with his cousin.

He summoned a waiter. "Has Sir Gabriel been here tonight?"

"No, my lord. If he appears, shall I mention that you were looking for him?"

Devon's mouth thinned. "Yes."

"No other message?"

"The rest I shall deliver in person."

As he left his old haunting ground and walked outside, he found he had been followed by Thurlew and his two companions. They stumbled up beside him on the way to their carriage. "Shall we drop you off somewhere?" Thurlew asked.

Lord Burnham laughed. "In the Thames, perhaps? Bad luck getting caught, by the way. Are you already so bored of your bride that you've escaped her this early in the game?"

An unbidden response came to his mind. *No, she's so* damn *appealing that I escaped to preserve my own sanity.* "Where are you idiots going, anyway?" he asked instead.

"Audrey Watson's," Thurlew said. "We've a mind to bring down Babylon."

He laughed. The most exclusive bordello in London would never admit this unsavory trio.

"That's a thought," the younger man said, swaying into Devon's side. "If we escort Boscastle there he might get us an invite upstairs."

Devon shook his head. "She'll have you tossed onto your drunken arses before you can knock at her door. But drive me there all the same. You've given me an idea about where Gabriel might have gone."

Jocelyn had drifted off into a light sleep after she and Devon had made love, not even wanting to talk. She was more than content savoring the warm intimacy of lying beside him. Surely this closeness would serve as a milestone in their marriage.

She opened one eye just as he rolled off the bed and donned his clothes, sneaking with his boots in one hand toward the door.

She sat up in disbelief. So much for intimacy and milestones.

Her impetuous husband had taken the pleasure she offered and given her pleasure back, only to leave her without a backward glance. For several moments she stewed in her simmering indignation until some glimmer of instinct brought a strange clarity. It didn't matter that he was more experienced in sexual matters then she. For even if she did not know where he had gone at this time of night, she thought it unlikely that he had quit her bed to seek another.

Unable to sleep, she rose to bathe before she went downstairs to await his return.

A few minutes later she found herself answering a quiet knock at the door. Utterly shocked, she stared up into the equally startled face of his cousin Gabriel.

She *never* answered the door herself.

She was not properly dressed to entertain, her gown hastily laced, no stockings on, her hair unbound.

"Goodness, Sir Gabriel," she said, "I thought

you were Devon else I would never have answered the door this—"

"He's not home?"

He had already invited himself into the hallway, she thought in disconcertment. Not that she wouldn't have allowed him entrance, but she certainly did not want to throw kindling on the fire of their old rivalry.

"I hope I haven't disturbed you," he said with the polished air of a contrite gentleman.

Jocelyn had to admire his aplomb. She stepped aside unthinkingly to allow him into the house. The servants would not go to bed for another half hour or so. She had no idea when her husband would return. She had not expected to entertain anyone else.

Daringly she had dressed in an opal-white silk gown unencumbered by either chemise, garters, or corset. She'd felt scandalous when she saw in the looking glass that by a certain sway of the hip, a trick of the light, the lines of her bare form showed. Scandalous and secretly delighted that she would greet her sensual husband at the door in an invitation he could hardly misinterpret.

However, she had not intended to greet his diabolical cousin in such inappropriate attire. She could only hope he had not noticed.

"May we retire to a more private place?" he asked in the most respectful manner possible.

She made a noncommittal sound in her throat,

which he appeared to interpret as assent and swept his cloaked presence through the vestibule.

Good heavens. All the men of this family displayed the most overwhelming sense of self-possession. Nonetheless, she was Devon's wife, and she would not be accused of mischief.

"Sir Gabriel, do you think it's wise for you to be here after the discord in the park today?"

The question seemed to be merited when, in the next moment, she caught a glimpse of his reflection in the hall mirror and realized he was studying her uncorseted silhouette with a wolfish smile.

But his face was wiped clean of wicked intentions when he turned around. Still, she could not trust that mirror-Gabriel. Was it a reflection of his true self or a distortion?

"Devon was apparently looking for me tonight at the club," he replied. "Instead of chasing each other all about London, I thought I would do him the favor of waiting for him to come home."

"Oh." She was relieved to learn that Devon had not gone out in search of some illicit pursuit.

She wondered if Gabriel was still involved with Lily Cranleigh, and if the widow was behind Devon's hunt for Gabriel tonight. Gabriel did not seem to be the complete villain Society thought him.

"You don't mind if I stay then?" he asked.

Before Jocelyn quite realized how it happened, she had taken his cloak and ushered him up to the private first-floor drawing room reserved for family.

The next thing she knew they were discussing his last visit to Paris; she was a little astonished to discover he was a patron of the arts; she'd rather thought that he and the other Boscastle males counted *l'amour* as their craft of personal calling.

Another hour flew by in surprisingly enjoyable conversation.

She almost forgot her informal state of attire.

Yet somehow she suspected Gabriel had devilishly contrived it, the very minute that Devon appeared in the drawing room, the situation lost its patina of innocence. She became instantly aware of her careless appearance, of the fact that Gabriel and she were sitting on the sofa shoulder to shoulder—

She threw him an annoyed look. They had not been sitting that close together before. The blackguard must have sneaked over a few inches the instant Devon came through the door. He and Devon lived to provoke each other, it would seem.

Of course, to accuse him of this mischief would only serve to draw Devon's attention to the fact. And if her husband had not seen Gabriel's underhanded play, it seemed wise, in the interest of family relations, not to bring it to his notice.

Naturally, he had noticed. He scrutinized her first with steady regard that seemed to assess every lace, hook, and eye of her informal gown.

Then his narrowed gaze contemplated the two glasses of cordial on the table.

The full power of his displeasure seemed reserved for Gabriel, however.

She rose hastily as if to stand as a buffer between him and his cousin. "It's nice of you to return home before dawn, Devon. Your cousin has been keeping me company while he waited—"

"What the hell are you doing in my house, Gabriel?" Devon demanded, staring right over Jocelyn's head to glower at his cousin.

Jocelyn cleared her throat. "It is my understanding that you were looking for Gab—"

Gabriel stood, his jaw tight. "I only thought to save you the trouble of looking for me."

"And I was merely sitting with him," Jocelyn began again, "until you returned from wherever—"

Devon practically lifted her out of his path to glare down his nose at his cousin. Gabriel was glaring right back at him.

Well, she thought, stepping behind the chair for good measure. So much for acting as a buffer. If the two of them were determined to kill each other, she might as well take precautions to protect herself. She was not about to be caught in their crossfire.

"I only came here because I was told at the club that you wished to see me," Gabriel said stonily.

Devon hesitated as if he had forgotten this fact. "That's true, but you were not told that I wished for you to seduce my wife, were you?"

"I beg your pardon," Jocelyn said. She knew it was unwise to interfere, but her husband's accusation did not show her in a becoming light. She was beginning to sound like a seductress. "Sir Gabriel did nothing of the kind."

Devon shot her a scornful look over his shoulder. "Not that *you* noticed. I know how his mind works."

"Well, I wish I knew how yours works," Gabriel said. "I was given a message that you had asked after me. I would not have come here otherwise, believe me, as pleasant as your wife's company proved to be."

Devon glanced at Jocelyn once again. "Would you mind leaving us alone?"

"I should be glad to." She edged around the chair, conscious of her bare skin beneath the gown, even though both men made a point of looking the other way to allow her exit, a courtesy that did not ease her embarrassment in the least. It was quite one thing to play the temptress in private with her husband, an altogether different matter when it involved another man.

The moment the door closed on Jocelyn's willowy form, Devon turned to subject his cousin to a cold stare. "Cousin or not," he said. "If you sit that close to her again, I'll—"

Gabriel held up his hand in a conciliatory gesture. "I admit it was a deliberate provocation on my part, and I apologize. Some evil impulse got the better of me when I heard you enter the house. Jocelyn was innocent of any mischief. I didn't mean anything."

Devon snorted. "I know that, but— I suppose I'm just not in the mood for our usual jokes."

Gabriel idly toyed with his pocket watch. "Fair enough."

Devon lowered himself into the chair opposite the sofa. "I was taken with the impulse, actually, to thank you."

"To thank me?" Gabriel's fingers tightened around the chain of his watch. "I must have misheard you."

"You meant to help today at the park," Devon said. "My bad temper had gotten the better of me."

"It was understandable."

Devon grimaced. "God, listen to the pair of us discussing moral obligations."

Gabriel lifted his brow. "Honesty is not always appreciated."

"Dishonesty is never so."

"Do I take this to mean you now realize that I was not the person who deceived you into meeting Jocelyn in the tower?" Gabriel asked.

"I never really believed it."

"Perhaps the time has come to uncover the truth," Gabriel said, rising with purpose. "You have met your duty to Jocelyn, and now you may seek your personal revenge."

"My appreciation in no way gives you carte blanche to uncover my wife," Devon added swiftly, his humor suddenly returning.

Gabriel grinned and picked up his cloak. "From what I saw today it is not my attention that need worry you in that regard."

"Just don't give me any reason to worry about you," Devon retorted.

Chapter Sixteen

❦ ❧

"Why did you allow him in the house this late at night?" Devon inquired of his wife in the privacy of their bedchamber as he unbuttoned his pantaloons for bed.

"For one thing," she said evenly, "Gabriel is a member of your family, and as such I do not feel secure enough in my position to close the door in his face. What was I supposed to do? I would not have turned Drake or Grayson away."

"Opening my house to Gabriel and practically sitting on his lap on the sofa are two different things."

"I do not argue that." She got up, taking his coat off his shoulders. "The fact is Gabriel wasn't sitting that close to me until you appeared."

"I am not faulting you, but you might be a little concerned that men are . . . seeking your company."

"Perhaps you shouldn't leave me alone as much," she said, her smile provoking him.

"Perhaps I—"

She crossed her arms beneath her uncorseted bosom, the tempting contours of which he could discern in enough detail to make his belly tighten with desire. "What happened to your corset?" he asked, staring at her incredulously.

"My—"

She broke off, laughing and lowering her arms, as he ran his hands in a swift but thorough search over her breasts and bottom. "Nothing," he said in a scandalized voice.

"That's right."

He drew his head back to regard her in astonishment. "You're not wearing anything beneath this gown? My wife . . . and you're not wearing all those things you usually wear?"

"I did not think I would be answering the door when I dressed," she said in vexation.

His eyes traveled over her several times. "You mean to tell me you entertained my cousin dressed, or undressed, like that?"

"I wasn't expecting visitors when I went downstairs."

"My God. No wonder Gabriel was sitting so close to you."

"It wasn't my fault."

"Well, whose was it then?"

They examined each other in the lapse of emotional silence that dropped between them. Devon was not entirely sure if this was the eye of the storm, or the start. He did know that he had never engaged in this sort of silly argument with any of his past lovers. His loss of control bothered him almost as much as did the thought of Gabriel sitting next to his wife's uncorseted form on the sofa, admiring those charms that he was still in the process of admiring himself.

The reminder unsettled his thoughts anew. "It would have been common sense," he said, "if not simple modesty, to put on a dressing robe while the two of you sat together."

"An invocation to modesty coming from your lips," she retorted. "Yes, a dressing robe would have been a fine idea, had he not taken me off guard—"

"You're both lucky that's all he took. Let Thistle answer the door next time."

"Fine." She put her hands on her hips. "Do you wish for your nightclothes?"

He stared blankly before realizing that he stood ranting about her immodest dress with only his shirt and stockings on.

"I've walked about in my bedchamber naked for years, and I don't mind if you do, either. Furthermore, I was getting ready for bed. And I would still like to know what you were getting ready for in that dress that displays more of you than it should."

She unlaced her gown and let it slide off her shoulders to her feet. Lowering her eyes, she let him look at her before she answered. "You."

His throat closed. God, how she tempted him.

A man could only take so much. Could only

pretend so much. He watched her walk naked to the bed, her hips undulating with a sensuality that made his bones ache.

Then he followed.

His gaze darkened. "What do you mean?" he asked intently.

"You left my bed. I didn't know where you'd gone, but I wanted to greet you at the door when you returned."

He stared at her, realizing what she was trying to say. "You thought to wait for me looking as desirable as you do?" he inquired, approval heating his voice.

She fought a smile. "Are you admitting that you find me desirable?"

His blue eyes warmed with wicked delight. "Are you admitting that you were hoping to seduce me?"

She moistened her lips. "That hope might have crossed my—"

He grinned and then, without warning, threw her over his shoulder and swung her down beneath him onto the bed. "I know of a way to make up after an argument," he whispered.

She closed her eyes, her breath catching. "Did we just have an argument?"

He brushed her hair from her shoulder. He heard her soft intake of breath, felt his body heat, then harden. His warm, sensual wife.

"Tell me again you were waiting up to seduce me."

"No . . . all right. I wanted to seduce you."

His white teeth flashed in a grin. "Do you object if I go first?"

"It looks as if you already have."

He leaned over her and kissed her deeply, gently, his hand caressing her face and shoulders. Did she guess? Did she have any idea how he desired her? No matter how calm and deliberate he tried to appear, his body betrayed him. He could not hide how urgently he wanted her. How he had come to crave the pleasure he knew only with her.

His gaze swept over her beautiful naked form then returned in male triumph to her face. "Mine," he said softly. He could see the answering fire, the invitation in her eyes. She had already seduced him, he realized, although at this rate he'd soon be begging on his knees for her favor.

Until that time, however, he knew how to make her beg. Slowly he stroked her breasts, her belly, her soft arse, the delta between her thighs until she was straining upward at her shoulders. He trailed his fingers languidly through her wet curls to tease her swollen labia, watching her writhe, making her whimper.

"You're torturing me," she whispered as he slid his large hands under her backside and lifted her.

"I'm torturing myself, believe me," he said raggedly, and then he spread her legs even farther and settled head and shoulders between her thighs.

She lay in frozen disbelief for several seconds before she hoisted herself onto one elbow and stared down at him in shocked comprehension. "What on earth—"

He gently pushed her back onto the bed. "Do you want to seduce me or not?"

"I—"

She never remembered what it was she'd meant to say. The touch of his sinful tongue like a brand at her sex robbed her of all reason. She groaned helplessly as he licked the most intimate recesses of her body. And aroused her beyond all reason.

She strained. She sobbed. But he did not stop. His tongue at turns licked and penetrated her body, wringing a climax from her that shattered her to the core.

He laid his head against the silky hollow of her thighs and breathed deeply of her scent. "Are you asleep?" he whispered.

She wriggled out from beneath him. "Devon?"

He glanced up at her face, framed in a tumble of dark brown hair. "What is it?"

"I said I wanted to seduce you."

"And you—"

He rolled onto his back as she suddenly straddled him, sliding down his belly to nestle her face between his legs. His heart thundered in his chest.

"What are you doing?"

"What you just did to me."

He hardened instantly. "Do you really want to?"

"Tell me how," she whispered.

"Lie between my legs upon the bed."

She obeyed, her heartbeat erratic, unsure of what he meant but determined to prove her dedication to what pleased him. She realized that men enjoyed the pleasure he had just given her, but the performance of it remained enshrouded in whispered rumor, the realm of the professional courtesan. "What next?" she asked unevenly.

"Let your mouth mimic the love act," he said, his heavily muscled thighs straddling her shoulders.

The love act. She knew that there was a rhythm to it, a give-and-take that pleased them both. He held himself in one hand and guided the knob of his engorged shaft into her mouth. She closed her lips and suckled him gently, feeling awkward and yet aroused as he moved against her mouth. He tasted of sex and salt and earthly desire. She raised even higher on her elbows, slowly encircling the bulbous crest with the tip of her tongue.

He fell back onto his elbows, panting. "Enough, or I'll flood your mouth."

She dug her fingers into his thighs and held him fast, as he had just done when pleasuring her in a similar fashion. She sensed a growing helplessness in his response that thrilled her. The movements of her mouth and tongue felt unskilled, lewd, and awkward; she was afraid she would injure him, although, considering the size of his organ, it seemed more likely he would choke her.

"Is it good?" she whispered against the pulsing length of him.

Was it good?

He spread his thighs, swallowing a groan at the silken caress of her lips upon his cock. He felt blood surging to his groin and resisted the urge to buck his hips. His wallflower of a wife would kill him if she kept that up. Her hands gripped his thighs even harder.

"More than good," he managed to groan, aware she awaited his answer, but, dear God, how could a man talk with that mouth sucking him so sweetly?

Her tongue circled his pulsing erection, then withdrew; he tensed and guessed that she was waiting for his instruction, his encouragement. She did not dream that her untutored act could have commanded a small fortune in the finest school of Venus. Sweet Christ, he'd pay her himself for this spine-tingling pleasure.

She lifted her gaze to his and gently ceased the suction of her lips. "I'm doing it properly?"

He nodded his head. He was shivering, not even able to answer.

Then before he could move, she set back to the task, refusing to stop again until his belly quivered and he spurted his seed into her mouth.

And when he could move again he leaned

down, wiped her glistening chin off with the sheet, and clasped her face in his hands. She smiled at him. And he smiled back.

God only knew what fate had befallen him and what yet loomed ahead. He knew only that its invisible threads had wrapped themselves insidiously around him in a web he had less and less desire to escape. And that even if his life had been turned inside out, he did not mind.

Jocelyn's bare toes ascended the instep of her husband's left foot before climbing his muscular calf to his warm groin. His eyes still closed, he smiled approvingly and locked his arms around her hips. She nestled against his bare chest. His stubbled chin abraded her shoulders before disappearing beneath her breasts.

"You look handsomely wicked when you have not shaved," she whispered.

He brought his knee between her thighs and forced an opening there. "And you like wicked men, do you?"

"I appear to have a weakness for one in particular." She shivered as he caressed her back. "You know, I've never asked, but I've always wondered: Is it true that you held up a coach and demanded kisses from the courtesan inside?"

He drew his head back and gave her a dark grin that sent chills all over her body. "Do you want me to wear a mask and tie you to the bed?"

She wasn't sure whether to jump at the offer or

pinch him. "Is this a performance that you give on command?" she asked archly.

His grin widened. "I have a domino under my bed if you require proof."

She gazed into the mirthful blue eyes that had seduced her body and soul. It was one thing to realize that the rumors of his rakehell past were well-founded, but to know that evidence of his past was beneath their very bed . . . "I take it that this is not the same domino you wore the night we were caught together in the tower?"

The rogue did not hesitate a heartbeat. "What difference would it make if I had a dozen of the things?"

"What difference—"

His deep kiss captured the protest that she would have uttered. "It worked, didn't it?" he asked mercilessly. "You came into your masked lover's arms that night with little hesitation."

"Thinking you were Adam," she whispered, unwisely perhaps, but annoyed at his male arrogance.

Which he proved remained intact as he imprisoned her between his iron-hard body and the bed. "I'll wager you haven't thought of being in his arms since."

She did not even bother to deny it.

Chapter Seventeen

It was past noon when Lord Devon and his well-seduced wife bestirred themselves from the bed, dressed between deep kisses, and plodded downstairs for the breakfast that the thoughtful Mrs. Hadley had kept warm in the kitchen. She had been quick to show her approval of their marriage by serving the most enormous breakfasts.

It was a ritual that Devon thought he might even learn to enjoy. A passionate romp with his wife, a late breakfast together, he sorting through his mail while she sipped tea and perused the newspapers and scandal sheets that, by this hour, had already entertained an unknown number of Londoners who relished a good dose of gossip before beginning their day.

"Anything interesting?" he asked, putting down his coffee to stare at her. She looked delectable after a night of lovemaking, and he wondered now why he'd so willingly come downstairs when they could have enjoyed breakfast in bed. And each other's company.

"As if you didn't know," she said in a voice of hurt disbelief that didn't sound anything like the lighthearted woman who'd warned him only minutes ago to behave himself at the table. He hadn't taken her favorite cup, had he? Forgotten her birthday? It couldn't be their wedding anniversary.

"What is it?" he asked in bafflement.

"Don't make me say it."

"Pardon me?"

"Not this time, you deceitful . . . deceiver."

He looked down at the paper. He'd hoped she was joking. The woman who was withdrawing from him before his very eyes was not his sweet, passionate wife. She looked betrayed—but surely not by him. "What have I done now?"

"Do not even bother to deny it," she said across the breakfast table at the precise moment the footman laid a silver platter of crisply fried bacon, sausages, and warm buttered scones between them.

"What exactly is in the paper?" he asked warily.

Her silver teaspoon clanked against her cup with an emphasis that challenged the integrity of the elegant bone china. "The gossip of London. Last night's gossip. The—"

"Gossip," he said, leaning back against one elbow in his chair. "I do not need the word hammered into my skull with a teaspoon to take your meaning. What sin am I accused of now?"

He thought a tear glistened in her eye. Her

voice, however, was quite even as she whisked the newspaper from the table and dropped it on the platter. "Pray read it yourself."

"And what is it that I'm supposed to read?"

"The charming piece entitled 'Wives and Concubines.'"

He picked up the paper, scowling, and read the article several times. He could feel Jocelyn studying his face as if to interpret every nuance of reaction. And in the end he was hard pressed to hide his own annoyance.

The unidentified correspondent of the piece had described in uncanny detail Devon's actions of the previous day and a good part of the night. This included a rendition of the encounter at the park between Jocelyn and a gallant.

A certain "Sir G's" chivalrous intervention was lauded when her husband appeared to have neglected to do his spousal duty. To further compound his lack of responsibility, this sinful nobleman had visited an infamous brothel later that same evening whereupon he was personally received by the proprietress of the exclusive Bruton Street establishment.

There was a ring of first-person authenticity to the account that brought his blood to a slow boil.

The last few lines, however, were what he realized had given his wife offense.

"It wasn't exactly a brothel," he said, which admittedly was not the best defense he could have presented.

"If it was not a brothel," Jocelyn said, her spoon tapping again, "then what was it?"

"It's more of an exclusive club than a brothel. And no matter what it was, I did not go there for pleasure. I came to you."

"There are women of easy virtue in a bordello, Devon."

"There are women of no virtue whatsoever," he said unwisely.

"And you think to visit these women without virtue after only a week or so of marriage?"

"I didn't think of them at all. I went there looking for Gabriel."

She stood, visibly upset, the quaver in her voice upsetting him. "You left my bed last night to go to a brothel?"

"Audrey Watson is a family friend."

"She is a votary of Venus, Devon."

"I don't deny what she is, but I only went to her house to look for Gabriel."

She swallowed. "But the paper said that this Watson woman took you into her private chamber to entertain you."

"Well, not exactly. We went into her chamber to talk. Audrey does not receive callers in front of an audience."

"You were alone with her."

He rose from his chair. "I came to you last night, Jocelyn. I merely talked to Audrey."

She backed away from the table. He had a

horrible feeling she wasn't listening to anything he was saying. "That's what my father always told my mother. And don't remind me. You warned me at the wedding."

He stared at her, his heart twisting in realization. "I won't tell you anything of the sort."

She nodded slowly. "It's not your fault. I know you didn't want to marry me."

He watched her helplessly. Suddenly he understood, or he thought he did, even if for several moments he was so insulted that she'd compare him to Gideon that he could not react. The pain in her voice reminded him that she had probably not been raised in the happiest of homes.

"I'm not like your father," he said carefully. "I'm not anything like my own father, for that matter. I was with you last night. I wanted—"

"Devon, it's all right."

"It damn well isn't. Not unless you say you believe me."

She gazed at him, biting her lip.

"Say it," he said, his voice urgent. "Say it, and mean it."

The door opened as she turned to leave, and Devon was prepared to chastise one of the servants for interrupting. The person who appeared to take Jocelyn's place, however, was none other than his older brother Grayson, who managed to enter the room between Jocelyn's escaping figure and the door.

"Did I arrive at an awkward moment?" Grayson

asked with a rueful glance in his disappearing sister-in-law's direction.

Devon shouldered him from his path. "Why would you think that? I've just been libeled wholesale in the papers, and my wife believes I am the incarnation of her father."

Grayson removed his gloves. "I don't suppose a private appointment with my jeweler on Ludgate Hill would help?"

"At this point," Devon muttered as he heard a door slam upstairs, "I'm not sure that an offer of the Crown Jewels would help."

Devon did not chase after his wife to offer another apology for a fictitious offense.

For now he had a more pressing matter to attend. Yes, he'd been gossiped about in the past, but not as maliciously as this. And he wasn't about to let it happen again.

Grayson followed him out into the vestibule. "Where are you going?"

"To find out who's slandering me."

"That sounds like a lively afternoon's entertainment. Do you care for company?"

Devon hesitated. He knew his brother meant well, but having Grayson on his shoulder like a stone gargoyle would only hinder his baser instincts. If Devon found the guilty party and wished to throttle him, he did not want his brother interfering. "We can call a family cabal, females excluded, later tonight to discuss the matter."

"You're doing this alone?" Grayson asked in his masterly marquess and patriarch-of-the-family tone of voice.

"I went off to war by myself, didn't I?"

Chapter Eighteen

❧ ☙

Viscountess Lyons came to call on Jocelyn only a half hour after Devon had left the house. To judge by the terse set of Emma's delicate shoulders, Jocelyn concluded that her sister-in-law had read the morning paper and was not amused.

For all of Emma's ladylike demeanor, she exuded the wrath of a warrior queen as she regarded the damning newspaper that still lay on the platter of eggs where Jocelyn had dropped it.

"This," Emma announced, picking up one corner of the paper between her thumb and forefinger, as if it were a live cockroach, "must be burned posthaste."

Jocelyn smiled wanly at this display of support and watched the viscountess march toward the coal fire in the grate. "There must be hundreds more where that came from," she said ruefully, unsure whether she meant the paper itself, or the vicious rumors it contained.

Emma shook her head in consternation. "I confess it is upsetting, but I know Devon. He is *not* guilty of these accusations. As I am sure he told you."

"Yes. He denied any infidelity."

Which should have been the end of the matter. In fact, Emma was looking at her as if she was expecting Jocelyn to announce that it was. It should have been. Deep inside, Jocelyn knew it was not fair to judge Devon by what her father had done.

Emma frowned; if she had any notion of Jocelyn's private turmoil, she was too tender-hearted to question it. "Of all the numerous sins to darken my brother's soul, I have never known him to lie. If he claims he is faithful, then he is. And although it pains me to admit this, Mrs. Watson has proven herself a true friend to my family. Not to me, of course," she added hastily. "I have never sought her company in my life."

Jocelyn stared out into the street, at the stream of carriages, carts, and vendors pushing barrows over the cobbles. London was a bewildering city to one unaccustomed to its throbbing undercurrents of life. "Perhaps," she said, glancing around at Emma, "your brother merely needs time to adjust to marriage."

Emma hesitated.

"Yes, perhaps. In the meantime, I have a proposal to make you. I am woefully understaffed at the academy, and the girls are staging an amateur theatrical for the benefit of our sponsors. I have already enlisted the assistance of Drake's wife, Eloise, whom I had once hoped to employ. Alas, my brother stole her away from me. Would you mind lending your supervision to my cause?"

Jocelyn could not find the words to refuse. She recognized a kindness when it was offered. Emma, like her younger sister Chloe, was clearly attempting to take her under her protective wings. Here was a chance to become part of her husband's family as well as to enlist another ally.

Indeed, one of the first lessons she had learned about the Boscastles was that there was really no denying them anything once they asked. Had she not been swept under her husband's spell?

Furthermore, she was a Boscastle now if only in name. Her children would carry their father's ancestry in their veins. It seemed obvious that she would by necessity become an irresistible herself, or wither on the vine.

Devon had resolved to trace the source of the slanderous article to the ends of the earth, which in terms of London's underworld meant he would probably be forced to scour the lowest dives in the slums of St. Giles. He didn't care. He couldn't forget the look on Jocelyn's face. He couldn't go home again until he'd made every attempt to prove that everything written in that paper had been a lie. He hadn't thought of another woman since he married her.

The pain in her eyes after she'd read that accursed article had ruined the most perfect morning of his life.

Home.

He urged his horse through the busy streets, reining in as a peddler pushing a wheelbarrow darted in his path. He cursed softly. Since when had he begun to crave the comforts of home? In the past, his bachelor abode had served as a boardinghouse for drunken friends, a place to rest between battles and entertainments, and even a shelter for his sister's academy.

But he had never thought of it as home.

"Bloody hell," a familiar voice said beside him. "Are you going to run down every beggar in the street?"

He glanced at the dark, broad-shouldered horseman who sat as easily astride his sorrel gelding as Devon did his gray.

"I don't have time for a family reunion, Drake."

His older brother shook his head. "How does it feel to be on the receiving end of Boscastle interference?"

"Has Eloise let you out of the house already?" he asked in reference to Drake's young wife.

"Has Jocelyn chased you out of yours?" Drake retorted with a rude grin. "I seem to recall that not long ago I could not rid myself of your company."

"Go bugger yourself."

Drake's shoulders shook with laughter. "Not in such a nice temper now that I'm the one playing nursemaid this time, are you? How does it feel to have a brother pester you incessantly?"

Devon drew his horse to an abrupt halt. "This is a personal affair. I realize that Grayson must have sent you after me. But there is no danger of a physical nature involved. Even if there was, I would handle it alone."

"Damnation, you have bedeviled me from the moment of your birth—"

"Alone."

Drake nodded in reluctant agreement. "As you wish. But remember that I'm more than willing to help."

For three centuries Fleet Street had provided residence to printers, booksellers, and publishers alike. At the moment of Devon Boscastle's arrival, indecent scandal sheets and reprints of Shakespeare's works were circulating in its surrounding taverns and coffeehouses.

It gave Devon pause to realize that public-house patrons were gorging their taste for gossip on nasty tidbits of his private life, half-true tidbits that they were. Were his affairs truly so provocative that strangers would pay a few pence to read about them?

It took him over five hours of threatening a number of Grub Street printers before he traced the source of the libelous column. The last editor he confronted, who never did admit his guilt, insisted that anonymity of his correspondents must remain protected.

Devon twisted the man's ink-stained shirtfront around his wrist. He wished belatedly for his brother Drake's presence, if only to keep him from homicide.

"All I want to know is who gave you the misinformation."

"I-I-wouldn't say even if I knew, m-my lord," the short, perspiring man stammered as Devon walked him backward into one of his paper-cluttered workrooms. "Most of my sources come from notes slipped under the doorsill late at night."

Devon contemplated this as he watched the man's spider-veined nose turn various shades of purple. "Then you assure anonymity but not accuracy?"

"Accuracy has little to do with the business of publishing, my lord."

Devon stared down into the man's empurpled face. "Then what exactly is the purpose of your business?"

"Entertaining the m-masses."

"I could think of a very inventive, violent way to entertain the masses at this precise moment," Devon said, tightening the man's soiled shirt to emphasize the threat.

An apprentice in an apron appeared from a back chamber. He took one look at Devon calmly choking the breath out of his employer and dropped the bundle of sheets he'd been carrying.

"I want your word that you will never defile my name again," Devon said. Then he shook the publisher a few times like a ferret for good measure.

"Upon my humble life, I swear I won't, my lord. And I don't know who the source was, but if I find out, I shall tell you, or may Satan smite me with sore boils."

Devon released him in disgust. The young apprentice who witnessed the encounter swayed against the wall with his hand pressed to his temple. "I will smite you myself if I discover that you have lied."

"I haven't."

Devon leaned over the counter and stared down in cold dispassion at the floor where the publisher had collapsed prostate upon a heap of scattered news sheets. "Good. Have a pleasant day."

The shaken man remained in his humiliating position until he was convinced the Boscastle devil had disappeared back into the inferno that had spawned him. "Well, don't just stand there like the village idiot," he shouted to his petrified assistant. "Go through the papers and find any reference to the damn, impudent fiend and remove them."

Unreasonably enough, Devon would have punched out any man who pointed out that this high-handed valor indicated he might be falling in love with his unchosen wife. He would have retorted that in the past he'd done as much to defend his own sisters.

He would have vehemently denied that there was reason to read any significance into his behavior. Or that he secretly viewed his wife as a budding goddess of sexual delight, a thorn in the side of his vanishing decadence.

He would have defended any damsel whose distress happened to catch his eye. He'd done so in the past and would continue into his dotage. Boscastle men were notoriously protective of the weaker sex.

Jocelyn belonged to him, didn't she? She was his wife. But had he taken her affection for granted? He'd practically warned her at the wedding altar that what he wanted was a marriage in name only. He'd never really given her a chance to express her wishes to him.

Well, except to let him know that she wouldn't put up with infidelity. As if he could look at another woman. As if he could spend every night of his life in her bed and not die a perfectly contented man.

What did he want from their marriage?

Her.

He wanted her.

They did not speak of the scandal sheet again, but to Devon's relief, Jocelyn was his warm, loving wife during the night. Perhaps it would take him forever to make her forget the hurt she had been dealt by her father. Perhaps it would take a lifetime. Late the next morning he took her to a breakfast party on the outskirts of town. He knew that several of his old friends were attending, and that he would be expected to explain how and why he had gotten married. Upon spending only a few minutes with them, however, he soon realized that their company bored him. He had lost sight of his wife, a fact that irritated him because he'd actually made an effort to keep her in his sight.

He wasn't about to let her think he was neglecting her today, not after what had happened in the park. Not after the papers made his private life sound lurid.

He strolled across the lawn and discovered her beneath a blue silk awning with several other young ladies and a rather snobbish French emigré, the Comte de Vauban, and his beautiful if unprincipled sister Solange. He could have picked better company for Jocelyn. He'd come to appreciate her wholesomeness in comparison to his world-weary friends.

He walked slowly toward their circle. Even from here he saw in a disconcerting flash what a subtle temptress his wife was becoming. His heart constricting, he admired the artless shrug of her graceful shoulders that she gave in response to something Solange whispered, her beguiling laugh as she turned to scold the taciturn French count, an aristocrat who was said to favor young men as his lovers, and who had been open in his criticism of English gentlewomen.

By the time Devon reached their group, Monsieur le Comte was pronouncing her *charmante*. "Solange and I have invited you both to the château this summer," Vauban announced as he glanced up to watch Devon approach.

Devon glanced past the silver-haired French aristocrat to his suddenly subdued wife. Did she think he would disapprove of her venturing out of her shell? "Did she accept?"

The count sniffed disapprovingly. "She said she had to ask you first. But I'm sure you won't be able to resist her request. The Corsican has made the roads better for travel."

"Of course, the château was ruined by Cossacks," Solange pointed out.

The count frowned. "At least the apple trees are still standing."

"It seems a long distance to travel for apple trees," Jocelyn murmured, casting Devon a side-long glance.

His heart stopped for a moment. The flirtatious gleam in her eye made him feel like pulling her to her feet and dragging her home for himself. Was she thinking about last night? Why had he brought her to this picnic, anyway? Couldn't he have paid attention to her at home?

The count let his quizzing-glass drop. "The trees of my family orchards yield forbidden fruit. There's nothing sweeter in my view."

Devon stared at his wife's face, awaiting her reaction. To his relief she merely laughed and rose. She was the sweetest thing he had ever seen, and he did not need another man to make him aware of the fact. Perhaps he *had* been neglectful of his duties as a husband, but he would change.

He and Jocelyn did not discuss the party on their way home. But it provoked Devon to no end. Was it possible she had always been possessed of this seductive charm but that he had not been willing to admit it?

He knew full well that she had been willing to love him on their wedding night. She'd worn her heart on her sleeve, and he'd resisted, refused to feel anything for as long as he could.

The benefits of his birthright had made him take amorous conquests for granted. But how did a man go about making a conquest of his wife? Because that was what he wanted. He meant to win her over, seduce her spirit, earn her trust.

"I saw little of you at the party today," she remarked, handing her gloves to Thistle as soon as she and Devon entered the town house. "Did you enjoy yourself with your friends?"

He stared slowly at her receding figure as she ascended the stairs. He noticed that she hadn't really waited for his answer. It might have been the polite inquiry one made to an acquaintance, not a husband. She was fashionably poised, aloof . . . alluring. "Bloody wonderful. The best."

"Oh, good," she said airily. "I had quite a

lovely time myself. The French have such an appreciation for life."

He followed her to the bottom of the stairs, realizing that what he had at the moment was an appreciation for his wife and little else. "The count does not like women, you know."

She glanced back, her smile taunting and mischievous. "So I've heard."

"He doesn't. It's true. A fact."

"Whatever you say, Devon."

Whatever you say, Devon?

He stood motionless as she disappeared into the hallway above.

He didn't give a damn what she said, Vauban took male lovers. Unless . . . He rubbed his hand over his face, grinning wryly. He refused to think about the "unless." If his wife was teasing him, he couldn't take it.

That same night he escorted her to a quiet supper party hosted by an old family friend, the Duke of Dunhill. His grace had been widowed for eleven years and showed no signs of replacing his beloved country-bred spouse with either a wife or mistress. Politics and social causes, primarily anti-slavery campaigns and prison reform, dominated his time.

He was a surly sixty-two-year-old aristocrat who grew a little ruder and more reclusive every time Devon saw him, which fortunately was not often. Devon admired his politics, but usually avoided his company.

Dunhill would predictably offend everyone invited to his house; Devon was afraid that Jocelyn would not know how to take his abrasive manner.

"The duke," he warned her as they awaited entrance to the house, "likes neither men nor women."

"What does he like, then?" she wondered.

"To be disagreeable."

"But he's invited us to supper."

"Only to disagree."

"So you've finally gotten caught, you young scoundrel," Dunhill said with malicious glee by way of a greeting to Devon and Jocelyn in his drafty drawing room. He was a pinchpenny who did not waste a candle nor a lump of coal. He snagged Jocelyn by the arm as the other guests filed out into the hall for supper.

"What do you know of dogs, madame?" he demanded, stooping to arrest the pug who came bounding across the room to sniff at her slippers.

The pug performed an acrobatic twist of its compact body in order to snuffle Jocelyn's dangling fingers as she sat down to pet it. "I know that I prefer a good deal of them to certain people."

"How did you trap young Boscastle?"

She looked up as if an arrow had pierced her heart. Mean old bastard. "Perhaps he trapped me."

"No, he didn't. I know the whole story. Does he treat you well?"

"He walks me regularly and doles out the occasional treat."

He snorted. "Throws you a juicy bone now and then?"

"I beg your pardon."

"The papers mentioned he spent an evening with that pretty procuress on Bruton Street. Audrey Watson."

Jocelyn's cheeks flamed, but through sheer will she did not avert her gaze. "The papers also said that you empty your chamberpot on passing carriages for entertainment."

"It's the truth. I hate the aristocracy. Always have. The most ill-behaved people in the world."

She glanced down into the pug's soulful eyes and smiled a little ruefully. "I imagine," she said, before she could stop the impulse, "that you're not exactly perpetuating the notion of a grand aristocracy by emptying your waste products upon the unsuspecting heads of the populace."

"You should see the expressions on their faces when the first volley is launched."

She allowed the dog to snuffle her hair before rising to her feet. "Silly little dog," she murmured. "Snorting little piglet. I do believe I could fall in love with your homely face."

The duke wrenched off his shoe and tossed it over the dog's head. The pug darted forth to retrieve the costly leather and dropped it promptly at Jocelyn's feet like a love offering, cocking its head appealingly. "Has nobody ever told you that it is unbecoming for a woman to be straightforward? Have you not been schooled to give no offense when you answer someone?"

She sighed. "More times than I can count."

He stared hard at her. "I detest straightforward females."

"Your grace, I can only apologize—"

"They remind me of my wife."

She met his gaze. "Your wife?"

"The only person on this wretched earth brave enough to tell me the truth. I miss her, you see. I ought to have gone before her."

"I am sorry."

"Oh, bugger it. How can you be sorry about a woman you've never even met?"

Jocelyn shook her head and turned to the door to find herself standing before Devon, who had separated himself from the other supper guests to fetch her. He gave her a curious glance before he looked back at his host, now sprawled on the sofa.

"Thank you for keeping my wife company, your grace," he said in a voice that even Jocelyn recognized as more thoughtful than his usual deep-pitched tone.

"I'll be damned until a sennight from Sunday," the duke remarked, "how you managed to get yourself a wife of her quality."

"Perhaps I'm *damned* lucky," Devon replied, firmly placing Jocelyn behind him.

"Guard her well," Dunhill said with a sigh. "Your wife is a woman of some wit."

Devon paused. "Yes."

"You notice I said wit, and not beauty. Beauty does not endure."

"I believe she is beautiful as well," Devon said without any hesitation.

"Of course she is," the duke snapped, nudging the dog away from his instep. "You are fortunate to have found her, and a blasted jinglebrains if you do not realize it. It would serve you right if she became a wanton."

"Your grace," Jocelyn said in dismay.

"I'll thank you not to refer to my wife in such a way," Devon exclaimed, not caring if he severed any old family tie or not.

"I didn't say she was one." The duke scowled at Devon. "Yet."

Devon studied Jocelyn in contemplative silence in the shifting darkness of the carriage. When the lantern light captured her face, she appeared as what he had always assumed her to be, a comely country miss with a subtle appeal. But when the wheels hit a rut and the shadows danced, she became an elusive beauty whose company he could not resist and whom he did not deserve.

A sharp, unrecognizable pain gripped him. It felt something like yearning, except that this was worse, and it had been building inside him with an intensity that he found intolerable ever since . . .

Ever since he had met Jocelyn again at the house party.

"You made another ally tonight," he said, to break the tension of his own thoughts. "I was afraid I'd left you alone and defenseless, and yet when I returned . . . "

She caught her underlip between her teeth. The unconscious gesture beguiled him, and yet her voice was completely guileless when she replied. "I cannot guess why. I only remarked on his habit of emptying his privy contents on pedestrians."

His eyebrows rose. One moment she was a temptress, the next she was simply his uncomplicated Jocelyn. "He admitted to that?"

"With unnatural pride," she said with a frown.

"Ah." He rested his head back on the seat.

He wasn't going to let himself touch her until they arrived home. No matter how much he wanted to. No matter that he had stared at her all night, that he couldn't remember what he'd eaten for supper, or if he had eaten anything at all.

He felt as if he could live on her company alone, her voice, her smile. And the realization shook him to the core.

Undoubtedly it would have helped his cause if he could have proven these feelings to her in some tangible way over the next few days. One could hardly make a conquest in absentia. As luck would have it, however, he saw little of his wife the following week, although not of his own volition.

When he and Jocelyn returned home from supper that same night, he found a message awaiting him that one of the officers in his old regiment had died; Devon's presence was respectfully requested to pay tribute.

The funeral was to be held in Brighton, which meant two days coming and going. As much as Devon would have welcomed Jocelyn's company in the carriage, the officer had died a bachelor. No other women were invited to the memorial service by the sea.

The few days apart from his wife only sharpened what he felt or what feelings he had denied. It was as if when apart from her the warmth slowly vanished from his life. His old friends seemed to be mere ghosts of his past existence.

He laughed with them. He mourned the death of one who had fought with him. But mostly he had longed to fulfill this sad obligation so that he could return home to hold his wife throughout the night and, well, to merely be himself.

When he returned to London, having traveled during the night, he was disappointed that she was not home to welcome him. The entire journey back he'd pictured her waiting at the door for his return. He imagined chasing her up into their room. Instead, he walked into a quiet house and sat down alone at the breakfast table where a fresh pot of coffee and the morning paper awaited his pleasure. "Where is my wife?" he asked of the housekeeper who flitted past the table.

Mrs. Hadley hesitated. "I believe she went to

the academy early this morning, my lord. At least that's what she said."

"Well, if that's what she *said*, I suppose that's where she is, isn't she?"

"I couldn't say."

"Then what—"

"Excuse me, my lord," Mrs. Hadley murmured, backing away from the table. "I think that's your toast I smell burning."

Her eagerness to escape should have put him on the alert that something was off.

The manner in which his footman tiptoed around the table a minute later to bring him his burnt toast was the second clue.

The ominous appearance of his butler, Thistle, brother to Weed, intimidating, senior footman to the marquess, provided the third and final clue. "Why does everyone in this house appear to be so morbidly inclined this morning? Has someone else died during my absence?"

Thistle straightened his spine with such precision that it pained Devon to watch him. "Someone dies every day, my lord."

"And what exactly does that mean?"

Thistle murmured an incoherent reply and drifted from the room.

When Devon read the morning paper, he found the question answered, and not at all to his liking.

The wife of "Lord D" had been accused of conducting an adulterous affair under his very nose. Devon read the charge three times before he realized that Jocelyn was the unfaithful spouse alluded to in the article and that his was the unknowing nose. The unnamed reporter went on to write that the country bride of "Lord D" had not only captured the interest of a widowed duke but was secretly conducting afternoon liaisons with a Welsh Latin instructor at the home of her unknowing husband's sister.

The offensive article was not printed by the obnoxious Grub Street publisher Devon had recently threatened. This unpalatable tidbit had been published by a rival gossipmonger in Whitefriars, a fact that led Devon to another troublesome conclusion.

Either he did indeed have an anonymous enemy who meant to ruin him, or, God forbid, Jocelyn *was* having an affair.

"She can't be," he thought aloud.

"Of course she isn't," Mrs. Hadley murmured, removing his plate of untouched toast from the table. "Vicious lies, that's what it is."

And even though he did not believe Jocelyn capable of betraying him, even though he had scolded her to ignore what was written in the scandal sheets, it still hurt.

This piece of gossip accused Jocelyn of adultery.

He wouldn't stand for it.

And then he stood so abruptly that the underfootman in attendance nearly dropped his tray.

"Are you going out, my lord?" he asked, recovering his platter and wits at the same time.

"Yes."

"Shall I be accompanying you?"

"No."

He was going to pay his wife a surprise visit, and God help them both if he discovered that there were grounds for the morning's gossip because the next story printed about him would be that he'd committed murder in Mayfair.

And it would be true.

His sister Emma granted him only a perfunctory if predictably polite greeting when she was called from her deportment class to admit him into the study of their older brother's home. Lord Heath Boscastle and his wife, Julia, were visiting friends in Scotland; Emma had moved her school into their house until they returned.

"I hope the girls don't see you, Devon," she said levelly. "You know that half of them fancy themselves in love with you. I can't have them sighing and swooning all day when I'm trying to hold their attention."

He grinned. "God bless them."

"And protect them from handsome young devils like you, my love." She drummed her tapered fingertips on her desk. "And now that we have prayed together, may I ask what you are doing here in the middle of the afternoon?"

"I would like to see my wife."

"Your wife?" she said blankly.

"Yes, please. I need to talk with her for a moment." She stared back at him as if he were babbling nonsense, and indeed, he felt like the king of fools. "It's about what was printed in the paper this morning," he added quietly.

She closed her eyes. "What has our family done this time?"

His mouth thinned. "Nothing. And it has nothing to do with me, so please don't ask."

"Well, thank heavens. What—"

"Where is my wife?"

"She's gone with Charlotte to hunt for costumes in the old trunk of clothes that have been donated to the academy."

"She's with Charlotte." He repeated this as if to reassure himself. Of course, Jocelyn was not up to any nonsense, not with Emma in the house. Why had he let a bit of scuttlebutt befool him? He should have known better. He'd scolded Jocelyn for believing gossip. Why couldn't he take his own advice?

"I can hear them thumping about now," Emma added. "Devon, are you all right?"

He smiled. His wife was with Charlotte, and there was nothing alarming or adulterous about that. "I should help them then, if the trunk is heavy." It seemed now that he would have to find an excuse to explain what he was doing here. He'd be damned if he would admit to Jocelyn that he'd been upset by gossip when he'd chided her for the same reaction.

"I sent Mr. Griffin up to help with the heavy work," Emma added, still watching him in concern.

"The Welshman?"

"Yes."

He swallowed. "Isn't he the Latin instructor?"

"Among other things," Emma replied, giving him a puzzled smile. "He's qualified in quite a few subjects if you must know."

He sent a covert glance up the empty staircase. He couldn't hear any of the aforementioned thumping, but he definitely detected laughter, gales and gales of unrestrained giggles followed by a man's deep lilting voice.

"It sounds as if someone is being amused," he remarked wryly.

"Perhaps someone is a little too amused for her own good," Emma retorted. "I'm afraid that her Boscastle blood is running true."

"She married me," he said darkly. "A wife can be influenced by bad behavior, but Jocelyn is not a blood relation."

She stared at him. "I was referring to Charlotte, Devon," she said softly. "Our cousin."

"I know who the bloody hell Charlotte is." But he didn't know who *he* was at this moment, or what he was becoming.

Emma rose from her desk. "I must return to

class. Will you ask your wife and Charlotte to go about their quest more quietly?"

He stood only moments later outside the first-floor library door, his hand raised to knock. The sound of Jocelyn's soft, refined voice made him hesitate.

" '. . . as a lover's pinch. / Which hurts, and is desire.' "

Desire, his arse.

The rational part of him realized there was nothing to worry about, and if he were wise, he would simply continue knocking until he was acknowledged.

But another part, unfortunately, that dominant instinct by which his forgotten ancestors had abducted their women and locked them away for lascivious purposes, proved to be stronger.

He pushed open the door without knocking.

His wife—well, the rear part of her—was bent over a trunk overflowing with costume props and clothing. Leaning against her shoulder was a young man who resembled a gypsy in a billowing shirt and black velvet trousers.

He coughed. Neither of them heard him. "Caught in the act," he said loudly, leaning his elbow against the door to observe them.

Jocelyn wiggled around in surprise. "Yes. It's act five, scene two of *Antony and Cleopatra,* to be precise." Her eyes brightened. "Devon, it's *you.* When did you come home?"

Her companion shot to his feet, mirth glittering

in his coal-black eyes. A ball of twine was wound around his wrist. "We were hunting for a snake to use in the play, my lord."

Devon smiled halfheartedly in response to the Welshman's warmth. "I shouldn't think she'd have to look far."

Mr. Griffin almost dropped his twine. Jocelyn straightened, her hair disheveled, the blush in her cheeks becoming. Clearly Devon's displeasure had been received, but he barely had time to decide whether it had been deserved before he noticed there was another person in the room. Which meant there had been a third witness to his behavior.

It was his cousin Charlotte, dressed in a sheet that he supposed was meant to be a toga, a gold headband tied crookedly across her high forehead. She was holding a basket of something that looked like old prunes.

"What the devil are you doing dressed like that?" he asked before he could stop himself.

"I'm playing the part of Charmian, Cleopatra's handmaiden."

Mr. Griffin cleared his throat, casting a hesitant look in Devon's direction. "Perhaps I should go back downstairs to assist Lady Lyons."

"Perhaps you should," Jocelyn said softly.

She turned slowly to look at Devon. The young Welshman made a wise exit. And Charlotte merely stared across the room in her ridiculous costume and said nothing, although her keen gaze seemed to absorb all.

Devon put his hand to his face. "I believe I just made an asp of myself."

Jocelyn shared an amused glance with Charlotte. "It must look rather odd—"

"It doesn't look odd at all," he said, his gaze on her face.

She pushed her hair from her eyes. "I'm glad you're back, Devon."

He smiled at her, wishing they were alone. "I'm glad I'm back, too."

Jocelyn could not decide what had changed about Devon in the past week or so. She'd missed him terribly while he was gone, of course, especially at night, although his family had made sure to occupy every hour of her days.

She'd been so busy at the academy, enjoying working with Emma and Charlotte, that it wasn't until later that evening that she remembered Devon wasn't supposed to come home for another two days.

She realized, after she ate supper alone and read the papers, that he must have returned early from Brighton and come straightaway to see her at Heath's house.

And what had he seen?

His wife buried in a trunk, and poor Mr. Griffin acting guiltily when he'd done nothing untoward at all. And then it occurred to her that Devon had been jealous. That he'd entered the library as if he'd expected to find—

Well, who knew what he'd expected to find? His wife engaging in an affair? The mere thought sent her into gales of silent laughter. Had she herself not allowed a scandal rag to arouse her own suspicions? Was that what had happened? Had Devon returned to the house from Brighton and read the gossip that had been written about Jocelyn and Mr. Griffin?

The entire situation with Mr. Griffin had been innocent. The scandal sheet had lied. And yet, it wasn't something she should admit, but she *had* savored that brief moment when it appeared that she and her rogue husband had swapped roles.

If Devon had rushed home to see her . . . if he hurried to Heath's house to tell her he was back, and she'd been shoulder-to-shoulder with another man—she sat back in her chair with a deep sigh of satisfaction.

Not for anything would she have provoked her husband into displaying his feelings for her. But she had seen the look on his face when she'd turned in surprise from the trunk.

And he looked like a man fighting some sort of private battle and losing badly. Why couldn't she have been home by herself when he'd returned?

Now he'd gone off again and she was sitting by herself. She sat forward decisively and rang for Mrs. Hadley, who missed little of what went on in her master's life, whether she approved of it or not.

"Did my husband read the scandal sheets this

morning, Mrs. Hadley? It was my understanding that he had banished them from the house."

"Indeed, he did, ma'am," the housekeeper replied in distress. "I thought I'd ridden the house of those you saw, but some instigator of evil apparently hid one in Lord Devon's personal papers."

"Why?" Jocelyn asked.

"I've no idea. Perhaps it's one of the trollops hoping to cause trouble in your marriage. I promise you it shall never happen again. Thistle and I have resolved henceforth to read all literature, not counting personal correspondences, of course, that comes to the house."

"Thank you, Mrs. Hadley."

The housekeeper walked to the door, then glanced back in hesitation. "People gossip about this family all the time, ma'am."

"Goodness, I can't imagine why."

"What can't you imagine?" Devon asked from the doorway.

She rose from her chair as he entered into the room. "You missed supper, Devon," she said quietly. "It was lamb and young peas. I can ask Mrs. Hadley to bring you something before she goes to bed if you're hungry."

"No. It's all right. I dined with Chloe and Dominic a short while ago. I hadn't meant to, but I stopped by to see her, and stayed."

She met his gaze, helping him out of his coat.

One of the things that she adored about him was that he cared for his family. "How is she?"

"Better, I think. I should have sent word that I would be late. I didn't mean to make you worry. But I thought . . . "

"Yes?"

He turned slowly, taking her into his arms. "I thought you would be angry at me for what happened today."

"I don't even know what happened," she exclaimed.

He caught her chin between his fingers. "Don't you?"

"You read the paper?" she asked softly.

"Tell me it was all lies."

She smiled. "Every word."

He bent his head to kiss her. "I know."

"Are you sure you don't want any supper?" she asked as his mouth captured hers in a deep, passionate kiss.

He laughed against her lips. "I don't care if I never eat another meal again in my life. I want *you*."

Chapter Nineteen

Grayson, the Marquess of Sedgecroft, had decided to give a small masquerade party at his Park Lane home at the urging of his sister Emma. Not that as a rule Grayson required a reason to entertain, or that he typically took the advice of the Dainty Dictator, as Emma was fondly called by the family.

He had become adept at ignoring Emma's socially enlightened suggestions over the years. Lord knew no one would derive any pleasure from life at all by listening to Emma's advice. Since the death of their mother, she had assumed the role of Boscastle's maternal conscience. If not that of the entire world. Where there was a wrong, Emma felt obligated to right it. She meant well, but, by damn, she drove her siblings half-insane with her interfering ways.

Emma had expressed concern, in her perceptive way, over their sister Chloe's lingering grief that she had miscarried her first child, as well as her own personal observation that the young marriage of Devon and Jocelyn might require a little support to withstand the barrage of rumors that had assailed them in recent days.

A bit of encouragement from the family, Emma suggested, might be all that was needed to make Devon and Jocelyn realize how well suited they were to each other.

Grayson could not argue either point, for his wife, Jane, wiser in such matters than he could ever be, shared the same opinion. Ironically, as it turned out, Jocelyn did not particularly wish to attend the ball, nor from what he could tell, did his brother Devon. This made it rather hard for Grayson to arrange a party in the hope of strengthening their union.

However, no one, family members included, could ever refuse the marquess, and so it was expected that once he issued the invite, it would be accepted.

Jocelyn descended from her husband's carriage and covertly adjusted her heavy golden silk headdress. Perhaps costuming herself as Cleopatra had not been the most inspired choice for her brother-in-law's ball, but it was the only costume on hand, and Devon had given her scant notice to make other preparations. He seemed as reluctant to attend the party as she did.

She didn't understand exactly why she felt so tired or reluctant to go out. Her menses, never entirely predictable, had been delayed this month.

This irregularity appeared to contribute to her subtle sense of fatigue. She wondered vaguely whether it also had something to do with the shifting of her moods.

Whenever Devon glanced at her, she was irrationally tempted to burst into tears. And when he did not look at her, she was even more prone to weep.

To make matters worse, he disappeared almost from the moment they entered his brother's elegant home and were announced at the party. She might have been more offended by his desertion had her sister-in-law Jane not taken her aside to confide that Devon and his brothers had congregated for a private brandy in Grayson's study as was their habit whenever the family met.

"They call it male discourse," Jane explained as she led Jocelyn into an antechamber behind the ballroom. "Which means they meet for vulgar jokes and great grunting slaps on the shoulder as if they were bears and not merely brothers. It does make one wonder about the course of human civilization."

Jocelyn could only envy the ease with which the marchioness accepted the customs and peculiar conduct of her husband. Even more so she envied the warm glances that Jane and Grayson had shared in the reception room while greeting their guests. Marriage had obviously not dimmed the passion between that pair.

"That is a provocative costume," Jane remarked

over her shoulder in reference to Jocelyn's white Egyptian-style dress. "Cleopatra?"

"Yes." Jocelyn frowned. "I feel rather bare, but it was all I had on hand."

"Why did Devon not dress as Marc Antony?" Jane asked. She looked ethereal and lovely herself as a woodland nymph in a diaphanous copper-green silk gown with silken leaves entwined in her hair. Grayson was rather incongruously dressed as a Roman gladiator.

Jocelyn trailed Jane down a long vestibule to the refreshment room. "I did not think to ask."

"At least he isn't dressed as a highwayman," Jane said in amusement.

Jocelyn paused. "Did you know him when—"

Before Jocelyn could complete the question, a cluster of guests spotted Jane and rushed to claim her attention. The marchioness had rapidly become one of London's most popular hostesses, and it was regarded as a sign of importance to be personally acknowledged at one of her parties.

Jocelyn stood at a loss until she glimpsed her sister-in-law Chloe waving for her to join the rest of the family in the ballroom.

She stepped forward only to feel a hard body brush against hers. Startled, she glanced around. A tall man costumed as a monk inclined his cowl-hooded face to her, his hand clasping the crucifix he wore.

"I beg your pardon, madam."

"It's quite all right. I think I walked into you."

From the edge of her eye she spied Grayson's senior footman, Weed, scrutinizing her down the long slope of his nose. For a mortifying moment she thought she was to be chastised by a footman for her clumsiness. She was accustomed to more informal country affairs where one guest bumped into another more often than not.

She was jarred by the feel of rough, unfamiliar fingers grasping her wrist. She turned in alarm, trying to pull free.

"How many miles to Babylon?" the monk asked her before he released her hand and melted back into the group of other guests.

How many miles to Babylon? What nonsense was this? And that voice. Those hard glistening eyes. Did she know him? If so, it could not have been a pleasant association.

"May I be of service in any way, my lady?" another voice inquired behind her.

She glanced back reluctantly. The stone-faced senior footman bowed before her, although his shrewd gaze was following the monk's rapid progress across the room.

Coloring, she wondered perchance whether Weed had read the scandal sheets and judged her unworthy of the family he served. Or perhaps her social awkwardness was obvious to even the footmen.

"I am on my way to the ballroom."

"May I escort you?" he inquired in an expressionless voice.

"That is not necessary."

"As you wish, madam," he murmured with a wooden bow.

Devon had just exited Grayson's study with his brother Drake when he recognized the footman Weed escorting a tall, curly-haired man through a private passageway. He stopped in astonishment.

"Bloody hell."

"This gentleman asked to see you, my lord," Weed said. "I took the liberty of admitting him. He insisted he talk to you tonight."

"Mr. Griffin," Devon said in an undertone. "If you are here to discuss what happened between us today, then let me speak first on the matter. I was entirely in the wrong to assume that you—"

"We can apologize to each other later," the young man said in a manner that Devon might have interpreted as brash had he not perceived the sense of panic beneath it. "I have come here about your wife, my lord."

"My wife? What about her?" he asked tightly, not appreciating the fact that Drake was listening with obvious relish to this discussion.

"Pray," the Latin master said in earnest appeal, "do not believe that I in any manner encouraged what I am about to show you." He reached into his vest pocket. "Nor do I believe for one instant that your wife wrote this."

Devon drew a breath. He could feel Drake at his back watching, as with a trembling hand, Mr.

Griffin pulled out a folded note and handed it to him. He opened it and read.

Know that my heart is yours, even as I pay for the regrettable mistake of my marriage. You have spoken of the wild beauty of Wales with such passion that I yearn to escape there with you. Will you challenge my husband for our freedom?
Your Cleopatra
J

"I swear to you upon my soul," the young man said in an earnest voice, "I did not encourage—"

Devon looked up with a flash of emotion, realizing that the fellow was afraid he would be accused of adultery. Well, no wonder, the way Devon had behaved toward him today. Still, even if he had been misled once by a forgery, he knew Jocelyn's handwriting now and he would not be deceived again. "My wife did not write this. Do you think for a moment I would be so easily deceived?"

Mr. Griffin practically collapsed with relief. "Who would conspire thus against such a good-hearted lady? Who would want to destroy innocent people?"

Silence fell. Devon stared distractedly out the window into the street as a bell-ringing zealot paused outside Grayson's mansion to mutter a warning to the Hell-bound guests within. Religious disciples had been targeting the Boscastle family ever since he could remember, generally to no avail. And it had not escaped his attention that the Latin instructor had remarked upon Jocelyn's good heart, but not that of her husband. Well, it was an omission well-deserved.

"How art thou fallen from heaven, O Lucifer, son of the morning!" the zealot outside cried up at the house. "How art thou—"

The cloaked figure had barely resumed his sermon before two liveried Boscastle footmen hoisted him up under the armpits and unceremoniously bore him off into the night. "I am a messenger of God. . . . "

"Well, brother of Lucifer," Drake said amusedly to Devon after a long moment passed, "it seems you have an enemy, indeed."

Devon looked away from the window. *Messenger of God.* The words echoed; a recollection stirred.

"I don't have any enemies," he said, shaking his head. "I only have friends. You said it yourself."

"Who?" Drake asked quietly. "Think hard. Review each moment in your memory for the answer."

"A messenger of God," Devon said slowly. " 'Wives and concubines.' That is what the gossip paper said of our family, and I do not think it is an original phrase."

"It is from the Bible, my lord," Mr. Griffin said. "The Book of Daniel, as I recall. Could this malefactor have connections to the church?"

"Most of Devon's acquaintances attend church only when eulogized after an early death," Drake remarked.

Devon frowned at him. "Yet I think Mr. Griffin is right. And I also think I know who the malefactor is. 'What say you we bring down Babylon?' "

Someone gave a loud cough behind them. Devon glanced around distractedly to see Gabriel dressed in the flowing royal-blue robes of a medieval wizard. "If Babylon has fallen," Gabriel said, obviously not grasping the gist of the conversation, "I will probably be blamed for it even though I have not been in London the past few days. I don't suppose anyone missed me while I was gone?"

Drake laughed. "I thought the town seemed rather quiet lately. What have you been up to, or shouldn't I inquire?"

Devon stepped forward to seize Gabriel by the arm. "It doesn't matter."

"Why not?" Gabriel demanded in mock alarm.

"Because you're coming with me."

"Am I?" Gabriel asked in surprise, lowering his twisted willow wand. "Let me make sure I understand this. Are you asking for *my* help?"

Drake's angular face darkened. "The hell he is. If anyone is going to help him, it's me."

"I need you to stay here and keep an eye on my wife, Drake." Devon nudged Gabriel toward the door.

Drake stared at him in astonishment. "What?"

"Don't take offense," Devon said. "You're a happily married man, and I don't trust Gabriel alone with my wife for a single moment."

Gabriel smiled mildly. "I wouldn't trust myself with her, either."

They drove southeast in Gabriel's carriage from Grayson's home to St. James's Street, Gabriel not asking unnecessary questions, yet willing to offer his support. Devon thought fleetingly that he did not know much about Gabriel's background, except for the fact that his cousin had apparently known some rough years. Gabriel never talked about himself, or his past.

"I appreciate your willingness to help me," he said as the carriage rolled to a halt over the cobbles. "I can't think of another person I could ask to help me—and who would agree without asking why."

"Better the devil you know?"

"From one devil to another," Devon conceded.

Gabriel nodded in good humor. "I'll take that as a compliment to my character. I don't receive many these days."

"May I assume that you'll be my accomplice if I commit murder?"

Gabriel shrugged beneath his costume. "You ask that as if it were my first time."

Devon shook his head.

"Who are we hunting tonight, by the way?" Gabriel inquired.

Devon's lips curled into a sneer. "Captain Matthew Thurlew."

"The pastor's eldest son?" Gabriel asked after a pause.

"Yes."

"Well, damn me. Wasn't his brother Daniel your accomplice in that botched highway robbery not long ago?"

Devon gave a snort of self-disgust. "I'd rather you didn't remind me. But, yes. You're right."

"Did you know his brother had taken to robbing coaches for a living until he was caught three months ago?" Gabriel asked almost conversationally. "I'd heard he killed a banker's clerk on Crawley Downs. Word is the damned idiot is due for an execution."

Devon shook his head again. "That I didn't know." But now that he knew, he supposed that Matthew Thurlew might blame him for leading his younger brother astray, although Daniel had never displayed much of a social conscience to begin with. He'd been an amusing if amoral young vandal when Devon had met him. They would not have remained friends for long under any circumstances.

"In my opinion," Gabriel remarked as they walked toward the entrance of the club, "there's nothing worse than hiding one's sins behind the shield of religion."

"I would venture to say that you and I have not bothered overmuch to hide our sins at all," Devon said.

"Perhaps if you and I had put our heads to-gether," Gabriel continued, "we might have realized that Thurlew was trying to destroy you all along. I might even have helped you."

Devon grunted. "You helped yourself to Lily Cranleigh, didn't you?"

"I really didn't think you'd mind."

"I didn't." He paused, scowling. "But my wife is another matter."

"Thurlew must have put those rumors in the scandal sheets."

"I expect so," Devon muttered.

"And the invitations to the tower."

Devon nodded grimly. "Yes."

Gabriel glanced at him. "It was Thurlew who planted the coffin at Fernshaw's party."

Devon nodded again, stone-faced, and started to walk toward the club. "Let's put an end to his pranks once and for all."

But to his frustration Captain Thurlew had not been seen at the club in the last two days, according to the waiters, one of whom informed Devon in private that the captain had moved his lodgings recently to a more decent Downing Street address.

"I remember he complained of the riffraff in his old neighborhood, my lord. Said it offended his morals."

"Morals," Gabriel mused under his voice as he and Devon exited the club and stood once again on the sidewalk. He glanced at his cousin. "Are you in love with your wife?"

"What business is it of yours if I am?" Devon asked indignantly, the question taking him completely off guard.

Gabriel gave a deep chuckle. "I thought you were."

"Sod off, would you?"

Chapter Twenty

Jocelyn smiled at each guest who was presented to her at Grayson's masquerade until her lips ached from doing so. She made excuses for Devon's absence until she ran out of both breath and conviction. She had no idea how to explain his disappearance; she only knew that his older brother Drake was watching her as if there were some mischief afoot.

Well, whatever the reason Devon had disappeared, there was definitely mischief at work inside her body. She was not at all herself, she realized in the middle of a waltz with one of Devon's cousins. She felt queasy and tempted to weep all of a sudden, prompting her young dance partner to stare at her in concern.

"Perhaps you ought to eat," he suggested under his breath. "They never feed you enough at these formal affairs. All this dancing works up the appetite."

"Perhaps a bite or two *would* help," she agreed,

surprised that the thought of food sounded tempting.

"Let's find Jane," he said, taking her hand. "There's no fun in waltzing about on an empty stomach."

A few minutes later Jane sought Jocelyn out in the refreshment room. "Why didn't you tell me?" she asked with a smile of concern, motioning the footmen in attendance to close the door.

Jocelyn put down the bowl of rose jelly she was in the process of finishing. "Tell you what?"

"I craved jellies like a fiend when I was carrying Rowan," Jane whispered. "And cake. And custard."

"But I can't be . . . it's too soon."

"No, it's not," Jane said with a wistful laugh. "As a matter of fact, we could announce it at the end of the party. Grayson loves that sort of surprise, although on second thought, perhaps we shouldn't. Not quite yet."

"When will I know?" Jocelyn wondered aloud.

"Soon enough, believe me," Jane replied. "I wonder whether you shall have a son or a daughter. There's an apothecary in town who swears he can tell what gender a child will be before it is born. But it does require passing water into a pan of ashes, I'm afraid. I never told Grayson that I went, mind you. I made Weed swear to keep it secret."

Jocelyn released her breath. Pregnant. She had conceived a child, one with a lustful appetite it would seem. At least that explained her moody reaction to Devon's behavior, but it did not explain *his* behavior at all. He wasn't enceinte, tearful, and eating like a battalion of soldiers. He simply wasn't here.

"It would not be kind to share such news while Chloe is still grieving her loss," she said reflectively.

Jane nodded. "And one never knows. Those first months are precarious as the baby takes hold in the womb. Oh, Jocelyn, I *am* happy for you—would you like to come up to the nursery and sit with my son? I shall send the nurse to the kitchen for pastry and chocolate for a private celebration."

Jocelyn could not refuse her sister-in-law's offer, even if pastry seemed a poor substitute for Devon's presence. "Let me tell Drake first where I am going. He's guarded me so diligently that I fear Eloise has been quite ignored."

Indeed, Drake was watching her from the doorway as she wended her way through the crowded room to inform him of her plans. Jocelyn had the sense that he had not taken her out of his sight for even a minute.

She understood that the Boscastle family only meant to protect her, to cover for Devon's absence, but all their attention only heightened her anxiety because she had no idea where her husband had gone. And then she overheard a group of young guests talking at the refreshment table, and her worry seemed to multiply.

"Where is Devon, anyway?"

"He and Gabriel went to the club."

"And he left his wife, looking as fetching as she does in that costume? Damned arrogant devil. He's asking for her to enter an affair."

"Well, he's made it no secret that he never considered himself a man for marriage. One wouldn't expect him to stay chained to her side."

Jocelyn backed away, straight into the arms of her brother-in-law Drake. He glanced at the guests standing around the table. The group fell into an awkward silence.

"Is anything wrong?" Drake inquired, his eyes narrowing as he guided her toward the door.

"No. I'm—" She did not trust herself to behave for another minute. She felt cross, concerned for her husband, and concerned that she was proving to be such a bother to the Boscastle family. "If you don't mind, I shall heft my ball and chain back upstairs to the nursery and remove my dull presence from the party."

"As you wish, Jocelyn." He sent a withering stare over his shoulder at the guests who still had not resumed their conversation at the table. "Although I do not think it is your presence that should be removed."

"I wish you'd all stop," she whispered as he began to walk her to the stairs.

He frowned. "Stop what?"

"Watching over me as if something is wrong. There isn't anything wrong, is there?"

He came to a halt at the bottom of the staircase. "Devon and Gabriel have gone to confront the man responsible for the personal attacks upon you and my brother. My brother is pursuing honor, not another woman, if that's what you were wondering."

"I wasn't wondering that at all. . . . Do I know this person?"

"I doubt it," Drake said somberly. "His name is Matthew Thurlew."

She strained her memory for only a moment before another thought beset her. "There won't be a physical confrontation between them, will there?" she asked, recalling how Devon had flown into the boughs at the park. "Shouldn't you have gone with him instead of watching over me?"

He guided her onto the staircase, a man evidently comfortable with calming females. "Will there be a physical confrontation? I should be surprised if there were not. Should I have gone with him? He deemed it more important that I stay with you." His blue eyes smoldered with dark humor. "And as deeply as it pains me to admit it, I believe that with Devon and Gabriel joining forces, I would only be in the way."

Devon and Gabriel drove southeast to Thurlew's Downing Street lodgings only to discover not their quarry in residence, but instead one of their mutual acquaintances, a harmless fop named

Gilbert Amherst, dozing on the sofa. He opened his eyes and swallowed in speechless horror upon realizing that a pair of pistols were pressed at the ready against either side of his head. "I don't have any cash," he whispered. "Nor jewels except for my grandmama's pearl ring sewn in my—"

"Shut up, you blithering idiot," Devon said between his teeth. "Where is Thurlew?"

"Boscastle?" He blinked and glanced from one corner of his eyes to the other in recognition. "And Boscastle? We're friends, aren't we? I've never done either of you a wrong. Aren't we all friends?"

Devon lowered the pistol in disgust.

Gabriel laughed. "That depends. Do you know where Thurlew is?"

Gilbert swallowed. "Isn't he here?"

"No," Devon said roughly. "He isn't, but if you know where he is you damned well better tell me."

"He must have gone to the masquerade," Gilbert said meekly, leaning his head back on the sofa.

Devon wrenched him up by the ruffles of his shirtfront. "What masquerade?"

"The-the one at your brother's house. You invited him, didn't you?" His lower lip quivered. "Shouldn't *you* be there?"

Devon released him instantly and sprang to his feet, Gabriel right behind him. "He's right. I should have stayed with her."

"Drake is there."

"So are a hundred other people, one of them Matthew Thurlew. And nobody invited the bastard, either."

Drake escorted Jocelyn to the nursery with a glance inside to note Mrs. O'Brien dozing in her chair by the low-burning fire, and Rowan asleep in his cradle. There was a pot of chocolate and a plate of orange-cream cake sitting on the two-tiered table.

He grinned. "Not exactly the makings of an exciting evening, but it looks safe enough."

Jocelyn smiled. "I don't mind the quiet."

"Well, just be warned that Mrs. O'Brien is prone to singing lullabies when the whimsy strikes. Jane and the baby find her crooning pleasant. Grayson does not."

Jocelyn settled down on the stool that sat beside the cradle. "I feel sleepy enough as it is. I should hate to shame myself by dozing off like an old dog."

"Another warning," Drake added, hesitating at the door. "Rowan is an infamous farter."

"A what?" she asked.

He rubbed the side of his nose. "For a small blighter, he breaks copious amounts of wind. I wouldn't want it to frighten you. He almost put out all the gaslights in the city not long ago."

She got up, trying not to laugh. He looked so serious. "I shall bear that warning in mind."

"Fine then. I suppose you're safe enough here. I'll send Weed or another footman up to stand outside for your convenience."

"Quietly, please," she said with an amused glance at the unmoving nursemaid. "I wouldn't want to awaken either of them."

She closed the door without a sound and returned to the cradle. She could not explain it, perhaps it was because she truly was pregnant, but the sight of Rowan in all his plump innocence lured her irresistibly to gaze upon him.

A child. She peered over the cradle into Rowan's blue eyes. His lids drifted downward as if he were fighting sleep. She wondered whether Devon's baby would be a boy or a girl, and how he would react to the news. Hadn't he warned her of the possibility on their wedding day? But then he'd grown up in a large family.

Unexpectedly, Rowan turned his head and looked up at her with an engaging smile. She put her finger to her lips, whispering, "Ssh. We don't want to wake up your nursemaid. She's—"

At the mention of her name Mrs. O'Brien moaned and made a weak attempt to raise her arm. The mug from which she'd been drinking fell from her lap to the floor.

Jocelyn's skin crawled with forewarning.

"Mrs. O'Brien?" she whispered, turning her head toward the woman's slumped form. "Are you all right?"

The nursemaid responded with another moan, a

deep-throated unnatural quaver of sound. Jocelyn placed her hand instinctively on the cradle, studying the shadows of the room. Something . . . somebody . . . was here.

The gold damask curtains rippled, firelight glinting in the deep folds. Jocelyn edged sideways to stand in front of Rowan's cradle. The shadowy movement was not, as she'd hoped, her imagination. There *was* someone by the window. Even if she could back to the door and cry for help, she could not leave the baby and Mrs. O'Brien at the mercy of whoever was hiding in the room.

She told herself to remain calm.

Jane or one of her sisters-in-law would come up in a minute to check on Rowan. All the women in the family doted on Grayson's cherub. No female could resist a Boscastle male.

And hadn't Drake promised to send a footman up to stand guard at the door?

Of course, he'd only just gone, and even if he hurried he'd barely had time to make it down the stairs himself, which left her to defend the baby.

And the child she carried.

She stopped her thoughts from running to the horrific. Perhaps this was just a drunken guest who had wandered upstairs by mistake, or who craved a bit of peace. It happened all the time at parties. But no one wandered into a nursery by mistake. There was nothing peaceful about a crying child and vigilant nursemaids.

"What do you want?" she demanded softly.

In truth, her throat was so constricted it was a miracle she could get the words out at all, let alone continue to sound as if she possessed any courage.

The hooded figure detached itself from the curtains. Her heart began to pound as she looked up into the mocking countenance of a man she knew only vaguely from her brother's stern warnings about avoiding bad company at parties.

"Captain Thurlew," she said.

His name is Matthew Thurlew.

She detected a glint of metal between the layers of his voluminous sleeve and robe. She could not discern whether it came from a dagger or a pistol. Certainly whatever the source, it was not part of a pious man's apparel.

A calm head, she thought, even as her nerves screamed and tension knotted her muscles into immobility. Strange that now, of all times, it was her father's voice that counseled her. *Calm head, girl, when approaching an unbroken horse. . . .* Why would it now be her father's memory that gave her strength? He had always made her feel weak—No, he had wanted to make her feel weak and easily cowed. But he'd failed. His bullying had forced her to stand up for herself.

"Are you perhaps lost, Captain Thurlew? May I help you find your way?"

He laughed. "To Babylon? 'Can I get there by candlelight?' "

She stood her ground, despite the fact that he was moving toward her, that her heart was thundering, and that Rowan had screwed up his face as if he were about to cry. "This is the nursery, Captain."

"And that is the nursemaid," he said with a mocking nod in Mrs. O'Brien's direction. "See how she sleeps all snores. She drank all her laudanum-laced chocolate like a good girl."

Drugged. That explained it. He had drugged Mrs. O'Brien. Unable to stop herself, she glanced back in horror at the child in the crib. He wouldn't have drugged the baby, would he? Rowan seemed so alert and wakeful.

"You didn't—"

She couldn't bring herself to ask. She was terrified to even draw his attention to Rowan. Better to lure him out of the room before he took it into his head to harm the helpless Boscastle heir.

Where was Drake?

Where was the footman he'd promised?

Why hadn't Jane come up to check on her son?

Why wasn't Devon here?

Rowan opened his guileless blue eyes and gurgled. She glanced down at him inadvertently only to look up and find Thurlew directly before her.

"If you have a grudge against me or my husband, sir," she managed to whisper, "pray let us remove ourselves to a more comfortable place than the nursery to discuss it."

"A grudge?"

She swallowed. Time. She needed time. "Wasn't it you who wrote those letters at Alton's party, Captain?"

At that moment Mrs. O'Brien released a low unearthly moan and gave a spasmodic kick with her left foot against the firescreen. It wobbled and fell to the hearth with a clatter.

Thurlew uttered a curse and caught hold of Jocelyn's bare elbow. Rowan whimpered in protest. She put her free hand back to comfort him, a gesture to which the baby responded with a full-bodied wail that surely would attract the notice of anyone approaching the hallway.

"You're right, of course." Thurlew jerked her away from the cradle. "We'll have to go somewhere more private, or that devil's spawn will cry the house down."

She was so grateful he seemed disinterested in hurting Rowan that she had little time to fear for herself. "Quickly," she said. "He's about to squall—"

"He'd better not," he said roughly.

"He's going to whether you like it or not."

He'd dragged her halfway across the nursery before she realized that his destination was not the door to the formal hallway used by the family.

In fact, it was only as he forced her against the wall that she perceived a concealed service door behind the curtains where he had been hiding.

She flinched as the heavy swathe of damask drapery threatened to smother her face.

A cry of anger, of raw fear rose in her throat.

"Don't," he whispered harshly, shoving her forward.

She twisted her wrist and hit him across the cheek. His hand lifted; she flinched, thinking he would strike her back. Then the length of rope he'd worn as a belt suddenly looped around her neck to subdue her.

No longer able to see his face, she demanded indignantly, "What is this thing around my neck? Where are we going? Why would you do this? What—"

He pushed her, and she stumbled, her senses disoriented, her thoughts arrested.

For a few moments of blind panic she fought the sense of falling into a void before her heel scraped a hard step; regaining her balance, she realized he was leading her down a private servants' staircase, which, by the musty smell that offended her nose, had seen little use in recent months.

He tugged the rope to prod her into moving. "Every royal prince has his secret escape route."

She swallowed against the band that constricted her throat. "You'll hang for this," she said, her foot catching in the hem of his robe. For good measure she lifted her knee up between his legs, but he drew back, thwarting her hope of disabling him.

His voice echoed in the hollow void. "Your husband is the one who should hang. His entire family should hang for their abuse of privilege and power."

"What did Devon ever do to cause you to hate him?"

Even as she asked, she remembered the rumors about Devon and Thurlew's younger brother. The gossip papers had thrived on their pranks, on the mayhem they had unleashed on the city of London, the most prominent incident being her husband's infamous if fleeting stint as a highwayman. To her recollection a footman had been wounded, but had survived.

Scandal had ensued, but she didn't think there had been any other violation of person or property. Devon and his friends had held up the wrong coach in the course of an ill-planned joke. She'd thought the whole affair had blown over.

"Madam," he said, his voice without inflection, "you would do better to ask what I intend to do to you than to dwell on the harm your husband has caused."

Chapter Twenty-one

❧ ❧

Devon did not waste a moment stopping to explain to the curious why he was rushing headlong through his brother's house in the middle of a sophisticated bal masqué. Several of the costumed guests he flew by merely laughed indulgently and stepped aside as if his wild entrance were part of the evening's entertainment. A few of the older attendants regarded him with fond disgruntlement and murmurs of "those young Boscastle lords."

Some appeared too taken aback to react one way or another, especially as four or five footmen came running up behind Lord Devon, one of them brandishing an ancient sword that had only moments before hung upon the wall.

"A prop," murmured one white-faced matron, "it must be a stage prop for a surprise performance. This family grows wilder by the year."

Not that Devon particularly noticed, or that he would have apologized if he had. He had burst into the house like Hell unleashed, Gabriel at his heels shouting to anyone who would listen, "The bastard is in the house somewhere, costumed as a monk! Stop him if you see him."

"Jocelyn went up to the nursery only a few minutes ago," a female voice responded, and Devon did not spare a glance to see who had spoken. It sounded as if it might have been his sister Chloe. Even if he did not pause to acknowledge her, the information took hold in his mind.

The nursery. Surely the nursery was the safest place in the entire house. The nursemaid never left Rowan unattended until another servant or a family member, usually Jane, relieved her. It was an absolute rule of the house. Common sense.

And hadn't Devon committed Jocelyn to the guard of his intimidating brother Drake? Everyone in the Boscastle household had been afraid of crossing Drake in his younger adult years. He kept telling himself that Drake wouldn't allow anyone to harm Jocelyn. There was something dark and fierce about Drake.

All the Boscastles were a little afraid of Drake. All the Boscastle men protected their family, would die doing so.

As he should have been protecting his wife. She'd been innocent from the start, and he had drawn her into the debts of his own misspent past.

His thoughts might have run together in these self-tortuous circles indefinitely had Jane not appeared on the stairs before him.

"Where in God's name is my wife?" he asked in bewilderment.

Jane's distressed face offered no comfort. "Not in the nursery. I think he's taken her down the back stairs through the servants' passageway. Weed has already blocked every possible exit, and Drake has gone after him." She closed her eyes. "So has Grayson."

The back stairs. That was the only phrase that he seemed to grasp. He wheeled and someone, dear Jesus, he dimly recognized his brother-in-law Dominic, thrust a silver-mounted pistol at him, retaining the mate in his own hand.

"The back passageway," he said. He turned again and found Gabriel in front of him. "Our old escape route."

But, of course, neither Gabriel nor Dominic had grown up in this house to understand what he meant, and he had no time to explain.

In the old days a tunnel had run from the kitchen into the garden to a sunken gate that led into the street from whence the servants could come and go on errands without disturbing those they served.

Devon knew that it was Grayson's custom to keep the main armorial gates of the mansion guarded during one of his frequent parties, for it was a common practice for the populace to beg entry or at least a peep into his lavish affairs.

What he did not know was whether his brother remembered the gate that they had used for secret escapes as children.

Or whether it would be too late to even matter at all.

It seemed to Jocelyn that time had not stopped but had merely slowed as if ticking to the beat of an invisible metronome. Her limbs moved as if weighted with lead. Every moment dragged out into an eternity, or perhaps she only wished it so.

At the end of this horrifying interlude, she would most likely die. The fact that her abductor, a tall menacing blur in the dark named Matthew Thurlew, could take her life on a mad whim, filled her with an anger she could not hide.

"Drag me like a docile cow to market?" she whispered in the voice of a Bedlam virago. "Place a rope around my neck and drug another innocent woman as she tends to an infant?"

For a moment he looked a little shocked that a lady could mount such a scathing defense. "I told you to hold your tongue," he said through his teeth.

She started to shake, not as much from fear now as from all the emotions she'd been holding inside. Her father might have struggled to subdue the militant streak in her soul, but he had failed. For better or for worse, she was the daughter of a soldier, and she would not go down without a fight.

They had almost reached the bottom of the staircase. She was unsure where the door below led. She did know, however, that once Thurlew managed to get her outside the house her chances of being rescued, of staying alive, would be greatly diminished. With all the noise of the party, no one would pay any attention to two people outside.

She heard Thurlew fumbling with the doorknob, the heavy rasp of his breath. She hoped he would find the door locked, although the prospect of being trapped alone with him in a dark stairwell did not bolster her dwindling courage.

"Open," he muttered. "O—"

She swung upward with her elbow and dealt his shoulder a hard blow at the moment the door opened onto an unlit passageway. He did not react at all, nor did she attempt to hit him again. She was more preoccupied with finding a means to escape. They seemed to be standing in a tunnel just beneath the scullery and kitchen. She could feel ash dust beneath her feet.

Perhaps a servant would be posted nearabouts. She could hear the echo of footsteps and conversation on the floorboards of the chamber above. If she could shout for help, someone might at least be tempted to investigate.

"No one can hear us down here," Thurlew said as if he had guessed her thoughts. "Even if anyone ventured into the basement, we are not staying long enough for it to matter to you."

Life or death. Revenge. Mercy. The rewards of Heaven, or the threat of Hell. A single moment, a random occurrence could change the entire course of his life. And his wife's. He should never have left her. Why hadn't he waited until morning? Why had he been so damned impatient to prove himself a hero when he should have been protecting her?

He didn't know what he expected to find when he ran through the garden to the small wooden gate, but it was surely not the sight of Jocelyn being dragged by a rope around her neck. Splotches of dirt or dust besmirched her white costume, and her hair fell in tangles over her shoulder. A rope. Around her beautiful throat.

He drew to a halt, his blood roaring.

His mind did not seem to function. Primal instinct took over in a welcome rush. He was aware of only one thought: the man who had hurt and degraded her did not deserve to live. Life or death. Revenge. Mercy. Heaven or Hell. He might not have come in time to save her life, and if he hadn't—

He waited until he had a clear shot and no chance of striking her before he raised his arm. A wordless prayer in his heart, he took aim.

Then in an instinctual act that seemed as vital to him as drawing his next breath, he pulled the trigger, fired, and waited. It seemed as if the moment were suspended in time, as if it took forever for the pistol to discharge.

He was not even sure Jocelyn realized he was standing behind her, but for a viciously satisfying instant he saw Captain Thurlew turn and look directly into his face. The bullet struck Thurlew in the chest; he knew who had fired the shot. He knew that he was paying the price for what he'd done to Devon's wife.

Uttering a soft groan, Thurlew lifted his hand and crumpled to the grass beneath a headless antique statuary of Hermes. Fortuitously, the shadows of the winged god concealed him from Jocelyn's shocked regard. Devon rushed forward to take her into his arms.

She looked up into his face with a relief that wrenched his heart. "You came," she said, raising her hands to pull at the rope around her neck.

He gripped her to him, finally able to breathe, willing the heat of his body into hers. She felt like a sculpture of ice. He rubbed his large hands over her shoulders and back, telling himself that he had come in time, that he was holding her.

"I was worried about you," she whispered, her face still hidden in the hollow of his shoulder.

"I should have been here," he said fiercely.

"But you came," she whispered back.

He shook his head, stroking her disheveled hair. "Barely in time."

"Devon—"

He stared up at the sky, fighting to stay in control. He could feel the warmth stealing back into her body, and with it a little of his own cold fear began to melt.

"Devon," she said softly, "we can't stay here."

He nodded. Even now she was trying to take care of him. "I should never have left you. And I won't ever again."

She drew back slightly. Her face looked pale, and tears shimmered in her soft brown eyes. "Do you think you killed him? There are people coming."

"I don't give a bloody damn who's coming," he said, his voice breaking. "I only care about you."

"But if he's dead, we'll have to explain why."

"I hope to God he's dead," he said dispassionately, and meant it.

"Please, Devon," she whispered. "I don't think I can talk to anyone else about this quite yet."

He dropped the pistol into the grass as her plea finally penetrated his mind. He wasn't about to lie to anyone. He bore no regret for what he had done or who had witnessed it.

If he hadn't killed Thurlew, it was only by accident or faulty aim.

Thurlew deserved to die for the degradation he had inflicted upon Jocelyn. In fact, now that Devon was reassured of her safety, he had to restrain himself from putting another bullet into the bastard. And then another.

But a stronger instinct urged him to consider her feelings; it was suddenly imperative that he remove her from the garden before she was besieged by curious guests.

He heard footsteps at the other end of the path, and saw his eldest brother running toward them.

As Grayson neared, Devon swiftly helped Jocelyn remove the offensive rope from around her neck.

He watched as his older brother gently guided her away from the sight of Thurlew sprawled in the grass, then had the presence of mind to motion a footman to stand guard over the body.

In the next moment Devon caught sight of Drake and Gabriel hurrying toward them. He kicked the rope viciously into the grass. That any man would abuse and intimidate his wife as if she were an animal sickened him.

He came up behind her, not willing to be parted from her again.

"Is Rowan all right?" she asked Grayson in an anxious voice. "And Mrs. O'Brien? He poisoned the poor woman's chocolate. He was hiding in the nursery."

Devon had only the vaguest notion what she meant. Indeed, it seemed that his mind had just begun to function again while his heart, well, his heart might never be the same.

The mention of poison, of Grayson's son, chilled him, and he was vastly relieved to hear Grayson reassure her by replying, "Rowan is fine, thanks be to your presence, Jocelyn. And Mrs. O'Brien will survive to torment us all for many years to come with her infernal lullabies."

"Thank heaven," she said.

Devon made enough sense of this exchange to wish again that he could have prolonged his revenge. This unashamedly brutal desire was dashed only a few seconds later when he heard Gabriel mutter, "Dammit. He's not dead. Look. The swine's moving his hand."

Drake stepped on Thurlew's wrist. "Not anymore."

To which Gabriel responded in a low voice as he crouched below the headless statue, "We'd better search him anyway to make sure he does not have a weapon concealed in his costume."

"Just get him the hell away from the house," Grayson said with a look of contempt in Thurlew's direction. "Or finish him off for that matter. The footmen can dump him alongside the other offal in the Thames."

"Come inside," Devon urged his wife, wrapping his arms tightly around her again. The men in his family tended to play rough when those they loved had been threatened. He did not disapprove. In fact, he would have gladly participated; it was the Boscastle way. He just would rather she not watch.

"He isn't dead?" she asked, turning her head in the direction of the beheaded Hermes.

Not because he hadn't tried to kill him, Devon thought, urging her in the other direction.

"Come home with me, please, before Grayson's guests are persuaded that his entertainment has moved outside."

"Go with him, Jocelyn," Grayson said. "Let your husband comfort you tonight. I will handle matters here."

And, of course, he did.

With the finesse of a man born to master his environs since the moment of his conception, Grayson Boscastle, the Most Honorable Marquess of Sedgecroft, managed to convince his guests that the melee in the garden was merely another mistimed family prank. In truth, most of his company had come to expect no less from a Boscastle affair.

Word of it never even reached the scandal-mongers, for if the marquess claimed that nothing of interest had happened in his garden, then it must be so. In the end the Boscastles took care of their own. Brother, sister. Husband and wife.

Devon did not have to do anything more than give himself permission to let his true nature guide him from now on.

He was profoundly grateful that it was not too late for another chance.

Chapter Twenty-two

❧❧

To Devon's surprise, Jocelyn fell asleep on the carriage ride home and did not awaken as he carried her upstairs to the bedchamber of their town house. Clearly alerted in advance of their arrival, Thistle and Mrs. Hadley brought brandy and warm blankets up behind their somber-face master, then discreetly melted away in unspoken concern. Devon nodded at them gratefully; he did not believe he would sleep at all.

There was a profound contentment in merely holding her against his shoulder, making promises to her in the dark that he meant to keep. He would have comforted her had she stirred, but she moved only once, without even a murmur, subsiding back into his arms.

He prayed that her dreams were undisturbed by what had happened tonight even as his own thoughts pained him deeply.

Perhaps tomorrow he would sleep.

In a week or so he might be able to close his

eyes and not see his wife being led by a hideous rope around her soft white neck that he had nuzzled in teasing affection. He might be able to forget his own stark fear that he would arrive too late.

Perhaps by morning he would find the words to explain to her what he felt. Or perhaps he would whisper his love to her while she slept.

How the fates must be laughing at his arrogance—he who had sworn he would never fall in love. Had he truly believed that his precious freedom meant he could live a life without meaning?

Reckless fool he for assuming that when, if ever, he fell in love, he would choose the time, the place, and the woman.

Why hadn't anyone ever explained to him that one had no choice?

It didn't matter.

He wouldn't have listened. Perhaps he had been told a thousand times before and the words never penetrated his thick skull.

He sighed at the fatuous illogic he had followed as his creed for too many years. There was nothing to be done for his behavior except to apologize for the mistakes he had unknowingly made.

If he could have foreseen that she would be punished in his place, he would have been there to protect her. If he had not been such a blind, headstrong ass, he would have been at her side where he belonged. And where he would remain.

He exhaled, smiling faintly at the notion. His wife wasn't going to be able to get rid of him now, and she certainly would never attend a party alone again. He would be her lover, friend, and protector for the rest of their days.

And when she woke up they would go downstairs for one of Mrs. Hadley's groaningly huge breakfasts, and they would laugh if anyone mentioned either of them in the papers again because the mere suggestion of any infidelity would be ridiculous.

She stirred.

"What time is it?" She levered up on her elbow to gaze in apparent confusion about the room. "How did I come to be in bed?"

"You fell asleep in the carriage on the way here," he said, frowning in concern. "I carried you up in my arms. Don't you remember?"

Her silence made his chest ache with anger. "I remember falling asleep. But . . . not coming here. Home. I don't think I ever want to leave."

"Jocelyn," he said hoarsely, his arms tightening around her. "It was my fault. It has all been my fault."

"Was it?" she questioned softly.

"Yes."

He noticed that she did not argue. Well, he decided he deserved that, too.

"I don't suppose it was all your fault," she conceded, her voice teasing him.

"No?"

She smiled, studying him in silence. "A little of it."

He laughed.

"But not all."

He closed his eyes. "Thank you."

"I don't blame you, Devon," she said quietly.

"Well, I damn well blame myself. If I had lost you . . . " He swallowed, his heart in his eyes.

He loved her.

She heard in his voice what he did not say. It would have been lovely for him to confess this. She longed for him to speak the words.

Yet she had seen the stark fear on his face when he'd fired the pistol. She remembered when he had championed her at Alton's tournament, and how she had wished with all her heart that his declaration of devotion would come true, for she had already been in love with him then even if she'd never told him.

Tonight he had answered her wish in a particularly graphic manner, perhaps, but he had proved himself to be her champion in every sense of the word.

He was everything she ever wanted, and now he wanted her.

She wound her arms around his strong neck and urged him down onto the bed. He seemed to hesitate, no doubt out of consideration for what she had undergone. She realized that he could not possibly understand how she needed his touch to make the nightmare of Matthew Thurlew recede.

She *needed* him. She needed his caresses to banish the vile memory, and she could not keep her hands off him at all. She stroked his broad shoulders, the muscular ridges of his back. Her champion. He had been hers all along. He had defended her.

He loved her.

"It's all right now," she whispered, burying her face beneath his jaw to kiss his strong throat. He seemed to require some consolation himself.

He tightened his arm around her and rubbed his unshaven cheek across her cheek. "Did he hurt you in . . . in any physical manner?"

She frowned, resenting the intrusion of Thurlew into her thoughts, even as she realized the question must have been gnawing at Devon since he had found her in the garden. "No," she said swiftly.

"Then may I—"

"I wouldn't think you'd have to ask."

"I was afraid it might be too soon," he said hesitantly.

"It can't be soon enough. I'm wild for you, Devon."

"I know." He gave a deep sigh. "I'm not sure why, though. I have been a fool. I should have suspected Thurlew. His brother was an odd sort. I should have paid closer attention to him at the party."

"How can one understand evil?" she whispered, kissing her way down his shoulder. "It's enough to overcome it. And it wasn't your fault. Please, Devon, no one is blaming you."

He rested his jaw upon the top of her head as she pressed soft, arousing kisses upon his shoulder, then his chest. He had undressed for bed, discarding his boots, his coat and waistcoat, everything except for his long-tailed white muslin shirt, tailored expressly for his lanky frame.

He disengaged her from their comfortable position and lowered her beneath him. As he bent to kiss her, she hooked one arm around his waist. The other slipped across his arse and belly to caress his stones with her fingertips. Of course, his cock responded, and the skin of his sac tightened at her delicate touch.

He had not been able to resist her from the night of their unplanned tryst in the tower.

He had wanted her then.

He wanted her even more now. He—

He groaned and shifted his body, covering hers. "Jocelyn."

"All I need is you," she said, her voice catching at the end. "I want us to be together like this, always."

"Always," he promised.

"Devon," she whispered.

"Always." He held her head in his hands and gave his heart to her in one deep, melting kiss after another.

"And I need to feel you inside me," she said when she could draw a breath.

God, how he understood. He needed physical reaffirmation perhaps even more than she did, certainly more than he could admit. He needed her to feel safe again, and he needed . . . her. It was a relief to admit the truth to himself, to realize he had another chance.

They kissed again and set upon each other like a pair of long-lost lovers who had been apart for years and not merely a few hours earlier in the evening.

The possibility of losing her tonight had forced him to confront how unbearable his life would be without her. She had a place in his heart that no one else could ever hold.

He leaned back briefly to pull off his shirt.

A moment later she was in his arms, moaning sweetly at his touch. He could have pumped his hard cock into her right then and there, but for now he would let her set the pace. He had no idea what depraved acts Thurlew might have threatened her with during his abduction. A black fury seized him that he had not been at her side to prevent her ordeal.

But he was with her now, by God, and no one would ever lay a hand on her again except him.

He caressed her body with gentle possession as if to seal the promise he'd made.

She arched her back in response. Slowly his hand glided over her ribs to her belly.

He felt her give a start as he brushed his palm over her soft abdomen, but he was too aroused to question why. His mouth closed around one tempting nipple and tongue-teased it into a taut peak. At her delicious whimper he reached lower to tweak the hooded bud that lay hidden under her nest of curls. The nubbin of sensitive nerves grew taut at his caress. He stroked her lazily as if they had all the time in the world.

She gasped and spread her thighs for him, shivering helplessly. He pressed his other palm against her plump mound to hold her immobile. His touch deft, he parted her bedewed lips and worked one finger at a time inside her cleft.

"You're always wet when I play with you, aren't you?" he whispered, his voice thick with desire.

"Then come play more," she whispered, rotating her hips in the rhythm of his finger-thrusts.

His entire body shook in anticipation. What a passionate woman he had married. He raised his head from her jutting breasts and raked her with an exultant glance.

"Are there any rules or restrictions that I must obey?"

She shifted herself up to stare down into his dark, handsome face. "None."

He gave her a merciless smile. "Don't say later that you didn't ask for it."

"Ask for—"

He returned to teasing her engorged pearl with his thumb and eased another finger inside her soaked passage. Time and again he brought her to the brink and ground his teeth to keep from spilling his seed onto the bed.

She bucked her hips. She cursed him. She begged, even as he withheld his touch only to return to her drenched slit in his game of sensual torment.

She groaned. "You cruel— Oh, my God. You're a heartless fiend. You're the worst man ever. You're—"

Her inner muscles contracted around his fingers like a glove as the convulsions of climax broke over her.

Devon stared down at her in unabashed lust, his knuckles coated with her sweet musk-scented come. Watching her uninhibited response dealt the final blow to his defenses. He could have devoured her in one wicked bite.

She fell back onto the pillows, her sobs gradually subsiding. "You rogue, Devon. I thought I was going to die."

"But, sweetheart—" He moved his large, lanky body over hers, his smile a study of masculine decadence, the gesture one of domination. "That was only a prelude."

She studied him as her breathing slowly resumed a more even rhythm. "Everyone warned me what a sinful man I was marrying."

"Oh, yes." He bent his head to kiss her lips.

"And if I'd known how sinful *you* were, we'd have been married all those years ago when your father wanted us to."

"Just think of what we missed."

"I have," he retorted. "And I fully intend to make up for the time we lost." He exhaled. "As long as you're willing to give me the chance."

"You say that as if I'd given up on you."

"I might have in your place."

Jocelyn was given little time to reflect on his welcome confession. Apparently ready to seek his own relief, he hooked her knees over his broad shoulders and guided his rampant penis in his hand to her cleft. She still ached pleasantly from his earlier onslaught, but instinct overcame her discomfort, and her hips lifted off the bed to draw him inside her.

"Shall I torment you as you tormented me?" she whispered, pressing herself against his silken length.

The decadent grin he gave her warned her he was not prepared to concede defeat. "We'll see," he said softly.

She wanted to prove that she could not so easily be played, but the seductive promise in his eyes penetrated her resolve. Even his voice weakened her. She had to bite the inside of her cheek to keep from writhing against him like a wanton. To merely look at him filled her with longing. His face reminded her of a sinfully beautiful Renaissance prince she had once seen in a painting.

His body might have tempted the same skilled artist to capture the light and shadow of the muscular contours and lithe, long-boned grace.

He bent a little lower, and her body clenched in expectation. "Did you want something?" he whispered.

"Stop . . . teasing me."

"I don't think I heard you."

"Devil."

"Was that my name?"

"It may as well be."

He smiled.

She shifted, impatient, but he eased only the knob of his engorged shaft inside her slit. Not enough. She needed all of him. This little torture of his only made her ache for him all the more. She moaned in frustration and slid her hand down his belly to guide him into her drenched sheath.

He grinned and withdrew, rubbing the entire length of his thick cock between her slick lips with a flagrant sexuality that made her shake.

"Deeper," she said, arching her back.

"How deep?" he whispered.

"I want to feel you—"

"How far?"

She sobbed. "Damn you, Devon. All the way—"

He reared back before she could finish, thrusting with a force that drove the breath from her body.

Bliss. Black velvet. A pleasure so intense it

pummeled her senses and brought her to the brink of oblivion. She gave herself to him.

And he took her without mercy until everything else ceased to exist, and they struggled to hold on to sanity, only to come apart in each other's arms, spent, kissing breathlessly.

She closed her eyes, surrendering to her contented exhaustion. Safe. Protected. Sated. Warm. He loved her.

When finally Devon relaxed his vigilance enough to fall asleep, it was for only two hours or so before a commotion on the ground floor filtered into his awareness. He sat up, stiff, cramped, and grinned at his reflection in the looking glass. His bare-arsed, lightly bearded image grinned back, Jocelyn's right arm knotted around his waist.

An errant ray of sunlight fell upon his wife's bare ankle. Her Egyptian costume lay in a lewd display on the carpet. He groaned as the voices downstairs began to assume an all-too-familiar tone.

Jocelyn stirred, lifting her flushed cheek from her pillow to murmur, "Someone is downstairs. It's too early for callers, isn't it?"

He grunted. He craved nothing more than to crawl beneath the covers beside her and go back to sleep. "Yes."

"Is it the authorities?" she asked in alarm, apparently wide awake herself. "*Did* you kill Thurlew last night?"

"Yes," he said unhappily to her first question.

"The authorities are here. And I can only hope Thurlew died."

She sat up, one pert breast peeking out from the sheet. "If there is going to be an inquiry, do you not think you should at least shave? Put on your pants? A dressing robe?"

He sank back beside her, his free arm folded behind his head. He was in no particular hurry to rush downstairs and face his uninvited visitors, although he doubted he could wait them out forever.

He had recognized the voices as those of Grayson and Emma, two of the three family elders. He supposed he should be grateful Heath was in Scotland.

"There's going to be an inquiry, all right," he said in resignation.

His wife wriggled out of his grasp. "Perhaps I should talk to the magistrate first," she said in rising panic. "I could explain how Thurlew drugged Mrs. O'Brien, then abducted me, and how I feared that he would harm the Boscastle heir. And that, you, assuming—" She stopped in midsentence. "I don't think you're taking this at all seriously. You could at least pretend to show respect for the judicial process."

He stretched his supple form, the muscles of his belly rippling like liquid steel. "Why?"

"I don't know how to answer that, Devon," she said in exasperation. "While I understand that you were justified in shooting Thurlew and will neither appear before a jury nor be sentenced to a penitentiary nor to picking oakum, you should at least assume an attitude of gravity. As well as a suit of clothes." She shook her head. "You look quite dissolute."

He yawned. "I'm going back to bed. Cease your chatter and kiss me."

"The devil I will."

He opened one eye to witness her leap from their bed, her breasts bobbing as she went on a wardrobe hunt for appropriate attire. His gaze drifted over her sunlit nudity. Owing to her consternation, she was granting him a deliciously immodest display of her curvaceous form.

He felt fresh craving for sex as he beheld the firm white globes of her rump raised in the air while she bent to pick up a stocking. His groin tightened. He debated taking her in that position, on her hands and knees in front of the looking glass, but with regret decided against it. They might get carried away and knock over some of the furniture in a frenzy of lust, thereby alarming the visitors below. He could just imagine explaining such noises to Emma.

Jocelyn straightened without warning, waving his waistcoat at him. "Are you waiting for me to dress before you summon your valet? Or are you going to loll about all day with that lustful grin on your face?"

He sat forward, willing his painful erection to subside. "Is it possible that your breasts have become larger in this last week, or have I never been allowed the pleasure of examining you in the daylight before?"

She dropped the waistcoat between his feet. "Would you like me to bring the matter of my breasts before the magistrate?"

"Not unless you'd like to witness me shoot him through the heart, too."

"Are you not going to be serious for once?"

"I'm very serious about this."

"About the size of my breasts?"

"Yes."

"Devon, for the love of—"

He stretched forward in one sinuous move to capture her hand and trap her between his hard-muscled thighs.

"Your nipples are darker too, aren't they?" He brushed his knuckle across one tender peak. "Surely I have not been that inattentive. Let me have a closer look."

She shivered as, with a tenderness that few women could resist, the handsome beast took her breasts in his hands and weighed them in his palms like ripe peaches at the market.

"Why did you not tell me?" he asked simply, lifting his gaze to her face.

She shook her head, submerging herself in the depths of his blue eyes, his low caressing voice. She should not have been surprised that a Boscastle male would perceive the early signs of pregnancy, being the sexual creatures that they were.

However, it did not please her to realize her husband had experiences in these frank matters when she had only the vaguest understanding of the facts of reproduction herself.

"How can you tell?" she asked somewhat resentfully.

He gave her a guileless smile. "How can I tell what?"

She swallowed, her emotions suddenly in turmoil. "Jane said that it is ill luck to talk of my condition until we are certain that it is true."

"Fine." He laid his broad palm protectively against the curve of her belly. "I won't tell anyone. Unless I'm asked, of course."

She glanced down at his dark head, her heart beating hard. How she loved him. "And what will you say if you're asked?"

"I don't think I should lie, do you?"

"Hmm. Perhaps not. I mean, it isn't the sort of secret that one can keep indefinitely. Perhaps for a little while longer."

He broke into a grin. "To hell with keeping it a secret. Let's tell everyone right now. We'll go to the park and stand on the corner, informing random passersby. I'll have a monument erected to proclaim our news in case anyone doesn't hear me shouting."

"Then you're pleased?" she asked, biting her lip.

"I am absolutely out of my mind with delight."

She sighed happily and tangled her fingers in his

thick black hair. "Should we not dress now to face the magistrate?"

He looked up at her with a rueful grin. "Didn't I correct you? It's the marquess who's downstairs, not the magistrate."

"The marquess?" she whispered in alarm, glancing over his shoulders at the door. "As in Grayson?"

"God, is there any other? The marquess and his major-general."

"His who?"

"The Dainty Dictator of the family. Emma."

He eased off the bed, the bones and the musculature of his body a tribute to youth and battle-hardened strength. "After she's done scolding me on not being a proper protector to you, I shall no doubt wish I had faced a magistrate and been sent to a solitary jail cell."

"So that I should raise our child alone?" she teased. Leaving the bed, she passed him the pantaloons that he had thrown upon a chair.

"Alone? In this family? Sweetheart, there's hardly any fear of that." He dressed, pausing to kiss her once before he put on his coat. "There's no fear of me abandoning our child, either. The Boscastles have their faults in spades, and I do not pretend to seek absolution for all my sins, but family always comes first, even among the worst of us."

"Emma means well, you know."

"I do know. And she's usually right, which

makes all the rest of us look shabby in comparison."

She nodded, feeling weepy all of a sudden again. It would not do to dissolve with the marquess and his sister waiting so patiently downstairs. The passionate loyalty of which Devon spoke was perhaps the facet of him she had loved first and now loved the most. There was no doubt in her mind that his capacity for devotion was a legacy of his dynamic ancestry.

And the child she thought she had conceived would most likely inherit the notoriety of its noble lineage.

"Unless I fight to intervene first," she thought aloud.

He pivoted at the door. "Did you say something?"

She regarded him with a wistful smile. Sinful he might be, but at least he had managed to dress himself and present a decent appearance while she sprawled about like a well-tumbled tart between their disheveled bed-sheets.

He cleared his throat and gave his crisp neckcloth a final tug. "You might want to dress before you face them."

"Splendid idea," she said drily.

He walked to the side of the bed and stared down at her, the devil in his deep blue eyes. "On second thought, perhaps you don't want to dress at all." He began to unfasten his neckcloth.

She laughed, scandalized. "What are you going to tell your brother?"

His eyes glittered. "Somehow I think Grayson will understand. God knows he wrote the book on seduction."

She subsided back onto the sheets. "Won't he be offended if we ignore him?"

"Not if we name our firstborn in his honor," he replied, tossing his coat back onto the chair.

"And if it's a girl?"

"Then we shall name her after Emma."

"Emma will *not* understand." She paused, her eyes widening as he peeled off his pantaloons and stood before her. "Emma," she continued, albeit her mind was suddenly not on her sister-in-law, "would not find our behavior listed under proper late-morning etiquette in any of the guidebooks she lives by."

He lowered himself onto the bed to kiss her. "Then I say we should write our own book on the subject."

"A literary endeavor? Now *that* I might consider, but as to the writing of it without our clothes—"

"Jocelyn." He laid his forehead against hers. "Hush a moment, I am inspired. I have a notion what the very first line shall be."

"Once upon—"

"I love you," he said.

She clung to him, letting the words sink in. He hadn't needed to tell her, but she was glad he had.

"With an opening like that, there's no question as to how the tale should end," she said softly.

"How?" he whispered.

"I love you, too."

He pressed her back onto the bed. "Then all that's left is for us to take care of the middle of our story. And I don't think either of us will have to look far to find inspiration."